PRAISE FOR
DANCER WITH ONE LEG

"FASCINATING, WELL-WRITTEN . . . COMPARES FAVORABLY WITH ED McBAIN'S 87TH PRECINCT SERIES."

—*Library Journal*

"THE . . . CHARACTERS ARE PRECISELY RIGHT, THE DIALOGUE IS POETIC, HARD-BOILED, AND WRY, AND THE DENOUEMENT A ZINGER."

—*The Washington Post Book World*

"GRITTILY DETAILED . . . AUTHENTIC MIXTURE OF ARSON DETECTION AND CHARACTER STUDY . . . HONEST AND STURDY."

—*Kirkus*

"TOUGH, GRITTY FARE, AND IT REALLY WORKS . . . THE SCENE IS SET FOR A TERRIFIC TALE."

—*Publishers Weekly*

"DOBYNS TELLS AN ASTONISHING AMOUNT ABOUT FIRES AND THE MEN WHO START AND STOP THEM, AND ALL OF IT IS FASCINATING . . . HIS WRITING IS HONEST, TOUGH-MINDED, AND AS UNCOMPROMISING AS HIS UNFORGETTABLE HERO . . . A PEACH OF A BOOK."

—*Lawrence Block*

Dancer with One Leg

Stephen Dobyns

BANTAM BOOKS

TORONTO · NEW YORK · LONDON · SYDNEY

*This low-priced Bantam Book
was printed from new plates. It contains the
complete text of the original hard-cover edition.*
NOT ONE WORD HAS BEEN OMITTED.

DANCER WITH ONE LEG

*A Bantam Book / published by arrangement with
E. P. Dutton Inc.*

PRINTING HISTORY

*E. P. Dutton edition published May 1983
Bantam edition / July 1984*

*Bantam Books are published by Bantam Books, Inc. Its trademark,
consisting of the words "Bantam Books" and the portrayal of a rooster,
is Registered in U.S. Patent and Trademark Office and in other
countries. Marca Registrada. Bantam Books, Inc., 666 Fifth Avenue,
New York, New York 10103.*

PRINTED IN THE UNITED STATES OF AMERICA

O   0 9 8 7 6 5 4 3 2 1

For Peter Roberts

I would like to thank members of the Boston Fire Department, the Boston Police Department, the Massachusetts State Fire Marshal's Office, the National Fire Protection Association and several private investigatory agencies, and especially James DeFuria, retired Massachusetts State Police lieutenant-detective, whose help and kindness made much of this book possible.

Dancer with One Leg

1

In the darkness, the Charles River seemed perfectly still. Lazard stood at its edge, his shoes squishing in the mud, feeling how the mud seemed to tug at his cane. To his left, the curve of the Boston University Bridge concealed much of the Boston skyline. Across the river, the red sign of a Cadillac dealership blinked on and off. It was shortly past 2 in the morning, Monday, April 19: Patriots' Day. Despite the time, Lazard had passed dozens of people on his walk to the river, presumably unable to sleep because of the heat. On the river, it felt cooler. A breeze blew in from the ocean, and Lazard could feel its coolness against his skin.

Since Thursday, the days had been getting steadily hotter and yesterday, Easter Sunday, the temperature had been in the mid-nineties, making it the hottest Easter Sunday on record. Lazard stood behind the backstop of a softball diamond in a small park bordering Memorial Drive. He didn't mind the heat and blamed his inability to sleep on his personal life or lack of it. As he stared at the river, he kept thinking of his wife's face as he had seen her in court Friday morning. It wasn't that she looked very different, apart from her short hair, but there had been something in the way she had regarded him, as if he no longer existed, as if he were dead. Lazard wasn't a reflective man, but he knew his separation from the focus of her life was a kind of death. And as he stood by the river's edge, he felt the absence of that focus and it seemed he was being carried forward in his life simply by momentum. He asked himself if he loved her, then left the question unanswered. After seventeen years of marriage, it seemed pointless to ask which was the bandage and which the wound.

From across the river, Lazard could hear sirens. A causal relationship appeared to exist between hot weather and false alarms, and over the Easter weekend there had been constant sirens. As he listened, Lazard began identifying the various engine and ladder companies, judging their speeds and the probable area of the alarm.

Lazard was a lieutenant with the Boston Fire Department. For the past six years, he had been assigned to the Arson Squad. He had joined the department in 1960, having come to Boston from East Lansing, Michigan, where he'd been raised. His wife had been a sociology major at Michigan State. He had just joined the Lansing Fire Department, and they met when she began interviewing firemen about something concerning fear response, he couldn't remember what. To Lazard, his ambitious twenty-two-year-old self was a different species, and he felt as separate from that self as if his young counterpart were a dark shape trying to signal him from the other side of the river. In any case, he had married. Elizabeth was from Boston and wanted to return there.

Lazard turned right and began walking along the riverbank. He held his cane almost flat against his right leg and when he walked, he swung the leg out and forward, then leaned heavily on the cane, which made him seem to weave from one side to the other. He was a tall thin man, and his stiffness, plus the slight weaving, made him resemble a tree in a wind—maybe a poplar.

Here the Charles River made a bend so that this section of Cambridge formed a peninsula. At moments in the darkness, the river became invisible and the space looked like a great gulf. Even the baseball field and park seemed a sort of gulf, while Memorial Drive with its streams of traffic looked like the actual river. Lazard could make out a few other people in the park: some sleeping, some wandering as he was. During the hot weather, there had also been a higher number of holdups and muggings, and Lazard wondered what risk these people were taking sleeping out in the open.

2

He thought about them a minute, then imagined them thinking about him, wondering about the tall thin man limping along the water's edge. In the dark, all that was visible was his white shirt, one of the many left over from when he was lieutenant in an engine company. He carried a few stones in his left hand and as he walked he tossed them into the water. Ahead of him, across the river, he could see a Coca-Cola sign blink the time, then the temperature, then the time: 2:27, 74 degrees. From somewhere he heard a dog barking.

Lazard knew he should go home, try to sleep. Despite Patriots' Day, he was scheduled to work, although he would be delayed because he had to see his lawyer to finish some business about the divorce. Elizabeth's lawyer would also be there, and when he had agreed to go Lazard had thought Elizabeth would be there too; then his lawyer told him she would rather they didn't meet.

Lazard had just begun to bend over to pick up some more stones when he heard a noise behind him, the quick sound of footsteps, as if someone were rushing at him. He straightened and spun around, swinging out with his cane. Even before he connected he realized his mistake. His cane smashed against the arm of a jogger—a young man in a white T-shirt and shorts—making him stumble to his left, cry out, and clutch his arm.

"Jesus, man, what the hell you doin'?"

"I'm sorry," said Lazard. He was startled at himself for striking out, had thought he'd been keeping himself under tighter control. "You surprised me. You should have given some warning."

The jogger circled Lazard warily, then began backing away. He held his hands at chest level as if expecting Lazard to swing at him again. "Warning! I'm just running, man. What the hell's wrong with you?"

2

By the light of the two flashlights, it looked like a living room that had grown cancerous and begun to expand: an area 35 by 100 feet crowded with couches, armchairs, coffee tables, bureaus, dressers, beds; some gathered to simulate actual room arrangements—two armchairs and a sofa against a coffee table—others piled up chair upon bureau upon table. To the left was a shop area where the spring and wood skeletons of several chairs waited for upholstery and padding, and a butcher block table tilted on three legs.

As the cones of light moved across the warehouse, the younger of the two men kept expecting to see someone: four people gathered around a table or someone dozing in a chair. All would be men and wear the gray fedoras of the police officers of his imagination.

"Great place for an orgy," he said.

"Let's get started," said the other. He was in his early fifties, nearly thirty years older than his companion, and he saw nothing but furniture. Both men wore dark blue coveralls and rubber gloves.

They stood in the doorway of an office at the rear of the warehouse. Behind them was an outside door leading to their car. A crowbar lay on the floor by the door. In the past few minutes, they had carried into the office two red five-gallon plastic containers and six wire milk crates each holding four half-gallon cartons. These were piled on the wooden desk along with a black vinyl attaché case.

The older man motioned toward the front with his flashlight. "The stairs are over there. Keep your light away from the windows. The shutoff valve's just to the right of the boiler."

He turned back to the office, put his flashlight on top of a file cabinet so it shone on the desk, and began carrying the milk crates into the main area of the warehouse. The desk was covered with papers and, once the crates were moved, the man pushed them onto the floor, clearing the desk of everything but a black business phone. Opening the attaché case, he removed a pine board to which was attached a series of transistors, fixed resistors, and other electronic paraphernalia joined by colored wire and ending in a relay connected to an electric squib: a small aluminum tube about an inch long. He placed the board on the desk by the phone, then took two nine-volt batteries from the attaché case, which he also put by the phone.

Taking the two five-gallon containers, he unscrewed the tops and withdrew from each the end of a quarter-inch white cotton sash cord. The room began to smell of kerosene. Still holding the ends of cord, the man fished about in the pockets of his coveralls until he found two shingle nails. He then retrieved the crowbar from near the door, stuck one nail through the end of each cord, and prepared to nail the cords to the center of the desk. He raised the crowbar and stopped. Wiping his forehead on his sleeve, he stared down at the nails. The right side of his face was lit by the flashlight; the left was dark. It was a square, craggy face with a small stub nose. Putting the crowbar across the ends of cord, he took a piece of paper from the floor, folded it several times, and again prepared to hammer the nails into the desk. This time, however, he put the folded piece of paper over each nail head, then struck each twice, driving them into the desk. By now the room smelled heavily of kerosene.

He straightened and turned to see the younger man entering the office. "Can you get a spark off a zinc nail?"

"Beats me. Who cares?" He noticed the board on the desk. "Jesus, you wanna blow us across the expressway?"

"It's dead."

"You sure? You're a great one for taking chances."

"It needs a charge, for crissake. Let's get started, it's too fuckin' hot'n here."

They each picked up one of the five-gallon containers and, carefully threading the cord out behind them, made their way back into the warehouse.

"It's hotter up here than it is back home. I never seen such a place," said the younger man. "You seen the TV? A fuckin' record, ninety-four degrees. What a day to be stuck in a motel."

"Whaddaya want, Revere Beach?"

"It's Easter Sunday, I shoulda gone to mass. I always go to mass on Easter Sunday."

"You could of seen it on TV."

"It's not the same. They like you to be there. If I didn't go to mass, least I coulda got laid. I still know a lotta broads, six years or no six years."

As the men talked, they moved through the warehouse placing the half-gallon cartons on chairs and couches, then wrapping the kerosene-saturated cord twice around each carton. The older man did it methodically and without thought. The younger was slower and now and then paused to inspect a piece of furniture. He seemed primarily interested in coffee tables and pressed down on one then another to see how sturdy they were. He had curly black hair that reached just past his collar. Each time he bent down, a lock of hair fell across his eyes and he flicked back his head in order to see.

"You know, there's some pretty nice stuff here. I could use some of it back home."

"It's all gonna look the same in a coupla hours. Come on, it'll be light soon."

They had taken three milk crates each and were dividing the cartons so they stretched in two zigzagging lines toward the front of the warehouse. The floor was wood, and when they set down the crates they made a hollow sound like a single knock on a door. Each man was careful to keep his light pointed at his feet and moved in a small circle of illumination. By the time the older man had placed all but two cartons, the younger still had six to go.

"I'm taking these last upstairs."

"Want me to come too?"

"What the fuck for? Just finish what you have."

The furniture on the second floor was either brand-new and still crated or old, out of fashion, and damaged. There had been no attempt to create home settings, and the pieces had been put wherever there was space. The furniture in crates was mostly piled against the left wall, covering the windows.

The man fed out the rest of the cord, which took him 15 feet from the stairs to a pile of couches. His flashlight was clamped under his arm and as he moved the light swung in arcs over the scattered furniture. Tying the end of the cord around the last two cartons, he poured the remaining kerosene on the couches and floor. Then he tossed the container aside. It made a hollow bumping sound. Before going back downstairs, he noticed he had spilled kerosene on his shiny black shoes and, taking a handkerchief from his coveralls, he carefully wiped them clean.

Downstairs the younger man had been moving more quickly. He disliked being alone. He began to wonder if he should have come, if he would be able to get back to the legal part of his life where he drove a truck and had several girlfriends. Putting the last carton in a dark blue armchair, he wrapped it twice with cord and stood up uncertainly. He still had 20 feet of cord. To his left at the front of the warehouse was a two-bay garage. The farther bay was empty, but in the first was a white delivery van. He shone his light on the van and read the words "Trieger Furniture Leasing Co.," written in black letters on its side. On a workbench in front of the van were tools, a battery, and about a dozen cans of Quaker State oil.

The older man came back down the stairs. "Hey, you want to take in some jai alai later? There's a matinee at noon."

"I gotta work. Anyway, they don't have matinees on Monday."

"Tonight then, whaddaya say?" He joined the younger man by the truck.

"I gotta work late. I can't see why you like that shit. Buncha Cubans bouncing a ball off a wall. What you want me to do with the end of this rope?"

The older man shone his light on the red container. "Stick it in the gas tank of the truck. I'll spread the rest of that stuff around the office." He picked up the container and started back through the warehouse.

The younger man unscrewed the gas cap of the van, then threaded 10 feet of kerosene-soaked cord into the tank. When he got back to the office, his companion was pouring the rest of the kerosene on the floor.

"Christ, don't walk in it, you'll track it all over. Shine your light on the desk while I attach the batteries."

The younger man moved back to the door. "This is the part I hate."

"You worry too much. You sure there's no matinee today? I could of sworn they had 'em Mondays." He attached the colored wires to the terminals, then stooped down and took one last package from the attaché case. He tore open one end.

"What's that stuff?"

"Little extra insurance."

Black powder fell in a thin stream onto the desktop and around the electric squib and two pieces of white cord.

When the package was empty, he crumpled it and tossed it into a corner. "Come on, let's go."

The two men had been in the warehouse exactly half an hour.

3

The heat and Hapgood's incontinence and itching had combined to give Raymond Farkus a restless night. The temperature had not gone below 70, and in his apartment in The Abbott it had remained above 80. The Abbott was suffering from what Raymond Farkus thought of as hot bricks: a condition rarely found before June and which usually required a heat spell of a week's duration. And here it was only April 19. Last Monday there had actually been snow. Well, flurries.

Before owning a bulldog, Raymond Farkus had assumed they were a sturdy sort of beast. Unfortunately, Hapgood was delicate. Sudden changes in the weather affected his bladder, and extreme heat caused a skin rash and wheezing. Therefore Hapgood too had had a restless night. About 5 o'clock he began scratching on the door, gradually becoming more frantic until at last Farkus got up to take the dog for what he called a business walk. As the two left The Abbott at 6:30, Farkus thought it particularly unfair to be waked so early on a holiday. Since it was Patriots' Day, the office supply store where he worked would be closed.

The Abbott was a five-story brick apartment building on East Canton between Albany and Harrison in Boston's South End. It was the third of four identical buildings all with pretentious names: The Groton, The Bigelow, The Abbott, The Lawrence. To Raymond Farkus, who had lived there for twenty years, they had a faded dignity. Many of the residents worked in the nearby medical complex.

The Boston University Medical Center was two blocks behind The Abbott. Left, to the west, were the rambling yellow brick buildings of the Cathedral housing project; to the east was the Southeast Expressway. North of The Abbott buildings had been torn down to provide parking for hospital staff, and for several blocks beyond more buildings and warehouses had been removed as part of some renovation program. Now there were vacant lots where all weekend children from the projects had been playing baseball and getting in trouble for uncapping a fire hydrant.

To Raymond Farkus these open blocks were a positive asset. Not only did he have a clear view as far as the brick warehouses on Plympton, but he could see beyond to the firehouse on Harrison, then the massive brown pile of the Cathedral of the Holy Cross, then the Hancock Tower and Boston skyline.

It was another perfect morning, but as he led Hapgood into the lot between Dedham and Plympton Farkus again thought of the basic wrongness of the season. It felt like midsummer, but trees had barely begun to leaf. There were few weeds in the lot, just rocks, broken bricks, tin cans, and trash where Hapgood was snuffling after an imaginary rabbit.

There was mud over by the fire hydrant and Hapgood appeared to be making his way toward it. Twice Saturday and twice Sunday the hydrant had been uncapped and dozens of screaming children had run through the water until each time the police came and stopped it. The last time rocks had been thrown and several teenage boys had been bundled into the back of a squad car. Farkus had been impressed by the perseverance of the police until he heard a landlord up the street brag that he had been the one to call them.

By now Hapgood had tired of mud and was exploring an interesting bit of lot near the corner. Farkus could see his brindled coat as the dog circled a mound of stones. Beyond the dog, the Hancock Tower rose over the cathedral. On cloudless days, its glass walls made it seem less like a building and more like a heavier piece of sky.

Farkus glanced at his watch and saw it was nearly quarter to seven. As he shuffled after his dog, he regretted he hadn't worn shoes instead of his slippers, which were gradually filling with dirt and bits of stone. Farkus was a tall man of about fifty, with a long thin face and long thin hands which he thought of as sensitive.

Hapgood crossed Plympton and trotted into the next vacant lot. He appeared to be making for the firehouse at Harrison and Wareham. A fireman had once given the dog a peanut butter sandwich, and ever since Hapgood seemed to view his morning and evening walks as gastronomical quests. Raymond Farkus whistled. The dog paused but continued to look toward the firehouse. It was a square two-story building of light gray stone.

As if in response to Farkus's whistle, a series of bells began to ring in the firehouse in an abrupt staccato pattern. Moments later a siren began, followed by a grumbling roar as a motor started. Another motor started and the two seemed to compete as each was revved up higher and higher. The doors slid open and both bells and motors grew louder. Now more sirens joined in, they too revving higher and higher. A fire engine slowly pulled out followed by the aerial tower truck. Both crossed Harrison onto Reynolds. Accelerating past the cathedral, they turned right onto Washington and the combined sounds of sirens, roaring, and honking began to diminish, although now Farkus could hear other sirens in the distance.

As Farkus turned back to look for his dog, he heard what sounded like a gunshot. It seemed to come from one of the warehouses to his right on Plympton. There were six: red brick, two and three stories, each separated from the next by empty lots or parking areas and all going back to a large five-story warehouse on Wareham, the next street. This taller building put the rear portions of the Plympton warehouses in shadow; and it was in a window in one of these shadowed areas that Raymond Farkus thought he saw flames.

It was a narrow two-story warehouse about a hundred yards away. Some of its windows had been bricked up, but on the west side were five grimy windows on the lower story and three on the second. There was a flash and now Farkus saw flames in two windows. He ran a few steps toward the warehouse, then stopped. He saw no people or cars on the street. He ran a few steps toward the firehouse, then stopped again. It was all confused. First the firemen left, then there was a fire, and now the firehouse was empty.

He remembered a fire call box on the corner of East Dedham and Albany, two blocks away. Looking again at the warehouse, he was certain he could see flames in all five downstairs windows. There was a crash and the sound of breaking glass as the rear window blew out. Flames and black smoke pushed through the window, and flames began licking the side of the warehouse. Farkus hurried back across the lot toward the alarm box. Having discovered the fire, he wanted to be first to sound the alarm.

Written in white on the red call box were the words "Please Pull Down The Hook." Under them was the number 1646. Farkus pulled down the hook and immediately there was a high, rattling noise like pebbles spinning in a clothes dryer. He looked around for Hapgood, but the dog was nowhere to be seen.

4

The clock was 3 feet in diameter, perfectly round, and had a white face with twelve black Roman numerals. It was suspended from the center skylight by a black metal rod 15 feet long. Its minute hand was black and ended in a rounded arrowhead. When the minute changed, the arrowhead jumped over an inch with a loud, two-syllable CLA-LACK.

The CLA-LACK was echoed by lesser clacks from two pendulum clocks hanging opposite each other in the middle of the side walls. Another clock was on the top of a circuit panel at the front of the room: an illuminated gray-metal, digital clock with the time given in 100-hours: black numbers on a white ground. On a side wall, 35 feet away, was a second digital clock: white numbers on a black ground.

Nearby, on a 20-track tape recorder, were two more digital clocks, one seven seconds behind the other. There were two recorders in a cabinet 7 feet tall. Both had 14-inch reels and automatically recorded every incoming and outgoing radio or telephone call. There were more clocks in each of the two switchboards, two radio consoles, and two alarm or box transmitters. Arranged in the front of the room, these were gray and looked like futuristic spinets.

Seven men usually worked in the room, although only four were there at present: the principal operator, two senior operators, and an operator: ranks corresponding to captain, lieutenant, and firefighter. All the men wore watches. At this moment, all the clocks in the room said 6:46 A.M.

The room was filled with sunlight streaming through the three skylights and twenty-seven windows located high in the 25-foot walls. The windows were covered with heavy grates, and from the outside Fire Alarm Headquarters looked like a giant Greco-Roman crypt. It had been built in the 1920s at the edge of the Back Bay Fens, 250 feet from the nearest building. Constructed of metal and stone, it was designed to be left standing after the rest of the city had burned down.

The day was going to be hot and the building had no air conditioning, just a blower in the basement. At the start of hot weather, the huge room stayed cool, but as the granite walls warmed the heat built up and the room remained hot for days after the temperature had dropped outside. Since Thursday, the temperature had passed 80 each day, and yesterday, Easter Sunday, it reached 94. Throughout the city, kids uncapped fifty hydrants.

John Lafferty hated hot weather. He was principal operator and would soon be going home. Hot weather meant more false alarms and during the past 24 hours there had been three hundred. He also hated to work in hot weather. He hated the feel of his clothes sticking to his skin and preferred cool nights when he could change into his flannel shirt.

Lafferty was a thin, electric man who had spent twenty of his twenty-two years as a fireman at Fire Alarm. He prided himself on his control and his great trial were his fingernails, which were chewed to the quick: a habit begun before memory and not, he said, a result of his profession. In any case, they led him to stand with his arms crossed or his hands in his pockets: anything to hide the destruction.

At the moment he stood with his arms folded in front of a 4-by-5 map of Boston mounted on fiberboard. Each firehouse was shown on the map and at each location was a small hook from which hung colored plastic chips a little smaller than a quarter. A white chip indicated an engine company; red, a ladder company;

14

blue, a district chief's car; green, rescue; rust, the aerial towers. Each chip bore the number of the corresponding company. When a piece of apparatus went out on an alarm, its chip was moved to a hook on the right side of the board. When it arrived, the chip was put on another hook. When it was returning, the chip was moved again.

The board showed six pieces of apparatus were out. Engine 37 had an automobile fire in Roxbury. Engines 7, 26, and 3, Ladder 17, Aerial Tower 1, and the District 4 chief's car were responding to Box 1616 at Shawmut and Herald. A minute earlier someone had called to report a fire in the Castle Square apartment complex, and Box 1616, the nearest fire alarm box, had been struck.

Lafferty was waiting for more calls reporting the fire and as none came he grew suspicious. Apart from the clocks, the room was quiet except when a driver reported his location on the radio. Behind the driver's voice, Lafferty heard the sirens and roar of the engine, but distantly like the sound of the sea in a seashell.

To Lafferty's left were the assignment cards: a brown file containing a yellow 5-by-8 card for each of the more than 2,400 alarm boxes in the city. These were filed by order of box number. Each card listed the box location, which companies responded to each alarm, and, after the second alarm, which companies covered for companies at the fire. Three engine and two ladder companies, plus the district chief, responded to the first alarm; four engine and two ladder companies to the second, four more engine and one ladder company responded to a third. In a five-alarm fire, fifty companies might be moving around the city.

Lafferty wrote the numbers of the companies responding to Box 1616 on the incident card, then the incident number for the year: 15,106. Sometimes, when he was off duty, he went to fires to remind himself what they were like: these disasters to which he had sent millions of firemen in apparatus that he kept imagining as so many plastic chips.

Circuit panels for sending and receiving alarms surrounded the room on three sides. Each panel was a gray marble slab 4 feet wide by 8 feet tall. They adjoined each other and were trimmed at the top and sides by what looked like dark oak but was actually metal painted to resemble wood. There was no real wood in the building.

At the top of each panel was a brass picture lamp that lit up when an alarm came in on any of the circuits on that panel. Beneath it was a horizontal row of ten red bull's-eye lights: one for each circuit. Beneath each light was a list of the alarm boxes covered by that circuit; then, in a vertical row, followed brass circuit switches, relays, Morse keys, and test switches. At the bottom of the panel was a sounder that amplified the clacking of the alarm.

Not long before, IBM had spent a year trying to computerize Fire Alarm's entire system. Each time they thought they had succeeded, the superintendant remembered something else until one day trucks pulled up and the computers were taken away, leaving nothing but piles of printout paper.

Lafferty liked that. He liked the brass and marble and clacking of the alarms. So what if the computers cut fifteen seconds from the response time? The average response time now was two minutes.

The radio crackled and the voice of the chief's driver came over channel 1. "We're at Box 1616. Nothing showing. Looks like a probable 710. They're still checking."

Malicious false alarm. Lafferty wrote the time of arrival—6:47 A.M.—on the incident card and moved the colored chips down to a lower series of hooks.

As he stepped away, he noticed the lamp light up on one of the panels to his left. Immediately a red bull's-eye began flashing the box number and in unison the sounder clacked out the series, striking three blows per second: 1646. The light flashed the number again and across the room on the mutual aid panel the ten lights flashed and the sounder clacked: 1646.

Laffery had already pulled the assignment card and stamped the incident card: 6:48 A.M., incident number 15,107. Box 1646 was at Albany and East Dedham. Assigned to the first alarm were Engines 3, 43, and 7, Ladder Company 13, and Aerial Tower 1, plus the chief of District 4. Lafferty knew that the chief, along with companies 3, 7, and the tower, were still at Box 1616. He hadn't heard from them and couldn't wait. He set the transmitter for Companies 43 and 13, then the companies reserved for the second alarm: Engines 22 and 24 and Ladder 4. If fire were showing, he'd send in the rest of the companies reserved for that alarm.

Lafferty turned the switch, striking the alarm. Immediately the twenty greenish-blue lights of the tapper transmitter system and the ten red lights of the mutual aid panel began to flash and the sounders clacked out the numbers twice: 1646.

Lafferty began moving chips on the map board. As he touched the board, it shook, jiggling the chips as if echoing the alarm sounding in firehouses across the city. Lafferty guessed that Engine 43 would arrive shortly before the other companies, but he didn't think it would make any difference. Then the phones began to ring.

5

Lieutenant Paul Harris was brushing his teeth when Box 1616 came over the taps. As it repeated a second time, the claxon began honking and Harris heard the rumble of the overhead doors.

"Engine 43 going out." Souza was on watch and his voice came over the loudspeaker.

When Harris hit the pole, he had an arm through one sleeve of his white shirt. The plates dropped away and he slid down to the apparatus floor. His boots were only a few feet from the pole. He pulled them on, then grabbed his helmet and fire coat from their hooks, and ran toward the pumper. The claxon was still honking.

Harris pulled himself into the cab. "Hey, Jimmy, got your pants on right?"

For a moment the motor had refused to catch, giving Jimmy Vernon a pain in his stomach. Now the cab trembled as he revved the motor higher and higher. As for the pants, several months before he'd put on his pants inside out in his rush to get to the pumper. He'd noticed it only several hours later when he couldn't find his pockets. He was tired of hearing about it.

"You got toothpaste on your chin, loo."

Harris glanced through the back window to make sure Roberts and McCarthy were on the jump seats. "Come on, let's go!"

Jimmy Vernon hit the siren and lights, and the engine jounced out of the barn, turning left on Mass. Ave., then immediately left again onto Glynn. Engine 43 was housed with Ladder Company 20 next to the Maintenance Division and directly behind Department Headquarters on Southampton. Some of the men didn't like being so close to headquarters, but Harris liked it and he had worked hard to get into this particular company. He was thirty-four and had been a lieutenant three years, having passed the exam five years before. He finished buttoning his shirt, then wiped his chin.

"Get some speed up, Jimmy, I want to be first."

The pumper turned left onto Southampton. It was a bright red 1970 Hahn and could pump 1,250 gallons a minute.

Harris had gotten out of bed when Box 1616, the false alarm, was struck five minutes before. Whenever he heard the tappers, he expected to go out, and the 1–6 combination, signifying the South End and hospital area, was enough to make him wide awake. He knew Engines 3 and 7 were still at Box 1616. If Vernon was fast enough, they could be putting water on the fire by the time the next engine arrived.

The district chief's driver came over channel 1: "All out in Box 1616. 710. Companies returning to quarters. We're on our way to Box 1646."

Fire Alarm acknowledged the message, then went on: "Box 1646 is a warehouse fire. Callers report flames showing."

Vernon began hitting the horn. There wasn't much traffic, but they were nearing the entrance to the expressway and cars were waiting to turn. Harris again glanced back at Roberts and McCarthy. Boston firefighters now rode inside on jump seats rather than standing on the back steps of the apparatus. Too many had been knocked off by the stones that some chiefs liked to call Irish confetti.

The pumper was approaching Boston City Hospital. Its flashing lights reflected on the windows and roofs of the cars around them. The height of the cab made the cars seem flat. Harris clipped up his fire coat. If they got there first, it would be his fire.

"I talked to Lou Kinsella this morning." Vernon had to shout over the roar of the engine.

"Yeah, who's that?"

"You know, he's that jake with Engine 14. They'd a fire off Blue Hill this morning, an empty house. A fuckin' chimney fell, injured four guys. Little ten-cent fire."

Harris didn't answer. The pumper turned onto Albany and he was looking for smoke. Anyway, there were more injuries than firemen. Last year more than 50 percent had lost time due to injuries.

There was more traffic on Albany, but the two streams were pulling over, leaving a clear lane like a tunnel down the center of the road. Vernon accelerated through it. The sound of the siren echoed off the buildings of the medical center.

"One jake, Charlie Powers, they figure his shoulder's broke in two-three places . . ."

"There's the smoke. Look at that shit. Come on, move it!"

As they passed the medical center, they saw black smoke rising like a massive black flower over the warehouses to their left. At the sight of the smoke, Harris caught his breath and it seemed that the time since his last fire had been only a long pause.

"I see the box," shouted Vernon.

A tall man with a dog was waving and pointing to the next street: Plympton. Jimmy Vernon braked and swung left, turning in front of the oncoming traffic.

Thick black smoke pushed from a two-story brick warehouse halfway up the block on their right. There were driveways on either side. No more than 15 feet behind it was a huge ramshackle five-story warehouse. If that caught, they could be here for days.

No other apparatus was on the street. "Stop at the building," said Harris. "We'll lay two 2½-inch lines."

As the pumper drew to a halt, Harris saw dark red flames forcing out through the side windows. Attached to the front of the building was a one-story, two-bay garage; left of it was a loading dock with a sliding door, then a small door with a window. The windows on the second floor were intact and showed no fire.

Harris took the microphone. "Engine 43 to Fire Alarm. We've arrived at Box 1646. The building is a two-story brick warehouse, fully involved, with flame showing at the downstairs windows. No life hazard. Unprotected exposures at the rear of the building. On the orders of Lieutenant Paul Harris strike a second alarm."

Harris barely heard the acknowledgment; he was helping Vernon drag 200 feet of 2½-inch line from the hose compartment. On the other side of the pumper McCarthy and Roberts were pulling another 200 feet from the second compartment. Dry, each weighed 232 pounds; filled with water, 650 pounds. Each line had a 1⅛-inch nozzle and could deliver 250 gallons per minute at 50 pounds nozzle pressure. Black smoke mushroomed high over the building.

"What're we going to do, loo," shouted McCarthy, "put this out ourselves?"

Vernon jumped back in the cab and, with McCarthy on the side, laid the lines to the hydrant 100 feet down the street.

Harris felt the heat on his face and neck. "We'll shoot through the window of the front door!" He had to shout over the noise of the fire.

Harris and Roberts left one line for the next arriving company, and began pulling the other toward the door. Although the glass was blown out, they could see no flame. Only the side windows and small broken panes of the garage door showed fire: cherry-red flame and smoke so thick and black that it looked like black drapery forced upward through the wrecked frames.

There were more sirens. Ladder Company 13 was coming down Plympton, followed by Engine 22.

Harris glanced back at his pumper. Vernon, who would work the pump, had connected the soft suction hose to the hydrant, opened the hydrant, and was charging the pump. McCarthy had connected both lines and was running back. His helmet was off and he wiped his face as he ran. His blond hair clung together in damp strands.

Harris left Roberts and ran to the senior man of Ladder 13. "Get that loading dock bay open and vent the roof. We'll start cooling it down, but get that bay open."

Before the man could answer, Harris had returned to take the tip of the 2½-inch line. The senior man—his name was Marino—ordered two of his men to grab the 35-foot ladder and get up to the roof. Then, taking a halligan bar, he got to work on the sliding door of the bay. First, however, he took off his glove and touched the door to see how hot it was.

By now McCarthy was holding the line behind Roberts. Harris shouted back to Jimmy Vernon at the pump, "Open the gate!" On his left he saw three firefighters taking up the other line. They would have to shoot through a side window. Beyond them, coming down Plympton, Harris saw Engine 24, Ladder 4, and the district chief's car.

Then the line began to twist and buck as it was charged with water. Harris lowered the tip. He felt Roberts pressing behind him with his arms around the line. Slowly, Harris shoved the lever forward. There was a high whoosh as the trapped air escaped from the charged line. The water sputtered, then blasted through the tip, crashing into the wire grill of the door, bending it back until it snapped. Harris struggled to steady the stream, pressing down with his arms. He heard a roaring from within the building as the water hit the flame, and the crackling and breaking of thousands of pieces of burning wood. He took a step forward and Roberts and McCarthy jockeyed the line behind him. Water blasted off the bricks back into their faces, bringing some relief from the heat.

To his right Harris saw two firefighters going up a ladder. The senior man from Ladder 13 and another man were still working on the sliding door with their halligan bars. Now another high whoosh to his left as someone cracked the tip of the second 2½-inch line. He heard the roar as water blasted through the side window onto the fire. From the front there was too much smoke to see any red. Harris glanced up again but no flames were visible in the second-story windows.

Shortly, the firefighters on the roof would have chopped a hole, venting the roof and drawing the fire upward. By putting water on the fire first and cooling it, Harris was preventing a back draft when the building was opened and fresh oxygen fed the flames. The main danger was a flashover on the second floor: the area bursting into flame when it received new oxygen and the temperature increased.

There was a crash as the men broke through the sliding door. Black smoke and heavy red flames pushed through the opening, forcing the truckmen away from the building.

"Let's go," shouted Harris. He turned the tip across the front toward the open bay. Water spattered back over the truckmen. Harris, coughing, pushed toward the bay. Roberts and McCarthy fed him line, crouching down behind him.

"Take up on the line!" shouted Harris. At this moment, he felt that he and the two men behind him, plus the line which seemed to fight them, were all one animal. He forced himself forward, keeping the stream on the red that still attempted to shove out through the bay.

They were 5 feet from the building. Crouched down, Harris was level with the loading dock. He kept trying to push forward as Roberts and McCarthy fed him line. Harris looked to see if there was fire on the second floor, but he couldn't tell because of the smoke. Another engine company now had a line to the front door on his left. Harris took another step, lifting the tip so water would crash into the ceiling and spray down onto the flames. There seemed to be less smoke.

"We're going in," he called, "give me more line!" He pushed forward to the loading dock. Roberts stumbled against him. Wrapping his arms around the nozzle, Harris flopped onto his stomach on the loading platform, then got to his knees. His arms ached. If he accidentally let go of the tip, it would whip back around, smashing anything nearby.

"More line!" He pushed forward again. Roberts was also on the dock. Harris forgot about the district chief and who arrived when. He felt the heat scorching his face, the pressure of Roberts against his back. The flames made a noise like a huge blowtorch, and the water smashed and hissed against the ceiling and what appeared to be furniture. Harris couldn't see much. He noticed a burning van to his right and turned the tip toward it. His arms hurt, but this was his fire and he meant to last longer. Actually, he'd been on the tip four minutes. He took another step toward the burning van. It was difficult to breathe. All three men were crouched down, bent nearly double, their arms wrapped around the line. Water smashed off the van and it began to go dark. Water from the other two lines was slowly darkening the other side of the warehouse. Harris began to see the burning furniture more clearly. He turned the tip toward a flaming sofa and it lifted up, fell onto its back. The hot steam from the water burned and stung his face. He took another step into the room. "Give me more line!"

He pulled the tip back and forth: tables, chairs, destroyed couches rose up and crashed over and over in a roar of sparks and steam. Small straight chairs flipped up toward the ceiling; coffee tables, lamps were flung by the weight of the water back into the burning portion of the warehouse. He took another step forward, bending as much as possible to get the cooler air from the floor. All his movements were painful.

Either his arms were growing numb or the nozzle pressure was decreasing. Even the sound of water hitting the furniture seemed diminished. The line felt lighter. "Hey," shouted Mc-

Carthy. Instantly the water stopped; the line went limp in their hands. Harris pulled the lever back and forth but to no effect. By the sound of shouting, he knew the other lines were also dead.

Immediately, the fire sprang forward, sweeping around the three men and behind them to the open bay.

Harris tried to yell, but when he took a breath heat scorched his lungs. They turned and ran for the door. At first Harris clung to the nozzle, then flung it aside. Roberts stumbled in front of him, fell to his knees. Harris stopped to help him, keeping low to the floor with his arm around Roberts's waist. He felt the skin blistering on his face and neck.

As he pulled Roberts toward the door, Harris heard a new crashing noise. He looked up. The ceiling was flaming and something was breaking through it. Harris dragged Roberts toward the door no more than 7 feet away. A burning piece of furniture, a sofa, broke through the ceiling; its cushions falling wrapped in flame. Staring up, Harris had no time to feel alarm and only experienced the beginnings of surprise.

McCarthy tumbled through the bay, fell into the street. Jumping up, he turned, looking for Harris and Roberts. When he saw they weren't coming, he began to go back. Someone grabbed his arm. Men were shouting. There was still no water. McCarthy saw the flaming sofa break through the ceiling, dangle for a second, dropping its burning cushions, then crash downward. Then more: chairs, tables, couches all bright with flame toppling through the hole, sending out showers of sparks, burning embers, swelling the roar of the fire.

Stumbling back, McCarthy saw dark red flames pushing through the second-floor windows. Black smoke billowed toward a cloudless blue sky. The edge of the roof was trimmed with copper, and where the fire crossed the copper, the flames turned green.

6

"It was like a little room. They found it washed up on the shore: half whale and half octopus. And the governor or somebody challenged him to escape from it. A sea monster! And they brought it up to Boston to Keiths Theater and cut open its stomach and bet he couldn't get out if they chained him inside."

.   The man talking was Andrew Pugliese, a twenty-nine-year-old state trooper assigned to the State Fire Marshal's Office. Minutes before, at 7:30, he had arrived at Fire Headquarters as Baxter and Theodore Quaid were getting out of the elevator to go down to the garage. Now all three were on their way to the fire on Plympton Street. Pugliese sat on the edge of the back seat. His voice was high and he spoke quickly.

Baxter drove. Beside him Quaid listened to the radio to learn who'd been killed. All he could tell was they were from Engine 43. Quaid guessed he knew the names of every man in Engine 43.

The car was a red 1974 Chevrolet with a flashing dome light that Pugliese called a gumball. Baxter used the siren only going through intersections. "I never heard of any Keiths Theater. When was this stuff?"

"In 1911. They put chains on Houdini's arms and legs, made

him get into the belly of this monster, then sewed up the stomach with a cable. Then they wrapped the monster with more chains and locked them. A sea monster!"

Baxter punched the siren button on the steering wheel as they approached the entrance to the expressway. "Sixty-five years, how you expect me to remember something that happened sixty-five years ago?" Unbuttoning his collar button, he loosened his narrow red and yellow striped tie.

"I'm not expecting you to remember it, for crissakes, I'm just telling you about it, that's all."

"So why tell me?" Baxter neither liked nor disliked Pugliese. Mostly Baxter didn't like anyone who wasn't a fireman. He couldn't imagine it. Baxter had joined the department in 1946. He was an inspector or private in the Arson Squad. Quaid was a lieutenant.

"I'm telling you because it's interesting. It took Houdini fifteen minutes to get out, and it nearly killed him because they'd poured arsenic in the monster's belly to keep it from rotting. Right here in Boston, so what if it happened sixty-five years ago?"

Although he had been a state policeman for five years, Pugliese had joined the marshal's office only eight months before. He had asked for the transfer and received a two-week course in arson investigation at the academy in Framingham before being posted to Springfield. After six months, he had been transferred to Boston on March 1. Since then he'd spent three or four days a week with the Boston Arson Squad learning how to look at fires. Pugliese was tall and brawny with dark brown curly hair. That morning he wore a light blue summer suit still wrinkled from having spent the winter in a suitcase.

"They still can't reach the bodies," said Quaid as Baxter turned onto Albany by the hospital. "Ceiling must have fallen."

The three men saw smoke ahead to their left. Quaid had switched to channel 2, which was used for communications at the fire scene. The commands were distorted on the car's speaker: an urgent chatter through which Quaid heard the noise of the fire, a small sound like someone clearing his throat over and over.

A third alarm had been struck at 7:05, but Quaid knew little else except that two men had been killed. The district chief had called for the Arson Squad at 7:15. At present there were eleven men in the squad: four teams of two men each who worked 24 hours on and 72 off, and three men in the office during the week for follow-up investigation. They were supposed to be under a captain, but their old captain, Charlie O'Neill, had suddenly retired six weeks before and moved to Tucson. O'Neill had had the reputation of listing more fires as being of accidental or undetermined origin than anyone, and his expensive habits and new cars had given rise to the rumor that he was often paid for this. Quaid knew it was more than a rumor but had tried to live with it. In any case, with O'Neill gone they took their orders from the city fire marshal until a new captain could be appointed.

Quaid usually worked in the office doing follow-up and today, because of Lazard's absence, he was glad of the chance to go out on an initial investigation. He had been with the squad for eleven years, having joined the department in 1948. Several inches under six feet, he was becoming pink and portly as he entered his fifties. He smoked a pipe, and his clothes were spotted with ashes and small burns from his habit of gently blowing into the stem when he was being thoughtful.

"One of those guys is the lieutenant from group two," said Quaid. "I don't know about the other."

"Who's that, Russell?"

"No, it's the young one. Harris."

"The hustler? Poor bastard."

Pugliese knew few firemen and the fact of two of them dead in a fire wasn't real to him. "Say, where's Lazard this morning?"

"Seeing some lawyers," said Quaid, still listening to the radio.

"What's he got?"

Baxter made a snorting noise. "He's got an ex-wife. They just got divorced."

"I thought he did that Friday."

"They were in court Friday," said Quaid, "but he had to finish up some stuff with his lawyer this morning."

"Some guys told me she was fooling around," said Pugliese.

Quaid shook his head. "Don't believe it." Lazard was his best friend, and he had always liked Elizabeth.

"No, these guys swore it was true. She's been seeing an assistant D.A., some guy over at Suffolk County Courthouse. Maybe Lazard can't get it up, you know, that bad leg."

Quaid glanced at Baxter. The inspector had a great loyalty for Lazard and Quaid doubted that Baxter would find the remark forgivable. Baxter was silent for a moment, then said, "Think of those guys running the Marathon. Twenty-six miles in 90-degree heat. Bet there're going to be some thin guys around." He touched his own large stomach thoughtfully. As a firefighter he'd been known as Ruby because of a gold ring with a small ruby he wore on the little finger of his left hand. People who didn't know him assumed it had some sentimental value, but more likely, Quaid had thought, Baxter had put it on in an evil moment, couldn't get it off, and decided to make the best of a bad situation.

Ruby Baxter turned onto Plympton and parked behind the Salvation Army truck where volunteers were passing out coffee to firemen. The street was full of apparatus, smoke, and flashing lights.

"Rocks, bottles, beer cans—you wouldn't believe the shit piled against that filter. Even a shoe. Completely stopped the water. The suction hose was packed with it. Took five minutes to clear it out. Had to come in from hydrants at either end of the block. Not that water would of helped Harris any. Roberts either. Ceiling and furniture fell all over them. Still can't get to them. You can see where they are, under that pile of stuff near the front. Over by those vultures."

District Chief Foster pointed across the street toward the building. The brick walls were standing, but the ceiling and part of the roof had collapsed. The way to the building was a confusion of fire engines and criss-crossing lines. Through the broken windows, Quaid and Pugliese could see flames toward the back. Toward the front was a pile of burned furniture, smoldering upholstery, charred legs of chairs and tables sticking up at random angles.

As close to the building as the heat would allow, a television crew and several photographers tried to get pictures. The photographers would run forward, take shots of the fallen ceiling, then run back. Two firefighters played streams of water over the pile with 1½-inch lines. Whether on purpose or by accident, they kept spattering the photographers, who would shout and cover their cameras with their hands.

"How'd the stuff get in the hydrant?" asked Pugliese.

"Somebody just opened it up and put it in." Foster was a heavy-set man of about fifty-five. He wore a white helmet and white fire coat. Black soot smeared his face and his nose was running. "Then it piled up against the filter in the pumper until the water stopped. Must of taken some time. Maybe somebody saw them."

Pugliese was balancing on a 4-inch supply line. When they had arrived, Quaid and Baxter took boots, fire coats, and helmets from the trunk of the red Chevrolet. Pugliese had no boots and the street was covered with an inch of water. He felt his socks, wet and squishy, bunching between his toes. Although he was listening to Foster, most of his attention was on the activity around the burning building.

Scattered around three sides of the warehouse were fifteen pieces of apparatus: pumpers, ladder trucks, rescue, and a white emergency ambulance with a horizontal orange stripe on each side. The bucket of Aerial Tower 1 reared high over the building, sending a thick stream of water onto the fire from the 3-inch line attached to its turret nozzle. To the left of the building, the Squirt, a nozzle attached to an articulated boom on the back of Engine 26, reached over the roof like a white skeletal arm. About forty firemen manning a dozen 2½-inch lines surrounded the building, moving forward or back, spraying water in high arcs or directly at the remaining flame. Because of the weakened walls, no one could enter the building. There was constant noise: the motors and generators of the apparatus, the rush of water, the static and voices over the radios, people shouting, officers giving commands, the fire itself: the sound of wind in a narrow space, a flapping sound, the breaking of millions of small sticks. Across the street, Foster, Quaid, and Pugliese stood close together and had to shout to be heard.

"Should never of gone in," said Foster, "but there was no fire showing upstairs so he must of thought it was okay. There had to be some accelerant up there and it ignited when they cracked the building. Soaked into the floors. Shit, lucky even McCarthy got out. Maybe even Harris would of made it if he hadn't stopped to help Roberts."

"What about sprinklers?" asked Quaid.

"They weren't working. I don't know why."

"You know who owns the building?"

Foster shook his head.

"What about alarm systems or guards?" Quaid unsnapped several of the hooks on his coat. His white shirt was soaked with sweat and he envied Pugliese his summer suit.

"Can't help you there either. We have the guy who pulled the hook. He's standing by Ladder 4, the older guy with the dog."

Quaid saw a man of about fifty with a bulldog on a short leash. The dog was growling at the people around him. At least a hundred bystanders lined the street. They showed no emotion and simply appeared to be waiting. A dozen kids ran through the water or tried to climb onto the apparatus. Police, newsmen, ambulance attendants, two men in black coats from Boston Gas, free-lance photographers—Quaid noticed the captain from the public information office instructing a couple of reporters. The three chaplains in their white coats walked around talking to firemen. Quaid was slightly amused by a system that called the Jewish and Protestant chaplains on the second alarm, and the Catholic chaplain on the third, when the majority of firemen were Catholic.

"Watch the guy with the dog, will you, Andy?" asked Quaid. He turned back to Foster. "What about windows and doors?"

"They had to force the front doors. The windows were all blown but they had steel grates. We took off a few. Must of poured a shitload of stuff in there for it to spread so fast. The back door, I don't know. Ladder 4 was back there. Better ask their senior man, that'd be Martinelli."

Baxter was just returning with McCarthy. Quaid asked him to find Martinelli. Baxter took a handkerchief from his pocket, wiped his face, then turned back toward the warehouse. Although a fat man, he walked lightly on the balls of his feet. The apparatus was parked at all different angles, making it impossible to walk anywhere in a straight line.

Quaid felt hot and dissatisfied. More than the noise and smells of the fire: the smoke, the odor of oil and diesel fuel, wet ashes and steam, ozone from the generators; beyond the general confusion was the confusion of the season. The 80-degree heat disturbed the balance of the morning, and this disturbance seemed duplicated in the events and people around him. Quaid certainly thought he saw it in McCarthy, weighted down by his friends' deaths and his own escape. Dirt and soot streaked his face, darkening the lines on his forehead and around his mouth and eyes. McCarthy was about thirty-five, but these marks made him seem like an actor made up to portray grief and old age. He leaned against Engine 43 and watched the photographers running up and taking pictures of the fallen ceiling and mound of debris.

"How much of the building was burning when you got here?" asked Quaid.

"Everything, the whole downstairs."

"Tell me about it."

"What's to say? The downstairs was fully involved. There's a truck in the garage, one of those carryvans. Its gas tank had blown. We didn't think there was any fire upstairs. The loo, I mean Harris, he was in a real hurry . . ." McCarthy glanced away toward the vacant lots where two groups of kids were throwing dirt clods at each other.

"Was there anyone around when you got here?"

"No. Well, there was an old guy by the box, and maybe some kids."

"Would you recognize the kids?"

"No."

"What was in the building?"

"What d'you mean?"

"The furniture. Was it old, new, was there a lot of it?"

"Furniture, that's all. Building was packed with it. Couldn't tell if it was old or new, I mean it was all burning. We were really knocking it down at first. Then nothing. The water just stopped. And the fire, it was climbing all over us . . "

"How'd you get in?"

"Some jakes from Ladder 13 forced the door."

After sending McCarthy back to his company, Quaid tried to imagine manning a line in the midst of a fire, then having the water stop. Then he tried to imagine the motivation of whoever had filled the hydrant with junk. Foster had gone off to talk to the Division 1 deputy chief. To Quaid's left, Pugliese stood near the tall man with the dog. Occasionally they eyed each other, then looked away. Sloshing across the street toward Quaid were Baxter and a young firefighter named Higgins. Over the years, Quaid had been active on the building committee at Florian Hall, the blood bank, and the credit union. Of the 2,000 department personnel, he guessed he knew the names of 90 percent.

He shook hands with Higgins, then turned to Baxter. "Check the people in these other buildings and see who owns or rents this place. Also, maybe there's a watchman or guard."

Baxter nodded. He had a pale, doughy face that looked even paler under his black helmet. "I've been going over the windows. It looks like all the grates were originally secure."

As Baxter left again, Quaid asked Higgins: "You opened that back door?"

"Kicked it in."

"Was it locked?"

"Can't help you there. I just kicked and jumped back."

"You didn't try the knob?"

"No, we saw red through the window so I figured the door'd be hot."

"Could you see anything in the room?"

"Lotta black smoke. Just seemed like a little room, maybe an office or something."

People began shouting. There was a rumbling noise from the warehouse as the back wall slowly gave way and toppled into the building, sending up a mass of sparks and smoke. Two free-lance photographers ran back toward the crash.

To Quaid the arson was obvious: the rapid spread, plus the red flame and black smoke, indicated the presence of gas or kerosene. But the who or why of it, Quaid hardly thought about. Statistically, there was one chance out of a hundred that whoever burned the warehouse would be convicted. Actually it was more like one out of four hundred. The previous year there had been about 25,000 fires in Boston. Although Quaid couldn't prove it, he strongly suspected that half were arson. Of those fires, about 6,500 involved automobiles or trucks and 99 percent of those were certainly arson. Conservatively, he guessed there had been 12,000 incidents of arson. During the year, there had been 92 arrests and 29 convictions. Some of those arrested would come to court this year, but some of the convictions had been held over from the year before. With 29 convictions out of 12,000 incidents of arson, it didn't pay for Quaid to measure his success by the number of arrests or even to worry if an arrest would be made.

Raymond Farkus had been about to go home. If the firemen weren't interested in what he had seen, he certainly wasn't going to insist they listen. Besides, Hapgood was behaving badly, snapping and growling at anyone who came near. Hapgood hated excitement: the enemy of sleep.

But now another fireman and the man who had been staring at him were approaching. The fireman was about his own age and had a pleasant, responsible face. His companion looked definitely suspicious. As if I'd started the fire, thought Farkus. He had thick curly brown hair and Farkus suspected it extended over most of his body. He could see tufts of it poking above the man's necktie.

"You turned in the alarm?" asked the fireman.

Farkus said he had and got a better grip on Hapgood's leash. The dog was beginning to pull. The fireman introduced himself as Theodore Quaid with the Arson Squad. Farkus knew he was with the Arson Squad since it was written in white letters on the shield of his helmet.

"When did you first see the fire?" asked Quaid.

"It must have been about quarter to seven. I was walking my dog and, well, this is my dog . . ." Farkus wore a yellow shirt and brown pants. They seemed several sizes too large and hung like drapery from his body.

"Could you tell me where you were when you first saw the fire? Let's walk over there."

The three men walked into the vacant lot. Hapgood kept pulling, trying to investigate Quaid's trousers. Farkus yanked the leash until the dog made a choking noise. "This is where I was." They were a hundred yards from the building, a little northwest of it.

"Where was the fire when you first saw it?"

"At the back of the building."

"You're sure?"

"Yes, that area was in shadow and I could see the flames in that back window near where those firemen are standing. Then there was an explosion."

"What kind of explosion?"

"I don't know, a sort of boom. Then there was more. There might have been a dozen."

Quaid made notes on a water-spotted pad. "Are you positive about the explosions?"

"At least a dozen, that's when I ran for the alarm box."

"Was there anyone else around?"

"No, no one."

"Did you stop and look?"

Farkus had gotten gravel in his slipper and was trying to rub his foot against his pant leg without falling. "Well, I didn't make a search, but Hapgood, that's my dog, he's quite picky and choosy and would have barked if he'd seen anyone."

Quaid looked at the dog thoughtfully. "How did you first happen to notice the fire?"

"The gunshot."

"The what?"

"There was a gunshot or what sounded like a gunshot and I looked over and in a moment I saw flames."

33

"What kind of gunshot?"

"I don't know, just a gunshot or maybe a large firecracker, like a cherry bomb."

"Could it have been a backfire?"

"No, there weren't any cars around."

"So first there was this gunshot, then you saw flames, then there was a series of explosions. Is that correct?"

"Yes, except it all happened quite fast."

"What do you think caused the fire?"

"I don't know. If it was a gunshot, then maybe the bullet hit something, you know, something explosive. But I couldn't help thinking it was the firemen who caused the fire."

"Oh?"

"Yes, you see that fire station over on Harrison? Sometimes the firemen give Hapgood food, but, well, just before the fire all the firemen jumped in their trucks and drove away. They drove away and the fire started. It's much closer to the station from here than to the alarm box. If they hadn't driven away, I would have gone there. So I can't help thinking, you know, that they were sort of responsible."

"How soon before the gunshot did the apparatus leave?"

"No more than a minute."

Quaid took his tobacco pouch from his pocket and began filling his pipe. When he spoke again, it was to ask Farkus where he lived, where he worked, and to take him back over the questions to see if he had anything further to add. But he didn't and shortly Quaid told him to go.

Quaid and Pugliese had begun to walk back when Farkus called after them: "Tell me, did the water stop because those children were playing in it?"

"What do you mean?" asked Quaid.

"Well, over the weekend some children turned on that hydrant about four times. The police came and at last I believe they made some arrests. The landlord in a building down the block called them. He said it lowered the water pressure and put all our buildings in danger, and I was wondering if it was low water pressure that made the water stop."

Quaid walked back to Farkus. His fire coat hung open and flapped against his legs. "Could you recognize any of those kids? Any of the ones around here now?"

About thirty children were watching the fire, running around and being minor nuisances. Farkus made an uncertain gesture with his hands. "No, I mean they were just kids. I didn't really pay attention. I thought they were from the projects. Some were colored. Actually, it was too far to see."

"What's the name of the landlord?"

"His name's Schacter and he owns an apartment building on Canton. You can see it from here." Farkus pointed. "That next to last one. He must have watched those kids all weekend. You think that caused the water to stop?"

"I don't know. We'll talk to him."

Walking back with Quaid, Pugliese said, "I thought the rocks stopped the water."

"Who put them there? Go find Ruby. We should talk to that landlord and I want to talk to these kids before they disappear."

Quaid crossed the street, pausing now and then to speak to a fireman. Several engine companies were rolling up and repacking hose, getting ready to leave, although half a dozen lines were still pouring water into the building. Usually after a fire, there was a lot of joking and banter. This morning Quaid was aware of firemen talking quietly in small groups: clusters of black coats and helmets.

Five men were digging into the pile of debris at the front of the warehouse. Quaid watched, then decided he had no wish to see the remains of Harris and Roberts pulled from the wreckage as photographers scrambled for good shots.

Fred Merrick, the department photographer, was crossing the street. Quaid called to him, "I want some pictures of the back."

Merrick also wore a black fire coat, helmet, and boots. He was a stocky man in his forties and had a steel pin in each ankle from when he had once jumped from a third-story window.

"That's a shame about Harris and Roberts."

Quaid agreed. They talked about it a little as they walked, not really knowing what to say, but feeling it necessary to speak. Whenever he thought about the deaths, Quaid felt a kind of hatred, but he wasn't even sure for what.

The rear wall of the warehouse had collapsed inward. It seemed to Quaid that if the fire had started in a back room, then any evidence was now covered by the ceiling and wall. This could be a piece of good luck since the debris might have protected it from the force of the water.

Quaid stopped to pick up a piece of window glass. It was an irregular, blocky-shaped piece about the size of his palm, and free of any carbon stains or soot. To Quaid it showed the intensity of the heat and meant the heat had broken the window from one to five minutes after the start of the fire, before carbon stains had a chance to form. All this indicated the presence of an accelerant. If the case ever got to court, they would first have to prove there had been a fire. Then the arson would have to be shown, and some of this glass would be submitted as evidence.

It was hotter behind the building and the smells of smoke and wet ash were abrasive. There was no sign of a back door. Quaid guessed it was under the debris. Even if entirely burned that wouldn't matter. Quaid had decided to sift the rear portion of the warehouse and eventually the locks would be found.

It was this poking around that Quaid liked best. He liked being alone in a burned building and bit by bit putting it back together in his mind, discovering the fire pattern and tracing it back to the point of the first spark.

When he was first learning about arson, one of Quaid's heroes had been an insurance investigator who'd had a case involving a burned clothing factory. Although there was no evidence of arson, the investigator doubted the inventory list given to him by the owner. He took a description of the clothing to a research chemist and learned that a certain type of button could not have burned. According to the inventory, there ought to have been thousands of these buttons buried in the debris.

The investigator sifted the entire factory through a screen. It took weeks but not a single button was found. Faced with this evidence, the factory owner confessed he had removed the stock, started the fire, and submitted a false insurance claim.

Quaid was thinking about sifting the warehouse when Ruby Baxter returned with Pugliese. "The building's owned by some realty company," said Baxter. "I don't have the name yet. But the guy that rents it is named Trieger, Howard Trieger. He owns a furniture leasing business and has a showroom downtown."

7

The office was 15 by 20 feet, smelled of wet ashes, and all four windows were smashed. Covering the floor was a water-soaked blue rug littered with papers, broken furniture, and the wreckage of a collection of tennis trophies: miniature arms and legs, heads, tiny racquets. In the corner opposite the doorway leading downstairs, a clothing rack lay twisted out of shape, surrounded by ashes and charred pieces of linen and silk. The room felt hot and steamy. It was 7 o'clock, half an hour after sunset, and although nearly dark there was still light enough to show the pictures of brides in their wedding dresses in rows on the side walls: 8-by-10 color photographs in cheap metal frames. There were fifty and in each frame the glass had been broken.

Between two windows stood a desk covered with account books and charred papers. Francis Lazard, wearing a black fire coat, boots, and a black helmet with the words Arson Squad written on the shield, leaned over the desk reading the papers by the light of a flashlight. Most contained columns of figures, and at the top of each was written "John's Bridal Boutique" in ornate script. In Lazard's right hand was a gray aluminum cane with a black rubber tip known in the department as "Lazard's working stick."

Although he was ostensibly reading the papers, Lazard hardly thought of them. He knew they would show a story of increasing debts and decreasing sales, until the owner, John Waters, tried to cut his losses with a fire that hadn't turned out as planned. Lazard could think of many such fires, and once he'd discovered the papers he could guess Waters's financial troubles, what he would say in his own reports, and how the case would end with the insurance company refusing to pay anything to John Waters's widow or heirs. This is not to say that Lazard was bored or in any way dissatisfied. Actually it was in surroundings such as these that he felt most comfortable. But because he could anticipate his actions in regard to this fire, he worked almost mechanically.

Instead of thinking of Waters, Lazard thought of Howard Trieger, whose burning warehouse had caused the deaths of two firemen that morning. It had taken him a short time to realize that he knew Trieger, although he hadn't seen him now for seven years. Trieger's wife, Norma, was Lazard's cousin. When Lazard moved to Boston in 1959, Norma was the only person he had known, apart from his wife's friends and family met at his own wedding a month before. Trieger and Norma had been married a week earlier. It created a kind of bond. Occasionally, he and Trieger had gone to Red Sox games together. Then their lives grew more complicated and they more separate until at last contact had been broken.

He hadn't known Trieger was in the furniture leasing business. When Lazard first knew him, he was assistant manager of a Woolworths in Central Square in Cambridge. At the time, Lazard had been a firefighter assigned to Engine 24 in North Dorchester. It surprised him that someone could go so completely out of his life. And since the death of his mother several years before, he had stopped hearing news of his cousin's family.

Lazard hadn't seen Trieger yet. Quaid had tried to contact him that morning, but learned Trieger and his family had spent the weekend at their cabin on Lake Sunapee in New Hampshire. The cabin had no telephone and Quaid called the New Hampshire State Police, to ask them to tell Trieger about the fire. Although Trieger had returned that afternoon, Lazard had been too busy to talk to him.

Lazard hadn't arrived at the warehouse until noon. Then, shortly after three, he and Baxter were called to a fire at an apartment house in Jamaica Plain. From there they went to a garage fire in Brighton. The Arson Squad covered all fires of a suspicious or undetermined origin, all multiple alarms, all fires involving a violation of the law or where people were killed or injured. Lazard and Baxter had returned to their office at six and spent nearly an hour writing up reports before being called to John's Bridal Boutique on Brookline Avenue.

Lazard limped to a file cabinet to the left of the desk. He had needed a cane ever since his leg had been badly injured in a fire seven years before. At first the doctors had said the cane would be temporary, but muscles and tendons had been permanently damaged, and now Lazard accepted the fact that he would always need it, that without it he would fall on his face.

As Lazard looked through the papers scattered on the floor around the file cabinet, he wondered how much Trieger had changed. He tried to remember what they had done together: a couple of picnics, a weekend on Cape Cod, dinners at Trieger's apartment in Brookline. Norma enjoyed bridge and they played a few times, even though Elizabeth disliked card games.

It was unsettling to remember a time when he had been happy with his wife. Friday in court had been the first time he had seen her in six months. He'd been struck by how attractive she was: how she looked like someone he would like to talk to. He had thought of himself as not missing her, except sometimes missing her body next to him in bed or missing someone to help with the housework. They had been married seventeen years and had no children. They hadn't grown antagonistic, simply indifferent, especially after Lazard's accident when it became obvious that his active career as a fireman was over and he began to turn inward. Sometimes he suspected her of being involved with another man, although he had no evidence. He didn't mind, didn't really care. But he was surprised by the simplicity of the divorce, like a thread being clipped. He expected no regrets, but now, although not exactly regretful, he didn't care to remember a time when he had been in love. Elizabeth's brown hair had nearly reached her waist. Usually she wore it piled on her head in an untidy bun. In court, the first thing Lazard noticed was it had been cut short.

Someone began climbing the stairs, and a light bobbed up out of the dark doorway. "You almost finished here?" asked Baxter.

"Almost. Where's Merrick, we need some pictures."

As Baxter entered, Lazard's light shone on his black fire coat. With his round unlined face and round body, Baxter looked like an overgrown six-year-old in costume. His boots made a squishing noise on the wet rug.

"He's on his way. Chief says people are talking about a bomb. Wants to know if he should call the state police."

"Gasoline vapor. What's the damage downstairs?" The business was in a small two-story building with the showroom on the first floor.

"Some water through the ceiling. Also a lotta mannequins and stuff got knocked over. You shoulda seen those guys being careful of those dummies in wedding dresses. By the way, they rang the 1015 on Harris and Roberts. The funeral's going to be Friday out of Holy Name Cathedral. We'll be working then."

Lazard didn't say anything. He was writing notes on his pad. By now the office was completely dark except for the two flashlights. The rotating red light of a pumper parked in back reflected dimly off the walls and the broken glass over the photographs of the brides. Baxter heard firefighters joking with each other as they put away their lines. A warm breeze blew through the window.

"We going to eat when we leave here?" asked Baxter.

"I want to see Trieger. We'll grab a sandwich on the way."

Baxter disliked grabbing sandwiches. "Can't he wait a bit? There's a delicatessen on Comm. Ave."

"Don't they have sandwiches?"

"Yeah, well, I don't feel I've really eaten unless I sit down to do it."

Lazard's flashlight illuminated the lower parts of his face, putting the upper parts in shadow and making it appear lean and cadaverous. It was a thin face with a high round forehead, a long straight nose, and a small chin: a thin balloon, narrow at the bottom, then expanding. He had light blue eyes and the circles under them seemed huge in the shadow.

"We have to go easy with this one, Ruby."

"The warehouse?"

"Harris had a lot of friends. We're not working for O'Neill anymore. This fire's getting a lot of attention."

Their old captain, Charlie O'Neill, had treated all cases the same, but Flanagan, the City Fire Marshal, had a great fear of politics and newspapers. In the six weeks since O'Neill's departure, Flanagan had been in charge of the Arson Squad, and often it seemed the attention given to a case depended on the publicity it received.

"You think there'll be overtime?" asked Baxter.

"No. Maybe they'll bring in Cassidy and keep Teddy working." Warren Cassidy was an inspector who worked in the office with Quaid and went out on follow-up investigations. "Anyway," said Lazard, "they'll keep us working as long as it stays in the papers."

"Least O'Neill didn't care about what some reporter said."

"O'Neill took bribes."

Baxter took off his helmet, looked in it, then put it back on. "Maybe now and then he took a little money on a case he could never get to court anyway. What difference did it make?"

Lazard didn't answer. He and Baxter had often had this conversation. Not only was Lazard sick of talking about it, but he had sworn to himself that he wouldn't mention it again.

"Well," said Baxter, "I'll see if Merrick's turned up." He started for the door. "By the way, I found another container of gasoline downstairs. I'll keep it for the insurance company. How much you think he poured in here?"

"Maybe eight gallons."

"He must of really flown." Baxter paused in the doorway, a black shape in the dark. "You see any of that Marathon on the news? It was 100 degrees out where they started. They had guys soaking down the runners with hoses. An American won it, some college kid. Least he was white. Two fuckin' hours and twenty minutes. Sometimes it takes me that long just to catch a cab."

Lazard returned to the desk to continue sorting through the papers. A combination of Marathon fans and the Patriots' Day parade had completely snarled Boston traffic that morning. Lazard had left his lawyer's office at eleven and it took him another hour to reach the Plympton Street warehouse. He disliked missing the beginning of an investigation. Although he trusted Quaid, it still gave Lazard an unsettled, incomplete feeling.

Together they had looked for the landlord who had complained about the kids opening the hydrant. They were told he was out of town and wouldn't be back until Tuesday. Pugliese had been chasing around after neighborhood kids. Most wouldn't talk to him. Earlier, however, Pugliese had discovered the name and home address of the private guard employed to watch several of the warehouses around Plympton. His name was Frank Toomey and he lived in South Boston. About one that afternoon, Lazard and Baxter had driven over to talk to him.

Toomey had worked the previous night and was still asleep. His wife went to wake him. In a few minutes he appeared in a brown bathrobe decorated with pictures of circus animals: elephants dancing, seals balancing balls. Toomey was a large man of fifty with a florid face and sad blue eyes.

"So they burned it after all. I figured that was a lotta crap."

"What d'you mean?" Lazard had asked.

"That extortion thing. I don't know much about it." Toomey yawned and scratched his head. "The cops said this guy Trieger got some letter. So they hung around five or six weeks but nothing happened."

"How'd they hang around?"

"Patrolled. They'd come down Plympton about six times a night. Kept me on my toes."

"How many times you check the door last night?" asked Lazard. They sat in Toomey's small living room. On every surface were ceramic souvenirs from Atlantic City, the White Mountains, Historic Quebec.

"About ten times. Believe me, tight as a drum."

"Is there an alarm in the building?" asked Baxter.

"Yeah. You think someone broke in there? No way."

"Where are you when you're not patrolling?"

"Either in my car or in that three-story warehouse up the street. I gotta little office in there."

Lazard guessed that Toomey was lazy, untruthful, and probably had this job after a long history of losing slightly better jobs. "What time do you eat?" he asked.

"Different time each night."

"You go out?"

"Mostly. There's a diner on Mass. Ave."

"And you go at different times?"

"Different time each night, I make a point of that. You think anything was took from there?"

"What was the last time you checked the doors?"

"About 6:30, just before I got off."

"And they were locked?"

"Like I say, tight as a drum."

"Who owns the building?"

"Some realty company. Mass. Mutual or Municipal. Something like that. Now there's something for you. I heard the president or someone killed himself Friday. That takes guts. If I was gonna put a bullet in my head, I sure wouldn't do it on Good Friday."

"Who told you this?"

"Same company owns the building where I have my office. Foreman told me. Maybe it was a clerk that shot himself. I don't know, clerk or president, Good Friday's still Good Friday."

Before leaving, Lazard asked for the name of the diner where Toomey usually ate. It was only a block from Fire Headquarters. They drove over and got the phone number of the night waitress. She had no trouble remembering Toomey.

"You mean that fat red-headed guard? He's in there every night from three to quarter to four. You could set your watch by him."

Lazard had just finished with the papers on the desk when he heard Baxter returning with Merrick.

"The chief's left," said Merrick. "You got much here?"

"No, get some shots of the desk and file cabinet. You develop the pictures of the Plympton Street fire?"

"I been running all day." Merrick carried a large Crown Graphic with a flash attachment. He took three pictures of the desk and two of the file cabinet while Lazard and Baxter waited.

"Anything else?"

"Take a shot of the light switch by the door."

Merrick took the picture. "How come you want the switch?"

"That's how he did it," said Baxter.

"What d'you mean?"

"He poured gasoline over the floor, then planned to ignite it with a string of rags from downstairs. When he left the room, he flicked the switch. Caused enough of a spark to ignite the vapor. That's how I like to catch these guys. No court time either. Fuckin' blew his ass downstairs. Neck broke."

Lazard had been reading a pamphlet on the dimensions of fire-hose-coupling screw threads when the tappers began to ring for what he ever afterward thought of as his last fire. Although he had been a lieutenant for less than two years, he was already preparing for the captain's exam and had begun his assault on the thousands of pages he would need to know by heart.

He had been sitting at the wooden desk in the officers' quarters of Engine 21, which was housed with the Second Division's Lighting Plant on Columbia Road in North Dorchester. It was 2 A.M. Thursday morning March 6 and Engine 21 had already been out twice that night on false alarms. The bells rang 1-2-3, 1, 1-2, 1-2-3-4-5-6: Box 3126, Richfield Street and Puritan Avenue. Even before the beginning of the last sequence, Lazard had pushed back his chair, knocking over the gooseneck lamp, and had run for the pole.

"We're going out," he shouted. As he hit the pole, he saw the lights flick on in the dormitory to his left. His hands had begun to sweat and as he slid down the pole they stuck and squeaked against the shiny brass.

Bells were ringing downstairs and Dave Peterson on watch announced over the loudspeakers: "Engine 21 going out."

Lazard was into his boots and fire coat before the first of his men had started down the pole. He ran to the driver's door of the fire engine, jumped in the cab, and began pumping the gas as he turned the key. It was a cold night, only a few degrees above zero, and he didn't want to waste the additional seconds it would take Harry Dwyer, his driver, to warm the engine.

Lazard was just revving the engine when Dwyer appeared at the door. "You goin' out by yourself, loo?"

Lazard grinned and slid over. "Figured you were havin' a wet-dream, Harry. Let's go." Even after nearly ten years in the department and thousands of false alarms, he still felt excited each time he left the barn. Looking out the back window, he saw Mike Felsch and Petey McQuire climbing onto their jump seats and clipping up their black coats. McQuire gave him a thumbs up.

The overhead doors were opened and the pumper, a 1968 Ward LaFrance capable of pumping 1,250 gallons per minute, pulled out and turned south on Columbia Road. Dwyer hit the horn and siren. Covering the road were large patches of ice and packed-down snow left from the February northeasters that had dumped more than fifty inches of snow on the Boston area. Along the curbs were shoulder-high piles of snow pushed there by the plows.

"Come on, Harry, give it some gas. Let's see if you can beat twenty-four this time. Shit, we're even closer to the box then they are."

Engine 24 had been first to both the false alarms that night. In fact, it was often first. Lazard blamed this not so much on the superior skill of Engine 24, but on the slowness of his own men. Although he joked with them and cared about them, the three men presently under Lazard remained skeptical. For one thing, he had been with Engine 21 less than a year; for another, he was an outsider, meaning not from Boston. Already one man had transferred and another—Felsch—had said he wanted to follow his old lieutenant to Engine 52.

Lazard also knew they thought he took too many chances and that made him angry. It was their business to take chances. But a month ago the fourth man under him, Jimmy DeRoche, had been seriously burned when they had pushed too fast into a blazing clothing store and the fire suddenly swept around them as they waited for water. Lazard felt the other men blamed him for this and that too made him angry. He wanted the best pumper in the city and what he saw as the excessive caution of his men was like a weight attached to his own eagerness and ambition.

"I'll betcha five bucks it's another 710," said Dwyer.

"So what?" said Lazard. "We still have to get there, false alarm or not."

"Hey, loo, you keep this up and I bet they make you commissioner next year. Commissioner, shit, I bet they make you the fuckin' mayor."

As it turned out, they weren't first or even second. Just as they had nearly reached Richfield Street, an old green Chevy slid toward them sideways across the ice out of the intersection at Hamilton.

"Jesus, Dwyer, watch out!"

Dwyer braked and swerved left, but then he too slid on the ice and the huge fire engine smashed through the piles of snow at the curb, knocked down a stop sign and bumped up against the brick wall of a hardware store.

The snow absorbed much of the impact, but Lazard had still been thrown off his seat. "See if you can back it up," he shouted.

"McQuire was knocked off."

Lazard was out of the cab and running back toward McQuire, who was limping toward him. The freezing air made Lazard catch his breath. The old Chevy had slid into some parked cars and the driver, a young black man, was standing by his crumpled right fender shaking his head.

"Just fell off, loo. Twisted my ankle. I'll be fine in a minute." McQuire was barely twenty-two and the man in the company whom Lazard liked best.

"You sure?"

McQuire nodded, although he was clearly in pain. He held his helmet in his left hand and his red hair stood up in spikes.

"Let's go then." Lazard helped McQuire back to the pumper, then jumped into the cab. "For crissakes, Harry, I told you to back it up."

"What about the guy in the Chevy?"

"Call it in. Otherwise fuck him. Now get moving, will you."

At first the wheels only spun against the ice, then slowly the fire engine pulled away from the wall. A few bricks fell to the sidewalk. The pumper backed around, then continued down Columbia Road. There was no other traffic. As they accelerated past the young black man with horn and siren blaring, he gave them the finger.

Dwyer reported the accident over the radio to Fire Alarm and the operator said he'd pass it along to the cops.

Just as Dwyer signed off, the voice of the district chief's driver came over the radio. "Box 3126. Fire showing. It's an old three-decker. Exposures on both sides with life hazard. Strike a second alarm."

"Son of a bitch," said Lazard. He began rolling the tops of his boots up over his knees.

"You know, loo, you're lucky you didn't go through the windshield back there."

"Sure, sure," said Lazard. Later he realized it would have been fortunate if he had.

8

"People come into the area for a short time. They rent a place. Why drag along a whole truckload of furniture? So they lease it from me. They like it. It's a change in their lives."

Howard Trieger paused in the doorway, rubbing the back of his neck, then continued to the kitchen to see if the coffee was ready. Lazard sat in a corner of a brown couch with his note pad. Baxter was by the fireplace in a mustard-colored reclining chair which he kept trying to adjust by heaving himself back, then yanking himself forward when he went back too far. It was a comfortable, well-furnished room with nothing very extravagant except a color television and stereo combination along one wall. Over the couch was a framed photograph of a covered bridge, while on the mantel were ten photographs of two girls at different ages; the most recent showing them about twelve and thirteen. The windows were open and through them came the sounds of boys playing basketball in a lighted driveway next door.

It was 8:30, and Baxter and Lazard had arrived a few minutes before. Trieger had taken Lazard's arm as if he were an old friend. He hadn't aged much in seven years and certainly didn't look forty-two. He was slightly over six feet and looked muscular under his

47

gray sweatshirt and khaki pants. Lazard had noticed several squash racquets in the front hall.

"So how long you been in arson?" Trieger called. His voice was eager and friendly, as it had always been, and it reminded Lazard what he himself had been like as a young firefighter with all his career before him.

"About six years," Lazard answered.

"Like it?"

"Well enough."

"Why'd you switch?"

"It was time to do something else." As if he'd had any choice, Lazard thought.

"Boy, I thought you'd stay in one of those firehouses forever." Trieger reentered the room carrying a tray with three mugs and a plate heaped with white cake. "Thought you really liked that. Got any more medals?"

"No." Lazard had received the Walter Scott Medal of Valor in 1965 for getting four children out of a burning house.

"How's Elizabeth?"

"Okay." It made Lazard uncomfortable to have his life dragged out in front of Baxter, who knew nothing about him, even though Lazard considered Baxter a friend.

"Say hello to her for me, will you? Try some of this cake. Norma made it this morning. She had a meeting at the school tonight. Damn, she'll be sorry she missed you, Frank."

"How's she been?"

"Pretty good. You know her mother died last year?"

"No, I'm sorry." Lazard sipped his coffee. He remembered Norma's mother as a heavy-set farm woman in a cotton print dress.

"And your leg," said Trieger, "did you hurt that working?" He seemed embarrassed at his question.

"That's right, it was an accident." Lazard touched his right leg as if surprised by its presence. "About seven years ago . . . How long you been leasing furniture?"

"I started in 'sixty-nine. I'd buy directly from the manufacturer, lease it, then sell it used. Right away, I had all the business I could handle. These big companies—Gillette, Polaroid, Raytheon, even the universities—they'd send people to me. They'd have someone coming in for six months or a year. What could he do? People don't like moving all the time."

48

Trieger's face grew animated. It was a slightly rectangular face with a straight nose, brown eyes, and tanned from being in the sun. His thinning brown hair lay flat across his head. He stood between Lazard and Baxter, and as he talked he held out his hands, palms up, as if expecting someone to toss him a ball.

"How much to rent a chair like this?" asked Baxter. He had succeeded in getting the recliner halfway back. His feet were up and he had a piece of cake in one hand and coffee in the other. White crumbs dotted his dark green suit coat. He looked like a fat boy enjoying an after-school snack.

"We usually just lease whole rooms. For instance, a bedroom set could run between $45 and $75 a month. Living room furniture as little as $25."

"How much inventory is out at any one time?" asked Lazard.

"About a third to half."

"How much was at the warehouse?" Lazard wanted a cigarette but he hadn't brought any. He was trying to cut down, not for reasons of health but because he disliked being dependent on a physical pleasure.

"I'm not sure, but it was pretty full. The books are at the showroom downtown."

"You keep much furniture in the showroom?"

"About ten different sets. There's not a lot of room. You know where it is? On School Street, just down from Old City Hall."

"You been over to the warehouse?" asked Baxter.

Trieger sat down in a bentwood rocker across from Lazard, then leaned forward with his hands on his knees. "I drove by this afternoon. I guess I don't want to think about it. I mean, you build something up . . . It was terrible."

"You got full insurance?"

"Yes."

"What else was at the warehouse?" asked Lazard.

"There was a shop for repairs, also a van."

"How many people worked there?"

"Three."

"Did they have keys?"

"Two of them, yes."

Lazard pushed himself up and limped over to Trieger, who glanced at his leg, then looked away. Lazard gave him a pencil and a piece of paper from his pad. "Write down the names of your employees and put checks next to the ones who have keys or access to keys. And let me have the name of your insurance agent."

Lazard returned to the couch. His aluminum cane was smudged with black soot from the bridal boutique fire. Baxter sat with his hands folded across his stomach staring at Trieger. Lazard glanced around the room. The wallpaper had a pattern of blue flowers and yellow vases. Each strip was matched perfectly to the one next to it.

"Here's the list." Trieger handed it to Lazard. "You can get the addresses from my office." There were seven names besides the insurance agent.

"What about this extortion business?" asked Lazard. Finishing his coffee, he put the mug on the floor. He hadn't eaten any cake.

"Six weeks ago I got a letter demanding $5,000 or my business would be burned."

"You have the letter?"

"I took it to the police."

"Who'd you talk to?"

"Lieutenant Natale in the intelligence section. The letter said I wasn't to call the police. What choice did I have? Natale said to contact him if I heard any more, but I didn't, I mean I heard nothing. He called me some and they increased patrols by the warehouse, but they didn't see anything. Natale said it wasn't uncommon for someone to make a threat and have no intention of carrying it out. If he gets the money, fine. If not, he moves on to someone else. Nice business."

"You think the warehouse was burned because of this extortion thing?" asked Baxter, dusting the crumbs off his coat.

"I've no idea. It's crazy."

"Can you think of someone else who might of done it?"

"No, no one."

"Anyone you've fired or had a fight with?" asked Lazard. "Someone you owe money to? Some kind of argument?"

Trieger raised his hands, then dropped them. He looked like a coach in his gray sweatshirt. "No one. Those guys've all worked for me at least a couple of years. I mean, I guess there're people who don't like me, but mostly I'm a pretty friendly guy."

"You know why the sprinklers didn't work?" asked Baxter.

"No idea."

"You keep gas or any inflammable stuff in the building?"

"Some paint remover and maybe some gas for the truck."

"Who owns the building?" asked Lazard.

"Mass-Prop."

"Pardon me?"

"Massachusetts Properties. They own a lot of places through there."

"You've rented from them all along?"

"I took a ten-year lease."

"You know about a suicide in the company?"

"No, who told you that?"

Lazard shook his head. "What'd you think when you got that extortion letter?"

"I guess I thought it was a joke. It was Norma that made me go to the police. I worried some but when nothing happened I sort of forgot about it."

"When did you go up to New Hampshire?"

"Friday. We decided to take advantage of the long weekend and open the place early. It was beautiful. Sunday Ellen, my older daughter, even went swimming."

"This is Lake Sunapee?"

"That's right, near Blodgett Landing. We've had it five years. It was a wreck at first but each year we fix it up more."

"What'd you do there?"

"Cleaned mostly. Fished as much as we could. Got out in the morning, then again at sunset. Beautiful perch and smallmouth bass. Brought back some to freeze. You do much fishing?"

"No. You've a phone up there?"

"Too much temptation to do business when I have a phone. Up there's where I become human again."

"When did you learn about the fire?"

"I don't know, we were still fishing when the trooper came by. I guess 10:30. We came down right away. It was terrible about those men. I guess . . . did they have families?"

"Sure they had families," said Baxter.

"I don't know what to say about that. If there's anything, well, if I could do anything . . ." There was a quality to Trieger's eyes that Lazard kept trying to define. They were large brown eyes and seemed not so much questioning as wondering, as if the world were constantly surprising to him.

"Who knew you were going up north?" asked Lazard.

"Lots of people, everyone in the office. You know anything about the fire, what caused it or anything?"

"Probably find out tomorrow when we go into the building. You ever had any other fires?"

"No, never."

"Business pretty good? That's a nice TV over there."

"My brother gave it to us for Christmas a year ago. Brought it up from Florida in a U-Haul. He's a great guy."

Lazard recalled that Trieger's brother had moved to Florida about the time he'd come to Boston. "Doesn't he have a restaurant or something?"

"He did for a while. Now he's got a motel."

"And your business," repeated Lazard, "it's pretty good?"

"Couldn't be better. Am I a suspect?"

"Sure. What'd you lose, $100,000? If you collect that much, then you're a suspect." Lazard tried to speak lightly but sounded harsher than he intended. The interview hadn't pleased him. He was sorry he had known Trieger, had ever been friendly with him. Trieger was definitely now on the defensive and Lazard wanted to say something which would appear more friendly. Then he recalled that each year Trieger made a point of going to the first Red Sox game.

"You go to the opener?"

Trieger glanced up. "No, I mean, I was too busy. Usually I go with Ellen, sometimes Joan too, but Ellen's the great fan. That's the main thing I regret about a prosperous business: I can't go to so many games. How 'bout you?"

Lazard shook his head. "I haven't seen a game in ten years, except on television."

"Christ, remember those games we went to?" Trieger turned to Baxter. "Frank and I, we'd make it to Fenway half-dozen times a season. Drink beer and shout a lot. I remember a doubleheader maybe in the spring of 'sixty-three. We were playing the Angels. Sox had a guy, Dick Stuart, played first base. Called him The Big Bomber. In the first game, Stuart hit a grand-slam homer smack into the left-field nets. Sox won both games.

"But in the first game the Angels got wild. Monbo was pitching and the Angel manager didn't like how he was faking with men on base, trying to trick 'em into stealing. He kept shouting and carrying on until the umpire threw him out of the game.

"Well, Monbo kept pulling these pitches and he caught a guy stealing to second and threw him out. One of their players, a guy named Thomas, first he started throwing towels out of the dugout, then he threw the ball bag, then he threw two bats, one right after the other, at the ump at second base. Shit, Frank here, I had to hold him down, he was yelling so loud. Well, they threw Thomas out too. We left there, we could hardly walk. That was the first time the Sox had beat the Angels at Fenway in something like ten games. Ellen, you'd like her, Frank, she can yell almost as good as you."

Twenty minutes later Baxter and Lazard were on their way back to Fire Headquarters. Baxter drove. They were on the Fenway, and Lazard stared out at the buildings of Simmons College and the Gardner Museum. He was thinking about Trieger.

"You really go to all those games?" asked Baxter.

"I guess so."

"Who's Monbo?" Baxter had worked with Lazard for six years and had never seen him shout at anything.

"Some pitcher."

"Colored? Sounds like a colored guy, you know, like Sambo."

"What'd you think of Trieger?"

"He seems okay. The sort of guy my Aunt Alice would call chatty."

"What about the extortion business?"

"It's happened before. Right?"

Baxter parked the red Chevrolet in the garage behind Fire Headquarters. They left their equipment in the trunk because they would probably go out again before getting off at eight. Baxter hated being waked for some ten-cent fire. Lazard didn't mind.

They walked through the empty building, then took the elevator to their office on the third floor. It gave Baxter great pleasure to be in a building where he rarely saw anyone he hadn't known for half his life.

An American flag decal was stuck to the glass of the green metal door below the words Arson Squad. From the knob hung a tag from the Sheraton Hotel saying, "Please Make Up This Room," in English, Spanish, French, and German.

The office was about 12 by 18 feet with a bank of windows facing north toward the Boston skyline. Two gray metal desks were back to back to the right of the door; around them were scattered seven metal and green Leatherette chairs. Opposite the desks was a row of gray file cabinets containing five years of cases. Files for three years before that were stored in liquor boxes balanced on top of the dozen green lockers along the south wall. The room was cluttered, green, and smelled of paper. It was lit by two long neon lights in yellowing metal frames.

Lazard put his radio into the recharger on the windowsill, then unlocked a closet in an alcove to the left of the door. He shared the closet with Quaid, but mostly it was full of Lazard's clothes. Somehow the smoke from any fire got under his fire coat and he always thought his clothes stank of it. Lazard stripped off his tie and white shirt, then put on a tan sport shirt that his wife had once given him. Although it was warm, he put on a dark red cardigan over the shirt.

Baxter was already at the first desk and had inserted the white form of the inspector's report into the typewriter. He'd put on a pair of black horn-rimmed reading glasses that had broken in the middle and were wound with layers of Scotch tape. They kept sliding down his nose.

Lazard took his seat at the other desk and rolled the activity sheet into the typewriter. Behind him on the wall was a tattered two-by-three-foot copy of the "Burke Procedural & Classification Chart For Arson Investigators" in five colors. It resembled the family tree of some small German duchy.

"What was the box number of that bridal place?" asked Lazard.

"2351. Incident number: 15,391."

Lazard typed out the numbers. Each time they returned to the office, they had to log where they had been, how long they'd spent, and the mileage driven: "22:34—Back in quarters."

Lazard took the four-page yellow arson report from the pile behind him and inserted it in the typewriter. "Did that place have sprinklers?"

"They'd been turned off."

Typing with two fingers, Lazard filled in the names of the first arriving engine and ladder companies, the groups working, the officer in charge, a description of the building, construction, origin of fire, the facts surrounding Waters's death, who owned the building, and who sustained the loss. On Friday he would find out about insurance and who had written the policies.

Although he had the next three days off, Lazard had to appear in court on two of them: a probable cause hearing on Tuesday in West Roxbury district court of a man accused of throwing a gasoline bomb into an abandoned house, and the arraignment on Thursday in Charlestown district court of a woman accused of setting fire to a beauty parlor she operated in the basement of her home. These could take most of the day.

Many firemen envied the extra money squad members received for going to court on their days off: time and a half for a minimum of four hours. But to Lazard the extra $1,500 a year wasn't worth it. He hated waiting around for some judge to get back from lunch.

When he finished rereading his report, Baxter went to his locker and removed two Chunky candy bars from a box on the top shelf. Putting them on his desk, he walked over to an old gray portable TV on the windowsill and turned it on. Nothing happened and Baxter thumped it several times until the voice of a news announcer blared into the room. Turning down the volume, Baxter made sure it was the channel that would soon present Johnny Carson and returned to his desk. He sat down and carefully unwrapped both Chunkies. He started to put one in his mouth, stopped, replaced it on the desk, and began massaging his right calf. Then he massaged his left while watching the TV, where a snappy man was talking about the weather. Baxter quickly picked up one of the Chunkies and ate it almost without chewing. Then he leaned back and continued to watch the weather, now and then glancing at the other Chunky as if to make sure it hadn't moved.

Lazard didn't look at the television. Instead he leafed through a 1971 *Fodor's Guide to Spain* he had found in a trash barrel on the first floor. Someday he meant to visit Spain and for the past year he'd been trying to teach himself Spanish, going so far as to enroll in a course taught at the Cambridge YMCA. His work schedule, however, and lack of real interest had caused him to miss several classes. Lazard had never been out of the country and part of him didn't believe in the existence of Spain. But he enjoyed the discipline of learning a language and in the past six months had forced himself to memorize a thousand words.

At midnight Baxter turned off the television and went to a large closet across the hall where five rollaway beds were stored. Lazard followed him and pushed one of the beds into the arson office. Baxter pushed another into the inspectors' office across the hall. For some minutes they were busy making the beds and getting out their pajamas. Lazard's bed in the middle of the office had yellow-orange sheets and dark green army blankets.

"You got everything you need?" he asked Baxter.

"Yeah. You thought any more about Trieger?"

"We'll go over his books Friday."

"You think he torched it?"

"I don't know."

Lazard shut the door and began changing into his pajamas. They were blue flannel with white checks and made him seem almost delicate despite his six feet three inches. He looked thin and gangly. The pajamas had no collar, making his neck and large head seem particularly balloonlike. His dark brown hair was cut in an uncombed Princeton. As he changed, he kept thinking about Trieger: not whether he had burned his warehouse, but that he had seemed the same as ever. It made Lazard realize what a different person he himself had become.

Putting out the light, Lazard limped to the windows that extended about 10 feet across the north side of the office. These were covered with one long venetian blind that was open and hung halfway down. The only sound came from the traffic on Southampton: buses turning at the light, then accelerating. Leaning on his cane, Lazard stared out at the skyline: the cluster of buildings downtown, then the Hancock and Prudential buildings off to the left by themselves.

Lazard opened the window, then got down on the floor and began his regimen of forty push-ups and forty sit-ups. The sound of his labored breathing was loud enough to be heard by Baxter across the hall, who was staring at the ceiling and wondering if he should try a little exercise someday. At last he turned over, hugged his pillow, and decided it was kid stuff. Besides, he liked being a large man. It pleased him.

When Lazard had finished, he pulled himself up by the corner of the desk and got into bed. The mattress was thin and his body sagged as if in a hammock. The light from the street through the venetian blind made a pattern of bars on the walls of the office. Lying there, Lazard thought about his ability to forget the past. It made him wonder if he had really gone to that ball game or if Trieger had simply made it up.

9

Bobby Dodge stood outside the Tropicana Discount Shop—Tienda de Descuento—on Washington near the corner of Mass. Ave. He was waiting for Roy Gibson, who managed the dry cleaners on his right. Of all Bobby Dodge's friends who earned money in a conventional manner, Gibson was most successful. Dodge hoped to get some of that money. It was 7:30 in the morning and Washington was full of people going to work.

In front of him, the elevated tracks of the Orange Line rose over the street on red trestles, providing some shade from what was becoming another hot day. There was constant noise from trains arriving and departing from the Northampton stop. Dodge had another friend, Pete Taylor, who'd been shot and killed outside the Rendezvous Cafe a few doors down. The trains had covered the gunshot and no one guessed what happened until they saw the blood.

Bobby Dodge knew who shot him, which was why he was eager to borrow the money from Roy Gibson. He knew people who made more money than Gibson, but they were just the ones who had caused his present problems. In his mind, he kept seeing them with Pete Taylor, friendly at card games and local bars.

57

Bobby Dodge kept shifting his weight from one foot to the other. His hands were tucked in the front pockets of his dark slacks and he kept looking up the street for some sign of Gibson. Dodge was a tall black man of twenty-six with a narrow face and a perfectly groomed afro. He wore a tan T-shirt and a thin brown jacket.

Partly he was nervous because each minute he waited made him later for his own job. He painted cars at a garage farther down Washington near Dudley. The owner, Leonard Quick, made a point of hiring parolees from Walpole. Dodge knew better than to think it was kindness. But if Quick fired him and his parole officer learned about the money . . . Well, if it came to that, he'd be halfway to Georgia before they knew he was gone.

Bobby Dodge felt ill-used. It seemed each time he got his life working, something came along to mess it up. This time it was Henry Pierce. He wouldn't have taken the money if he'd known Pierce would want it back so soon. Twelve hundred was nothing. Once in Saigon he'd won $5,000 playing seven-card, before losing it to some Marine. Even now he could see the green diamond pattern on the backs of the cards. Roy Gibson had been there. Anyone call him a liar, they could talk to Roy.

But worse than wanting the money, Henry Pierce wanted him to deal narcotics. Dodge didn't see even how he'd ended up owing Pierce so much. Several card games, sure, then he'd been drinking and they'd done a little coke because Dionne kept asking. Pierce had asked if maybe he needed a little more money to get through the evening, just a relaxed deal between friends.

Roy Gibson didn't arrive until eight. He was a tall black man a few years older than Dodge and getting fat around the middle. He wore a rust-colored double-knit suit. Bobby Dodge touched his arm.

"Where you been, man? I been waiting an hour."

"The sign on the door says I open at eight. It's eight. You got something on your mind?" He looked at his friend critically.

"You let me have some money?"

"Is Cecilia all right?" Cecilia was Bobby Dodge's wife. They had been married six months and she was pregnant.

"This don't concern Cecilia."

"How much you need?"

"Twelve hundred."

Dropping his head, Gibson turned away. "Shit, boy, you never going to learn nothing. Who you into?"

"Henry Pierce."

Gibson went over and unlocked the front door of the dry cleaners. Then he looked back at the traffic on Washington before he said anything. "I'll give you a hundred, that's all I got. Man, you just got your life going again. You don't need no girlfriends and card games. You're an ex-con."

Quaid tamped the tobacco down in his pipe with his finger, then checked his pockets for matches. Before him stretched the ruin of the warehouse on Plympton. The rest of the roof and side walls had been knocked down that morning by wreckers from the Boston Building Department. Where the warehouse had stood were mounds of bricks, debris from the roof, and charred beams sticking into the air like black fingers. From one pile came a thin wisp of smoke which two small boys across the street watched hopefully.

At the rear of the building a group of eight workmen shoveled bricks and parts of the roof into wheelbarrows, then dumped them where a yellow backhoe could ladle the debris into a truck. Earlier that morning, Quaid had seen Trieger and got a diagram of the layout of the warehouse. What had been the office was now roped off and the workmen confined their digging to that area.

A few feet to Quaid's left was a 4-by-6 mesh screen resting on a pair of trestles. As yet the workmen hadn't reached the level of the office, but they were deep enough for Quaid to decide to stop his canvass of the neighborhood and attend to the sifting. Pugliese had been canvassing with him, but at the moment was looking for the landlord who had reported the kids for uncapping the hydrant.

It was just past 1 o'clock. For most of the morning, Quaid and Pugliese had been going door to door through the Cathedral housing project asking people if they had seen anyone tampering with the hydrant or if they had seen a vehicle parked near the warehouse between 3:00 and 3:45 Monday morning.

It was not yet certain that any vehicle had been near the warehouse. The accelerant might have been spread around during the day. But if not, then Quaid and Lazard had agreed it must have been put in the building while the guard was at the diner.

Quaid and Pugliese had probably knocked on fifty doors. Mostly they talked to women. All claimed to have seen nothing. Perhaps that was true. The project was a long block from the warehouse and on the other side of Harrison. But in between was only one ramshackle building and many project windows faced Plympton.

The difficulty was that no one wanted to talk. Not that they were necessarily hiding anything, but to admit knowledge meant possible problems, such as appearing in court or seeming too friendly with the law. This irritated and depressed Pugliese, who had an overdeveloped sense of civic duty, but Quaid had seen it too often to think much about it.

Quaid stood on a small pile of bricks and boards, which not only gave him a better view of the workmen but also protected his shoes from the mud. He watched a starling land on the tip of one of the beams sticking from the rubble. It was the same color as the beam and the sight of the bird pleased Quaid. He searched for another match and relit his pipe. Quaid wore a maroon sport coat and gray slacks. His blue tie had pictures of small white cats chasing their tails. He wore the tie because it was his daughter's favorite.

"Hey," shouted one of the men, "you interested in a crowbar?"

"Where'd you find it?"

"Sort of by the door."

"Bring it over."

As he turned the crowbar over in his hands, Quaid saw that although the paint had been burned off, there were no nicks in the metal. The crowbar appeared new. Later he would ask Trieger if he was accustomed to keeping a crowbar in the office. As Quaid put it down, he saw Pugliese returning with a short balding man in his mid-fifties.

Usually it was Quaid who asked the questions. Not being a policeman, he had more freedom in what he said. Members of the Arson Squad had no police powers and couldn't make an arrest. Some privately carried guns, especially the photographers, but it wasn't officially known and the commissioner never mentioned it unless it was brought to his attention. Quaid remembered Warren Cassidy saying, "Whenever I go into his lordship's office, I just button my coat. He's happy and I'm happy."

Having found Schacter, Pugliese wanted to get rid of him. He seemed limited to two topics: one, that his tenants didn't appreciate him; two, that the changing neighborhood kept him from getting the tenants he deserved. Schacter said he had spent the previous day scrounging around scrap yards north of Boston for parts to fix the plumbing in his building.

"Think these Ricans care? They'd as soon shit in a tin can."

Schacter had a round face, puggy nose, and his pink complexion turned red when he grew angry. Every few minutes he pulled out a white handkerchief and mopped the back of his neck. He wore a short-sleeved white shirt with a pack of Pall Malls in the breast pocket.

"Where's this guy I'm supposed to talk to?"

"Standing over on those bricks. The man with the pipe."

Pugliese made the introductions, then walked away. He found it more interesting to watch the workmen. Always it fascinated him to follow Quaid as he poked through the debris of a fire. The previous week Quaid had taken a few drops of brass from an iron electrical conduit as proof that a fire wasn't the result of a short circuit, but rather the cause of it. The fire had melted the zinc used in galvanizing the conduit, and the molten zinc had burned the insulation from the wire. When the zinc touched the copper wire, brass was formed. The hot brass then fused several wires together, causing the short circuit.

"You called the police about those kids?" asked Quaid.

"That's right."

"How many times you call?"

"Maybe a dozen."

"How many times did the police come?"

Schacter rubbed the back of his neck. He had small brown eyes and kept glancing at the workmen. "Maybe four times, twice Saturday, twice Sunday. The last time these kids started throwing rocks. No time at all three more cars pull up. I call, they drag their feet. They call, Bingo. I shoulda said I was a cop."

"They arrested some kids?"

"About five of them."

"Anything else?" Quaid poked in the bowl of his pipe with a dead match, then tapped the pipe against the heel of his shoe.

"Yeah, round dark I saw some kids fuckin' with the hydrant."

"What d'you mean?"

"Well, they didn't turn it on so I didn't call the cops. I don't know, they were just fooling with it. It was too dark to see much. I forgot about it until I heard it'd been packed with rocks."

"Just where were you watching from?"

"My place on East Canton."

"And you saw their faces from two blocks away?"

Schacter glanced at Quaid a foot above him on the pile of bricks. "I've a pair of binoculars. Gotta good look. Colored, all three. Whaddaya expect? Fuckin' monkies."

"And you're certain you could recognize them?"

"Yeah, when they left, they walked right under that streetlight." Schacter pointed to a light halfway toward Harrison. "I don't know their names, but I seen 'em around."

"You watch the other kids with your binoculars?"

"Sure, the whole shebang."

"You own that building?" Quaid had taken out a pad and began to make notes.

"That's right. Also gotta coupla houses in Dorchester."

Quaid talked to Schacter a little longer, then told him to call the arson office if he saw the boys who had opened the hydrant. After Schacter left, Quaid asked Pugliese, "Why don't you check the police about those kids they arrested. They're probably juveniles, but if you get their names, I'll talk to them."

"Think they'll tell you anything?"

"I doubt it."

For several hours that afternoon, the workmen shoveled debris onto the screen. Quaid pawed through it and occasionally set aside bits that to Pugliese looked identical to the bits he threw away. The two men also helped remove bricks from the office and dug out the remains of the desk and file cabinets. The debris from the top of the desk included a melted telephone, some brittle and blackened wires and the remains of one or more batteries. The desk itself was charred to different depths with the deepest being two grooves running from the edge to two melted zinc nails.

Quaid called the photographer and had him take pictures of the floorboards, desktop, the location of the desk in the office, and the burned wires. Although the desk was badly burned, it had protected the floor beneath, enabling Quaid to see where it had stood.

When they took up part of the floor, Quaid saw the building didn't have a full basement. Under the office was dirt. He took several samples, hoping the state police chemist could find traces of accelerant. The remains of the back door showed the lock had been secure. However, they also found a number of keys, two of which fit the lock. Possibly someone had unlocked the door, then pretended to have forced it with the crowbar.

Around four, Quaid and Pugliese took the electronic debris and samples of dirt to John Lakin, the senior chemist at the Department of Public Safety at 1010 Commonwealth Avenue. Lakin promised to have the results the next day. Coming back, Quaid went out of his way by taking Commonwealth to the Public Gardens. He enjoyed seeing the magnolia trees, and their creamy pink blossoms were in full bloom in front of the brownstones.

Each April when Quaid was a child his father would choose some Sunday afternoon and the whole family would walk from their West End flat through the Common and the Public Gardens, then along the mall on Commonwealth just to look at the magnolias. Quaid's father had been a driver on the Green Line of the MBTA. As a child Quaid often went down to the Park Street station and waited for his father to come through. Then, when he saw his father, he'd tug someone's coattail and say, "See that guy driving the train? That's my old man."

Pugliese didn't notice the magnolias. He was describing to Quaid a trick of Houdini's, called The Flight of Venus, which consisted of the disappearance of a woman lying on a sheet of glass carried by two Hindu assistants. A cloth, not long enough to touch the floor, is held briefly in front of the woman. When it's flicked away, the girl is gone.

"The trick is," said Pugliese, "that the first Hindu is a dummy, I mean he's hollow. When they hold up the cloth, the girl jumps inside him. Take the cloth away, shazam, no girl. Then she strolls off inside the dummy and carrying the sheet of glass. Of course, there's the problem of how to get the dummy carrying his half in the first place. Houdini unfortunately never did this trick. When he died, he was just figuring he needed four Hindus, and the dummy would be really riding on the plate of glass. I don't know, for this to work those Hindus would have to be tigers."

Quaid made responsive noises but mostly looked at the magnolias. He was used to Pugliese's enthusiasms, which changed each week. A brief interest in popular literature had led Pugliese to read part of a novel in which Houdini was a character, which led him to read part of a biography of Houdini, which led him to a book on Houdini's escapes and magic, which he was now in the process of discarding for a book on carnivals and circus acts. This enthusiasm helped rather than hindered his work in the State Fire Marshal's Office. He could spend only a little time on each case and the rapid transition from one unfinished case to the next kept him from growing bored.

Even as he spoke, Pugliese wasn't really thinking about Houdini. He disliked riding in silence and so he talked. Actually, he was thinking about his fiancée, Ginny Lufkin. He hoped he wouldn't find her waiting for him in the arson office. It embarrassed him to see the office full of men trying to look at her legs.

Pugliese kept urging Ginny to set a date for their marriage. As it stood now, it was "sometime." She taught junior high school in Salem. He didn't care if she kept teaching, but if they were going to have kids, well, you can't teach and have kids at the same time. To his mind it was barely an engagement. Sometimes she went out with other men and at Christmas she'd flown to Jamaica for a week by herself.

When Quaid and Pugliese entered the office, the only person they saw was Fatback Tucker, who was keeper of the records and occasionally went out on follow-up investigations unless he could wangle out of it. Tucker had spent two years as a policeman in Cambridge after the Korean War, and the name Fatback had been given him by a rummy in Central Square who used to shout after him each afternoon as Tucker hurried to work: "What's the time, Fatback?" Soon everyone called him Fatback. They couldn't imagine calling him anything else.

Fatback Tucker was a large, slow firefighter who had served with an engine company in the North End until part of a wall fell on him in 1970, breaking his arm and shoulder. If he hadn't been quite so slow, the wall wouldn't have hit him. Transferred to Arson, he now spent most of his time in the office like a pallid plant. However, he kept adequate records and had read enough about arson to sound intelligent when reporters called for information. He had a thick, low voice that exuded certitude, and so along with keeping the records he had become Arson Squad spokesman.

The two men assigned to that shift were out "feeding their faces," according to Fatback, while Warren Cassidy had left for the day. That pleased Pugliese, who was somewhat afraid of Cassidy. He had once been foolish enough to call Cassidy "Butch," and had been rewarded with a look of such scorn that Pugliese now couldn't talk to him without stuttering.

"Flanagan wants to see you," said Fatback as they entered. "I don't know what he wants but he said if you come in before five, then he wants to see you. You too, Pugliese."

The City Fire Marshal's Office was across from the elevator. They found Flanagan leaning against his desk looking out at the Boston skyline. He was a tall, white-haired man with the habit of pulling his fingers until the joints cracked. Like all uniformed officers, he wore dark pants and a white shirt.

"You get anything out of the warehouse today?"

Quaid described what they had found. Flanagan nodded but continued to look out the window.

"You seen the *Globe?* They made a big deal outta that fire, talked to Harris's wife. I guess she was pretty bitter. Fuckin' reporters been calling all day. Know what that means? It means pressure from every asshole in city government right up to the mayor. Goddamn governor'll be calling next. Like they figure I can just run out and solve this by myself. I don't know what the fuck Harris's old lady's complaining to the papers for. I mean, he's a lieutenant and she's the wife of a lieutenant." He paused, then pinched the bridge of his nose between his thumb and index finger. "I talked to the commissioner. He wants you to stick with the hydrant. Lazard and Ruby will keep the furniture guy and realty company. But the commissioner thinks this extortion thing is a possibility so I'm giving it to Cassidy. If he needs any help, Pugliese, maybe you can give it to him, while helping Quaid too, of course. The commissioner suggested we ask for a real guy from 1010, but I don't know. Sometimes they attract publicity."

By a "real guy" Flanagan meant a lieutenant-detective from the fire marshal's office, and not just an inexperienced trooper like Pugliese himself. Quaid looked to see if Pugliese had been hurt by the remark, but Pugliese hadn't heard. He was thinking instead about having to work with Cassidy.

The last time he'd worked with Cassidy had been four weeks before when Cassidy had been told to "show Pugliese the ropes." Cassidy was a tall, muscular man with light brown hair and a long, angular face. Throughout the day, Pugliese had felt he was being treated as a stupid child. Later he discovered Cassidy treated everyone like that. Cassidy's most obvious quirk was his refusal to ride in elevators. In 1964 he'd been stuck in an elevator during a fire and badly burned.

It was at a fire on Columbia Road that Pugliese had been particularly unnerved. The building was a three-story Victorian house divided into small apartments. The fire had started on the second floor, then destroyed much of the third. Pugliese had trailed after Cassidy, who was rummaging around the second floor looking for the point of origin. There appeared to be several. Pugliese wasn't paying much attention. Mostly he was trying to protect his clothes from the debris underfoot and the water dripping from the ceiling. Cassidy wore his black fire coat, helmet, and boots. It was late afternoon and sunlight had streamed through the broken windows.

It was Pugliese who had found the body. He'd stepped on it and yelled. It was badly charred and he couldn't tell if it was male or female, young or old. The body lay stretched out in the middle of the floor covered with pieces of ceiling. Pugliese had been hurrying out of the room for he didn't know what, perhaps an ambulance, when Cassidy stopped him.

"Hey, you should be interested. I bet he was murdered."

Pugliese paused by the door. "How d'you know?"

"See where he's lying? Most people killed in a fire try to hide. Maybe they're curled up under the bed. This guy's stretched out like he's taking a snooze."

Cassidy had crouched down beside the body and was removing pieces of plaster. Pugliese looked at it, then looked away. "Won't an autopsy show if he was dead before the fire?"

"That takes time. You think you gotta murder investigation, you can't doodle around. I'll show you how to find out faster."

Pugliese took a few steps into the room. There was the smell of burned meat and the sour-sweet smell of smoke and wet ash.

"A fire causes blisters. Don't matter if the guy's living or dead. But if he was living, then there's a little fluid under the blister. If he was dead, it's dry. So you try to find some part that's not charred too much, maybe the inside of the thigh down near the floor. Follow me? Watch this." Pushing back his helmet, Cassidy took a penknife from his pocket, then brushed the rest of the debris from the legs. It was difficult to tell what belonged to the body and what to the ceiling.

"See, there're some blisters. How the fuck can you see standing over there? Okay, so you take the knife and slit a blister just like this and, what'd I tell you, dry as a goddamn bone. Hey, Pugsy, where you going?"

10

Lazard decided that she must have seen him on the street or heard him walking across the room to answer the door. Perhaps he had stood in some telling way as they talked. He put the yellow plastic flower in the pocket of his gray corduroy jacket and returned to the kitchen, where he had been getting breakfast before being interrupted by the doorbell.

He didn't think of himself as having a memory for faces but was certain he would have remembered her if he'd seen her before: an old black woman in a dark blue coat and blue straw hat. Her wrinkled face was almond shaped, with a few white hairs on her chin. Most noticeably she was several inches under five feet. During the time they talked, Lazard didn't think she once raised her eyes above his lower ribs, as if refusing to admit the possibility of people taller than herself. She had said she was raising money for what sounded like the sisters of furnishings. Lazard asked several times and each time it still sounded like the sisters of furnishings.

Normally he didn't give away money, but she nudged him from habitual action by calling him Sonny: "Good morning, Sonny,

I'm collecting for the sisters of furnishings." She mumbled, and all he was really sure of was the Sonny.

After asking her to repeat herself, Lazard had said, "No, thanks," somewhat meaninglessly, but instead of going away, she again told him: "I'm collecting for the sisters of furnishings." She held out a red heart-shaped box of the sort that often contains Valentine candy, using both hands as if it were heavy. Lazard dug in his pockets for spare change.

When the woman opened the box, Lazard saw it was empty. He dropped his change into the box. Embarrassingly, it was mostly pennies. Lazard apologized, reached for his wallet, and took out a dollar.

"Here, take this." He was tempted to retrieve his change, in which he now noticed some silver.

"Thank you, Sonny, you're very kind."

Again, Sonny was the only word of which he was certain. He wanted to correct her, tell her he was thirty-eight and aging quickly. Lazard had left his cane in the kitchen and was leaning against the door. Opening her pocketbook, which was small and covered with dark blue beads, the woman handed him a yellow plastic flower wrapped in cellophane.

"That's okay, never mind."

She continued to hold out the flower until, after several seconds, he took it. Her hands were like small brown claws.

Then she had said something else and once more Sonny was the only audible word.

"What was that?"

And, quite clearly: "I'll pray for your leg, Sonny."

Lazard poured himself a cup of coffee, then took from the refrigerator a bag of six doughnuts purchased the night before. He wore slippers and as he walked into the living room he listened to discern if his limp made any obvious noise. There seemed to be no noise at all. He put the doughnuts and coffee down on the card table, pulled up a gray metal folding chair, and sat down to eat.

Lazard lived in a three-room apartment on the third floor of a brick apartment house on Hancock Street in Cambridge. He had moved there in January after selling his house in Brighton. Although he'd been there three months, the apartment looked almost unoccupied.

In the bedroom was a mattress on the floor and two footlockers in which Lazard kept his clothes. There was also a gray metal folding chair. He had purchased eight of these from the fire department, thinking they would be useful if he had people over for card games. But since moving, he'd had no card games, and the chairs made his living room seem like a lobby.

His main purchase had been a round shag rug, eight feet in diameter, with green and light blue threads, which lay between the two front windows. On the rug were small piles of Lazard's books, primarily war histories. The only comfortable chair was a squat brown chair next to a standing lamp. In a half ring around it were dirty coffee cups, news magazines, copies of the *Globe*, and a history of the Boston Red Sox which Lazard had borrowed from the library the day before. The yellow walls were bare except for a large map of metropolitan Boston. Along one wall, between the bedroom and kitchen doors, was an inexpensive Panasonic stereo and a pile of records: jazz from the '20s and '30s. In the bedroom was a small portable TV.

Lazard found the apartment neither comfortable nor uncomfortable. So far he hadn't committed himself to staying and considered the apartment as no more than an oversize hotel room. He had moved to Cambridge because he saw it as a town of single people, possibly making it easier to meet women. He partly blamed his divorce on the indifference he had come to feel for Elizabeth, and although he felt kindly toward her, he believed he had no interest in anything in her life, not even her infidelity. In moving to Cambridge, he hoped to prove his indifference was to Elizabeth in particular and not women or people in general.

It didn't take Lazard long to realize he'd made a mistake. Although in good physical condition, he was still fifteen years older than most of the people he saw. Also, he was nonintellectual and basically silent. Cambridge was probably the worst place he could have gone to meet single women. Realizing this, he accepted it without much feeling.

Lazard's social life primarily consisted of weekly dinners at Quaid's. In fact, he was intending to go that evening. They would talk a little and watch a movie on television. Quaid had one child, Geraldine, who was eleven years old and mentally retarded.

Lazard finished his coffee and returned the remaining three

doughnuts to the refrigerator. He told himself that if he could decide either to sell the books stacked on the rug or buy a bookcase, then his apartment would be comfortable enough.

When he had first moved in, there had been voices, actually one voice: a high, male voice that spoke quickly and urgently. He heard it only late at night when the rest of the building was quiet. Lazard had tried to make out the words, but they seemed just below the level of hearing. Always as he was about to give up, he would hear a specific word or name which would again make him listen. It was the urgency that impressed him, a kind of urgent monotone.

This had continued for a month. Then one night when the voice was louder than usual, Lazard discovered it was caused by the trickling of water in the bathroom pipes. He felt embarrassed, but also disappointed, as if he had been let down in some way. Even now, when he'd grown used to the sound and knew it was water, he would sometimes grow alert, thinking he had heard a name.

Lazard had just begun to pick up the coffee cups around the brown chair when the telephone rang. It was a red phone on the floor by the entrance to the kitchen.

"Frank, this is Howard. I'd a devil of a time getting your number from the Fire Department. Say, the reason I'm calling is that Norma and I wondered if you and Elizabeth would like to come over for dinner tomorrow night. Sorry about the short notice."

Lazard wasn't sure how to answer. "Thanks, Howard, I guess I should have said. Elizabeth and I split up. We're divorced."

There was a silence, then Trieger said more slowly, "I'm sorry, Frank, I didn't know." He paused again, then said: "Look, come anyway. It'd just be the three of us. Norma'd love to see you."

Lazard knew he had ambivalent feelings about Trieger. Ever since seeing him, he'd been recalling his life before his accident and it made him realize how much he had changed. He had once told himself that he had merely grown more subdued, but he knew it was more than that. Trieger seemed unchanged, was as energetic as ever, and seeing him Lazard felt envious. He also knew that he could probably destroy Trieger if he chose.

"I'm not sure, Howard," Lazard said at last.

"Come on, why not? You working late or something?"

"No, I'm off tomorrow."

"Then it's all settled. Let's say six-thirty. We'll be expecting you."

It was nearly dark when Lazard parked his Ford in front of Quaid's house in Brookline that evening. A single bat swooped and fluttered between two streetlights. Quaid lived in a small gabled brick house that had a front porch with a swing. Lazard saw it move and guessed Geraldine was waiting for him. The day had been cloudy and cooler; rain was expected tomorrow, almost the first in a month.

When Geraldine heard the car door slam, she hurried to the top of the steps. She was a chubby girl whose brown hair was cut in a severe Dutchboy style. Her mother dressed her in bright clothes, which she made herself, as if preparing her for a party. Geraldine knew no words but had a variety of responsive sounds.

She was especially fond of Lazard, and he was touched by her affection but felt guilty for seeing her as some form of superior pet. Sometimes she would cry desperately as if suddenly aware of how different she was and of the vacancy in her head. This evening she wore a red dress and a string of large green beads. She had round red cheeks and deepset brown eyes.

As Lazard climbed the steps, Geraldine made a happy cooing noise. He kissed her cheek and they went inside where they found Quaid in the living room reading the paper.

"She's been waiting an hour. I warned you about bringing her presents."

Lazard patted the pockets of his gray sport coat. "Well, I forgot to bring anything this time." He could never get used to talking as if Geraldine weren't in the room. Feeling something in his pocket, Lazard drew out the yellow flower the old woman had given him that morning. He handed it to Geraldine.

She took it carefully. Stripping off the cellophane, she sniffed the plastic, then showed it to Quaid, who smiled. She made another cooing noise and hurried into the kitchen to show the flower to her mother.

"I'll get you a drink," said Quaid.

The house smelled of corn beef and cabbage. Lazard sat down on a loveseat with a pattern of green leaves. He was using a plain wooden cane tonight and he put it on the rug near his feet. It was a comfortable living room, and it had taken Lazard some time to realize that part of the comfort came from there being no sharp edges, no straight chairs or tables. Geraldine fell easily and occasionally wore a helmet. The furniture was soft with thick cushions, and there was a thick brown rug strewn with Geraldine's cloth dolls. Made by her mother, these were also dressed in bright colors and looked like small versions of Geraldine herself. On the wall above the couch were photographs of Quaid's wife's Irish relatives.

Quaid returned and handed Lazard a whiskey and water. "That guy Trieger get hold of you?"

"He invited me to dinner tomorrow night."

"Didn't you used to be friends?"

"His wife's my cousin."

"You going?"

Lazard sipped his drink. "Why not?"

"Just wondered. You think he's involved with burning his warehouse?"

"I don't know."

Quaid looked at Lazard for a moment. "You know, Flanagan's under a lot of pressure to solve this case."

"Sure," said Lazard. "That's because no one's getting paid off not to investigate."

"Flanagan's never been involved with anything like that."

"How do you know? Look at the promotion scandal."

Not long before, it had become public knowledge that certain chiefs were selling lieutenants' and captains' ranks to men who had passed their exams, were on the waiting list for promotion, and would probably remain on the waiting list for some years if they hadn't coughed up money for a bribe.

"A lot of guys were doing pretty well off that," said Lazard, "including some I thought were honest."

"I still say Flanagan's all right," said Quaid.

"Maybe he's just got a higher price."

Geraldine came back into the room. She had put the flower in a small blue plastic vase. Sitting down next to Lazard, she leaned her head against his arm.

Quaid looked at her kindly. She was both his bane and joy. For years it had been dreadful to have a retarded child. But as she grew older, he came to see her as the only completely loving and forgiving human being he'd ever known. Now, beyond simply loving her, he cherished her as incorruptible. There were no complications in her face.

"Finish canvassing today?" asked Lazard.

"Almost finished in the projects. I talked to Lakin on my way home. He's completed his analysis but won't have the reports written until tomorrow. Steam-distillation of the dirt turned up traces of kerosene."

"What about the electronic stuff?"

Quaid paused to light his pipe. "Wires, a couple of nine-volt batteries. The main thing Lakin found was the metal shell of a carbon microphone, least that's what he thinks it is."

"So, what does that mean?"

"It means the gunshot noise was set off by the telephone."

"Was it wired to the phone?"

"Doesn't need to be. When the phone rings, it sets up a responsive vibration in the mike which becomes a faint current. This is boosted until it's strong enough to set off a spark or a piece of dynamite. Probably the phone set off a squib and the squib ignited the kerosene."

"How complicated is it?"

"Pretty simple. Lakin said if you had the plans you could make one without knowing much about electronics."

"And it can be set off from anywhere?"

"Sure, you only need to call the number."

Lazard had thought the presence of kerosene might make the investigation easier. Most arsonists are one-time offenders and their mistakes are due to lack of experience. Kerosene is less volatile than gasoline and has a higher flashpoint, making it a safer and more effective accelerant. But being more difficult to buy, it's easier to trace. The presence of the carbon microphone, however, implied experience, and Lazard doubted the arsonist had been clumsy in his purchase of kerosene.

"What about those kids the cops picked up?" asked Lazard.

"There were five. Pugliese got their names. We talked to them at their school. You know the type: little tough guys. They claimed not to know anything."

"What will you do now?"

Quaid blew gently into his pipe, sending a thin column of smoke toward the ceiling and a few sparks onto his brown cardigan. He patted them out. "I'll see those kids again and Schacter may turn up something. And we still haven't finished the canvass."

"Maybe if you saw the kids without Pugliese."

"I don't think anyone could get them to talk."

"You get much help from Pugliese?"

"He's all right. Maybe a little eager. You don't like him?"

Lazard's right hand hung over the side of the loveseat. As he spoke, he kept rubbing his thumb quickly over all four fingers, making a faint fluttering noise. It was a constant gesture and contradicted the stillness with which he sat.

"I get tired of his talking." Lazard thought about it and realized that what he disliked was Pugliese's enthusiasm. "I guess he's all right. Cassidy start on that extortion stuff?"

"Tomorrow. He's got more to do on that Newbury Street fire. Flanagan's still talking about getting a lieutenant from 1010. Soon we'll be hearing about a Plympton Street task force."

"It won't last. The funeral's Friday? I bet he starts reassigning you next week."

"They say Harris'll get the Medal of Valor next spring. McCarthy said he could have gotten out but went back for Roberts."

"That should make everybody happy," said Lazard, still snapping his fingers.

Dinner was excellent, although as usual Lazard ate little despite Rose's warnings about starvation. She and Quaid had been married in 1962, having met at a parish dinner. Both had reconciled themselves to remaining single and still saw their marriage as a surprising gift. She had been a secretary with Prudential and continued working until she became pregnant. Sometimes she felt guilty about Geraldine, thinking that at thirty-five she'd been too old to have a child. She was a small round woman with red hair braided into a thick bun.

After dinner they watched a movie on television. Geraldine preferred action movies because it meant more running which made it all seem more important. Quaid's wife knitted. Mostly she knitted Irish fishermen's sweaters which she gave to a Catholic charity that sent them to Ireland. Lazard found this disconcerting, thinking of Ireland as an exporter rather than an importer of sweaters. It occurred to him that the Irish sweaters sold in stores might have been knitted by American women like Mrs. Quaid, then shipped to Ireland only to be reshipped to the United States.

Rose had once offered to knit Lazard a sweater. This too had disconcerted him. His clothes were all of a conventional type and he saw fishermen's sweaters as somewhat flashy. He had told Rose he would be delighted, but she had seen through him and no more was said. Lazard knew if he changed his mind, he only had to ask. He couldn't imagine changing his mind.

Rose Quaid's maiden name was Carbery and her family had come to Boston from a small town in north Leinster in the late 1890s. The Irish name was O'Cairbre. Over the years Rose had made six visits to Ireland, meeting her cousins, with whom she still kept in correspondence. Once she told Lazard how the O'Cairbres were originally a sept belonging to County Westmeath. They were chiefs in the barony of Clononan but had fallen on hard times because of their support of James II.

Lazard knew nothing about his own family other than that they had been farmers around Mason and Charlotte. He knew nothing of the name Lazard or where his people had come from or what sort of people they might have been: generous or miserly, kind or cruel. Looking at the photographs of Rose's relatives, he remembered similar photographs on his grandfather's walls. The men were bearded and the women wore bonnets. All had stern, expressionless faces.

11

Thursday morning a bomb exploded at 9:12 in the office of the State Probation Department on the second floor of the Suffolk County Courthouse in Pemberton Square. Nineteen persons were injured, two critically.

Preliminary investigation was carried out by a police homicide unit, a state police special investigative unit, the State Fire Marshal's Office, and agents from the Bureau of Alcohol, Tobacco and Firearms. The police intelligence section was also represented, as were the FBI and the Arson Squad. It turned out there had been an anonymous phone call at 8:53 A.M. telling of the bomb but no warning was given.

All criminal records were stored with the Probation Department. This was one of several factors that added to the frustration of Warren Cassidy's search for possible extortionists.

At 2:30 P.M. Cassidy was in Jacob Wirth's restaurant, listening to Joseph, his usual waiter, describe the explosion. "One guy's foot was completely blown off, whaddaya say about that?"

Joseph wore a black suit and a long white apron. A folded white napkin lay neatly across his shoulder. That pleased Cassidy. He liked it that the waiters had dressed the same for over a hundred years. Cassidy took a forkful of sauerkraut and chewed it slowly.

He had big red hands, a red face, and wore a dark green shirt and a tie with diagonal yellow and green stripes. Cassidy's light green sport coat hung behind him on a brass coat rack. He was a man who always seemed at the edge of rage, as if he were about to leap up and smash every stick of furniture in the restaurant. Actually, he saw himself as mild-mannered and believed that only a very few things could make him angry—things like people disagreeing with him and those assholes who thought they knew all the answers.

"I don't know why they blew the place up," said Cassidy, "but they couldn't of caused me more trouble if they'd done it to irritate me on purpose. Foot or no foot. Get me a dark, will you?"

Cassidy had eaten at Jacob Wirth's nearly once a week for twenty years. He liked the brass railings and dark wood paneling, the huge bar with the gold-colored bas-relief of Jacob Wirth's head over the words *Suum Cuique:* to each his own. No matter how busy he was, Cassidy always tried to have a decent lunch. The way he saw it, you had to be kind to yourself. Some of his colleagues put the job over everything else. Lazard, for instance, would get more and more wrought up the longer he stayed on a case. To Cassidy, this was crazy. A man had to know how to relax.

Joseph returned with his dark beer. Although Cassidy's third, he felt he had earned it. For nearly six hours, he had been rushing around trying to scratch the wart on Flanagan's ass, as he called it, meaning he had started to investigate the extortion threat against Trieger's warehouse. He had begun that morning by first going to the intelligence section at police headquarters to see the extortion letter itself.

It was a short note typed on half a sheet of cheap white paper: "Pay $5,000 or we will burn your business. Don't call the police. We will contact you."

"Get many of these?" Cassidy had asked. He had talked to a Lieutenant Natale. It was a small office crowded with ten desks.

Natale was balding and overweight. Leaning back in his chair, he stuck his thumbs in his waistband and gazed at the wall above Cassidy's head. "Not many, I couldn't say we saw many."

"You see any?" Cassidy wiped his nose on the back of his hand and looked at it. Policemen were one of the categories of people he didn't like.

"In this office, we see everything."

"Does it often happen like this, that nothing happens?"

"Sometimes. A guy demands money, says he's goin' to smash your face. He's not really goin' to smash your face. You don't pay, he just tries someone else."

"You do anything about this letter?"

"What could we do? We increased a few patrols."

"What about the envelope?"

"A regular cheap envelope mailed in Boston."

"You have a list of people who been involved in extortion?"

Natale got up and walked to a file cabinet. There were five other men in the room. Three were talking about a Red Sox game. Two were reading the paper. It was warm in the office, although the day was cool and it looked like it might rain.

The telephone rang as Natale was returning with the card file. "Intelligence, Lieutenant Natale." The policeman's face began to look strained or, as Cassidy later described it to Joseph the waiter: he looked like he was trying to pass a broken beer bottle.

"You're jokin'," said Natale. "Come on, you're kiddin' me. No, sir, okay, sir. Right away." He covered the mouthpiece with his hand. The other detectives glanced up at him. "They just blew up Suffolk County Courthouse."

"The whole thing?"

"Just a hole in it."

For the next few minutes Natale gave orders to his men, who began making phone calls and hurrying out of the office. Cassidy considered telling them they needed a few weeks in a firehouse to learn how to behave efficiently under stress, but since they were only cops he didn't see why he should bother.

Natale noticed Cassidy sitting quietly and said, "Lucas, give this file to the fireman and see if he needs anything."

Cassidy took the file, waved Lucas away, and began to look through it. The file contained about a hundred names, but Cassidy soon found they included people who were in jail, dead, or had disappeared. Still, after an hour he had made up a list of forty persons who might conceivably have sent the letter. He then went down to the identification section, where he rechecked the addresses and was able to drop eight names. Cassidy had no faith in the list, but he'd never been much of a believer and so didn't let it bother him.

Leaving police headquarters at 11, he drove to 1010 Commonwealth Avenue, to see if he could get more names from the state police. He went to the State Fire Marshal's Office first. It was on the fifth floor and Cassidy walked. "Look," said Lieutenant-detective Hoffness, "how can I help you? Even the marshal's over there. You know the trouble we got?"

Cassidy looked out the window up Commonwealth Avenue toward the Hancock Building. He was bored with cops telling him their troubles. Although bigger than the arson office, this one was cluttered with more desks. On the other hand, it had two female clerks and a better view. He looked at the two women and decided they were heftier than he liked. He turned back to Hoffness.

"Half an hour. I need some names. I also gotta talk to someone in investigation. When have I ever turned you down?"

Two hours later Cassidy had reduced his list to thirty names. He had cut the police list to twenty-three and added seven. Now he wanted to go back to Police Headquarters and check the addresses of the seven. What he needed most were the files at the State Probation Department office, but because of the bomb he saw no way to do it until next week.

"Whaddaya think of that explosion?" asked Hoffness. "Takes the cake, right?"

"Live like animals and whaddaya expect?"

Cassidy returned to Police Headquarters, checked the seven names, and at the end still had thirty. None seemed particularly likely suspects. He then drove to Jacob Wirth's restaurant on Stuart Street to have lunch and talk to Joseph. Along with Cassidy's brother, who was an assistant parish priest in South Boston, Cassidy thought the waiter was one of the most sensible people he knew.

When he had finished his pigs' knuckles and sauerkraut, Cassidy reread his list, then divided it in two: those who had used or threatened to use fire and those who hadn't. What he thought of as his active list consisted of six names: five men and a woman.

The first person Cassidy decided to see was Henry Venuti. It was an address on Agawam just past Wonderland Park Dog Track in Revere. Cassidy chose him because it would give him a chance to see the ocean from a different perspective. Each morning he saw it from Fort Independence when he ran out to Castle Island.

Venuti had been involved in a loan-shark operation and was suspected of burning a number of buildings belonging to people who hadn't paid. That had been five years before. Since then he had spent three years in jail for income tax fraud.

Now he lived with his sister on the second floor of a brick apartment building on a hill above Revere Beach. Cassidy parked down the block. He hadn't called because he wanted to make sure he saw the ocean. Hopefully, Venuti's apartment had a decent view. He stood outside a moment opening a pack of Juicy Fruit gum. Then he put three sticks in his mouth and rang the bell.

Venuti's sister let him in. Although the apartment faced the ocean, the venetian blinds were down and the curtains drawn. The sister, a middle-aged woman in a black dress, was on her way to the store.

"Don't let Henry do anything he shouldn't," she said.

Cassidy snapped his gum and winked. "He's safe with me," he said.

Venuti had watched Cassidy enter the living room. He was a fat man in a gray bathrobe sitting in an armchair. His fingers were folded across his stomach. He had thin lips and Cassidy thought his mouth looked like a rip in some pale fabric.

"I don't know who you been talkin' to, but I ain't been outta here and it don't look like I will unless they make Carmine put me in a hospital."

The room was dark and utterly quiet. Cassidy thought he could just hear the sound of the waves. Perhaps he imagined it. He sat down on another low armchair across from Venuti. Both chairs were covered with a yellow plush material with red baroque designs.

"What's the problem?" he asked.

Venuti raised his right hand, then lowered it gently to his stomach. "They won't say for sure, but who they shittin'? Each day I gotta little less stomach. Carmine, she means well, but you should use what gut you got for havin' a good time. Right? Carrot juice, that's her idea of a good time. I mean, if I gotta rot here, I hate to do it on carrot juice. You a drinking man?"

Cassidy went out to bars twice a week. Although he talked more than drank, he considered himself a drinking man. "Who ain't?" he said.

"I'm a Scotch drinker myself. Don't know that I've had any in four months. Trouble with my line of work. Nobody wants to see someone die."

"You know anything about extortion in the city?" Cassidy told him a little about the warehouse.

"Nah, that's a twerp's job. Junkies. Somethin' like that, it's too public. And the pick-up, they always get you sooner or later."

"You ever look out at the ocean?" asked Cassidy.

"Hurts my eyes, all that space."

After he left, Cassidy found a liquor store and bought Venuti a bottle of Chivas Regal, but since he thought someone with stomach cancer shouldn't drink, he bought him only a half pint.

One man had told Bobby Dodge that Harvey Butters had gone to Chicago, another said he'd gone to New York. All agreed that he wasn't in Boston, which was a shame because this was when Dodge needed him most. Sometimes when he was feeling right, Butters had been known to take out a hundred-dollar bill, give it to a kid on the street, and say, "Here, boy, go buy some shoes."

Bobby Dodge was walking down Blue Hill Avenue on his way to the apartment of one of Butters's girlfriends. She wasn't one of his main girlfriends and Dodge had heard they'd split up, but he'd tried every place else and didn't know what else to do. It was 6 o'clock Thursday evening and the sky was beginning to clear. Earlier in the afternoon it had rained a little.

What had been a bad situation two days before had grown worse. From two other friends, Dodge had received another $100. Those had been two out of twenty asked. One friend drove a cab, the other worked in a record store in Roxbury. In each case Dodge felt he had sold their friendship or at least their goodwill for $50 each.

On Wednesday he had seen his probation officer, Allen Hahn. Normally he liked Hahn, who, though overworked, remained decent. Was everything going all right? Sure. How was his wife? Fine. Been having any problems? No. Leonard Quick said he'd missed work a couple of times, why was that? His wife had been sick. Staying away from drugs? Sure.

His worst moment had been when he had tried to get money from his mother. It hadn't been worth the bad words. His mother, Loreen Lewis, was a proud woman whose new husband drove a bus. Dodge's father had died in 1962 when the family lived in Washington. Instead of returning to Georgia, Loreen had moved to Roxbury, sending two of her seven children down to Georgia to live with her mother. Dodge liked his grandmother and regretted he hadn't gone as well.

When she saw him, she knew right away he was in trouble. She was large and big-boned with a thick Georgia accent that rose an octave when she got angry. "Boy, can't you keep your life straight? Wasn't four years in jail enough for you? You're a grown man with a nice wife and a family on the way. You still got that habit?"

Bobby Dodge stood in his mother's kitchen and tried to scowl back at her. "Believe me, I don't do that anymore."

"Then why do you need the money?"

"I just do, that's all."

"You tell me or you get nothing."

So he had told her about Henry Pierce. He didn't mention Dionne but thought she guessed well enough. Instead of bawling him out, she went to a cupboard, took five twenties from a coffee can, then gave him the money without even looking at him she was so mad.

As he walked along the sidewalk, Dodge told himself that if it weren't for Cecilia, he would have left town days ago. A lot of men would have left her, pregnant or not. But he had stayed even though someone had told her about Dionne and she kept yammering at him about it. And today he'd missed work to find Harvey Butters, and his boss had called home, and now Cecilia thought he'd spent the day with Dionne. If his grandmother hadn't died while he was in Walpole, he'd have left for Georgia already. Cecilia or no Cecilia.

Bobby Dodge was still brooding about his luck when a gray Cadillac drew up to the curb beside him just as he had crossed the corner at Woodbine. By the time he noticed, three men had gotten out. Even if he'd seen them in time, he wouldn't have run. He'd have been too scared.

"Hello, Bobby, been thinking about my offer?"

Henry Pierce was a short, dapper man with a shaved head. To match his Cadillac, he wore a gray suit with wide lapels. On either side of Bobby Dodge was one of Pierce's men. Dodge knew the man on his left: John Gains. They'd been in the same tenth-grade math class at Burke High School and Gaines had let Dodge copy his answers on tests.

Bobby Dodge stood with his back to a mailbox. "I'm not dealing smack. I don't care what you say." A mongrel dog paused to look at them, then hurried across the street.

Henry Pierce smiled. "You raised that money? I been worrying, Bobby. I hate to see a boy in trouble."

"I can give you $300 now."

Pierce glanced at Gaines as if to indicate he had never heard anything so ignorant. "I been good to you, boy. What you want to insult me for? I don't wanna see you hurt or sent back to Walpole. What'd your probation officer do if he knew about this trouble? You do a little dealing and this'll all get straightened out. Right? Meantime, don't trouble me with pennies."

It was still daylight and there was a lot of traffic on Blue Hill Avenue. Dodge thought he was fortunate they hadn't found him on some isolated street. As he was thinking this, John Gaines turned and hit him in the stomach, doubling him up and making him gag. Then the other man hit him in the stomach and Bobby Dodge fell to the sidewalk. Then the two men kicked him several times, got back into the gray Cadillac, and drove away.

As Bobby Dodge was getting beaten up on Blue Hill Avenue, Lazard was driving to Howard Trieger's house in Brookline. Lazard was angry and would have canceled the dinner engagement if he hadn't decided that it was connected with his job. He had spent the day in Charlestown District Court waiting for the arraignment of the woman accused of burning her beauty parlor. The woman never appeared and a new date had to be set.

Trieger lived in a two-story, white Victorian house surrounded by shrubbery. Lazard parked his Ford behind a new Pontiac in the driveway. As he limped up the drive, he saw three boys about twelve years old grouped around one of the small windows in the garage door. They were arguing and didn't hear him approach.

"What's up?" Lazard had meant to sound friendly, but the boys looked startled when they turned to face him. All three wore blue baseball jackets and had sunburnt faces.

"Just looking at the car," said one. "I say it's new but Timmy says he's seen it before."

"Timmy's wrong," said another boy, "if that car'd been there before I'd of seen it."

"I swear I saw it before," said Timmy. "Twice."

Lazard bent down to look through the garage window. Parked beside a Ford station wagon was a 1950 red TD-Type MG Midget with a black leather interior. The car was highly polished and appeared new. As he stared at the car, Lazard recalled that Trieger used to have an old MG which he worked on and rarely drove. He seemed to remember that Trieger had been given the car by his brother, who won it in a card game. He was sure of the card game and, as he thought about it, equally sure the car had been a gift. Although it had happened fifteen years before, Lazard remembered his surprise at learning that someone could win such a car, then give it away.

"Why do you think it's new?" asked Lazard.

" 'Cause it's only been here a coupla weeks," said the first boy. "Sure it's new."

Lazard turned to see Trieger watching him from the front steps.

"Frank, good to see you. Come in and have a drink."

Lazard followed him inside. The car had set him thinking and he wondered how Trieger would explain it. Before the front door was a red rubber mat with the words "Welcome to the Triegers."

"What can I get you?" asked Trieger, looking pleased to see him. He wore a dark blue shirt and gray double-knit slacks.

"Whiskey is okay. A couple of ice cubes. That the same MG you used to have?"

"Sure is. It's only got 35,000 miles. I can hardly stand to take it out, afraid some guy's going to bash it." As he spoke about the car, his eyes widened, and Lazard was again struck by what he thought of as their amazement at the world.

"You been keeping it at the warehouse?"

Trieger had walked to the liquor cabinet in the dining room and had begun making drinks. His back was to Lazard. "That's right, had a whole shop there. I'd go down on weekends and tinker with it."

"When did you bring it here?"

" 'Bout three weeks ago. Here's your whiskey. Look, we don't have to stand around. That armchair's the most comfortable." Trieger pointed to the recliner that had given Baxter so much trouble, then he sat down on the couch. Lazard sat down at the other end of the couch.

"Why'd you move the car here?"

Trieger stirred the ice in his glass with his finger, then wiped his finger on his pants. "That extortion thing was bothering me."

"I thought you got that at the beginning of March."

"Well, I didn't think much of it at first. Then I started worrying and finally I just felt better with the car here."

"Is it insured?"

"Yeah, but you can't replace a car like that."

"Where's the nearest phone to your place up north?"

"There's a gas station about half a mile away. Then some of the neighbors have phones."

Lazard was kept from further questions by Norma, who came in from the kitchen. She was a thin woman, about six inches shorter than her husband, with a thin face which emphasized the sharp line of her jaw. She had small dark eyes like a bird.

"Frank, I'm so glad you could come."

Lazard kissed her cheek, but clumsily, bumping against her ear.

"Why didn't you tell me Frank was here?" She looked at his cane, then looked away. Lazard wondered how long it would be before she asked him about it.

"He's been keeping me busy with questions. Like a drink?"

"I was sorry to hear about your mother," said Lazard.

Norma wrinkled her brow, then smiled. "She was very sick. It was a blessing in a way. How's your father?"

"Okay. I talked to him in January on his birthday. He had to retire last year." Lazard's father had worked for the John Deere Company in Lansing. It was odd to think of someone in Boston who knew his family. "You get back there at all?"

"Every year or so. I was hoping we could drive back this summer but Howard hates to give up any time at the cottage." She laughed and Lazard found himself remembering Fourth of July picnics at his grandmother's farm in Charlotte. Norma was two years older and there had been a period when Lazard was in his early teens that he had spent a lot of time trying to attract her attention.

Dinner was roast lamb. They sat at a round oak table and through dinner Trieger talked about what they had done together years before: a trip to Cape Cod, a picnic at Crane Beach. Lazard's memory was vague. It was as if they were talking about some third person. No mention was made of Lazard's ex-wife, and although

Trieger nearly said her name several times, he made it sound as if only the three of them had been together.

It was Norma who finally mentioned her. "Do you hear from Elizabeth at all?"

"She calls every couple of weeks. Likes her job. I guess she's been meeting some people."

Trieger looked embarrassed but curious. Norma seemed more sympathetic. It bothered Lazard that he couldn't think of anything else to say. "We sort of just got tired of each other. I don't know, we still like each other well enough."

"You seem different," said Trieger.

"How d'you mean?"

"You're a lot quieter. Probably because we're getting older. Norma says I get stubborner every day." Trieger pushed a piece of bread back and forth on his plate. "Christ, remember how we'd be after a game? That time we got thrown out of that bar in Kenmore Square?"

Lazard found himself getting angry at Trieger. "Maybe I'm more content," he said.

After dinner they went back to the living room and drank coffee. Trieger talked primarily about his cottage and how he planned to add on a room. "One thing about my business, it makes it cheap to furnish a place."

Lazard wished he could open Trieger's head and see what he was thinking. He couldn't imagine why they'd invited him to dinner. "I thought you wanted a hardware store," he said.

"Yeah, well, you were hot to be a district chief. The furniture leasing thing looked good and my brother let me have some money. Since then I haven't had a chance to look at anything else."

"He goes into hardware stores all the time," said Norma, "and won't come out till he's picked up each tool and held it a few seconds."

"I like to pinch them," said Trieger, laughing.

It wasn't until late that Lazard's leg was mentioned. He knew Trieger was curious, but the more curious he became, the more he seemed to repress his desire to ask. Lazard was just returning from the bathroom. He felt them watching and, as always, he grew angry at his dependence on a cane.

"Frank," asked Norma, "how did you hurt your leg?"

Lazard lowered himself down to his place on the couch. "In a fire about seven years ago."

"What happened?" asked Trieger.

Lazard didn't want to talk about it but didn't see how to avoid it without simply refusing. "It was a burning three-decker. I was on the third floor seeing if anyone was there. A woman told me that a crippled kid was up there in a bedroom." Lazard was about to go on, then didn't.

"Did it take long to heal?" asked Norma.

Lazard looked at Trieger and his wife, their concerned faces. He was struck by the sincerity of their interest, then he told himself that it wasn't important, that none of it mattered. "I was out for a year. They said I was lucky to keep the leg."

Engines 17 and 24 and Ladder 7 were already on the scene and working when Harry Dwyer pulled Engine 21 up to the wooden three-decker on Puritan. Peering from the cab, Lazard saw that far back on the right side of the second floor several windows had blown and cherry flame was lapping up the side of the building. Thick black smoke pushed into a blacker sky.

It was a narrow street with houses and three-deckers built close together. The three pumpers, Ladder 7, and the district chief's car were all parked at different angles in front of the burning building, while the noise of the fire, men shouting, engine noise, and static from the radios seemed to fill every available space.

Jumping from the cab, Lazard was hit again by the freezing air heavy with diesel fumes and smoke—that mixture of burning wood with plaster and paint. Some of the truckmen had a ladder at the side of the building and were beginning to vent the windows.

Jakes from Engine 17 were directing water from a 2½-inch line into side windows on the second floor. Already ice was forming on the clapboards. Three men from Engine 24 had gone through the front door and were apparently waiting for water because their line was still flat.

"How's your ankle, McQuire?" shouted Lazard.

"Right as rain, loo."

"Then let's get with it."

Lazard ran to a side compartment on the pumper, began pull-

ing out air packs, and handed two to McQuire and Felsch. Strapping his own tank to his back, he let the mask dangle over his shoulder. Then, climbing into the pumper, he took the nozzle and first 50-foot length of 2½-inch line. McQuire took the second and Felsch the third as Dwyer began to hook up to the hydrant. Glancing at McQuire, Lazard saw he wasn't limping and after a moment he forgot about him.

Duffey, the district chief, wearing a white fire coat, ran up as Lazard and his men were pulling the line across the street toward the front door of the three-decker.

"Take it upstairs after twenty-four. The fire's in a couple of middle rooms. Be careful, it looks like gasoline. God knows what else's in there. A couple of men from seven are getting people out the back. Where the hell you been?"

"Accident." Lazard wanted to explain that it wasn't his fault, but knew he couldn't make excuses. Nothing would be worse than Duffey's distrust, especially if Lazard ever hoped to make captain. Looking away, he saw Ladder 23 just pulling up, followed by Engine 52 and Rescue 2 from the second alarm. He glanced back at Duffey and realized that the chief was still regarding him critically, and Lazard knew he would now have to work all the harder. The revolving red lights sent waves of color across their faces.

Then Duffey slapped his shoulder and said, "All right, get going."

As Lazard again began to pull the line toward the front door, he saw the first line manned by Engine 24 surge and swell as it was charged with water. People were trying to push their way out of the building carrying clothes, boxes, a lamp. One man was staggering under a large color TV as his wife ran behind him calling, "You'll drop it, you'll drop it."

Glancing up, Lazard saw flames in the front windows on the second floor, then he heard a whoosh as someone cracked the tip of the line running into the house.

Moments later there was a crash, followed by shouting, then more crashing. Lazard left McQuire and Felsch with the uncharged line and ran ahead through the front door.

Rushing into the darkened hall, Lazard pulled a flashlight from his pocket, flicked it on, and stopped. Several of the boards on the stairs had given way and two men from Engine 24 had fallen through, letting go of the line, which was now discharging 250 gallons a minute at 50 pounds of nozzle pressure. The third man on the line had been knocked back down the stairs but was still managing to hold on even though his hands were over a foot from the nozzle. The force of the water was heaving him first against the wall, then against the banister, which broke apart under his weight, then smashed him against the wall again. As it hit the wall, the nozzle sent chunks of plaster flying through the small space. A woman, crouched down in a corner, kept screaming.

Almost without thought, Lazard dropped his flashlight and flung himself past the other man and onto the nozzle, which had just smashed against the stairs, then bounced back against Lazard's chest. He wrapped his arms around it as he was thrown backward, and as he fell his hands found the lever and pushed it shut. Seconds later he landed nearly on top of the other firefighter. He lay there a moment hanging onto the charged line, hardly aware of the other man half beneath him. A sudden screaming from the stairs made him scramble to his feet.

Several men pointed their flashlights, settling them on the senior man from Engine 24 who was lying on his back headfirst down the stairs. His mouth was open and he screamed one short scream over and over. At first Lazard thought he had been hit by the nozzle, then he saw how his left leg was tucked back under him, broken at the knee. There was no sign of the other firefighter and Lazard guessed he had fallen through to the basement stairs. By the light of the flashlights, Lazard saw that several boards of the stairs had been cut away, then covered with carpeting to make them look safe.

Lazard turned to the firefighter from 24 who was still hanging onto the line behind him. "Hey, Schultz, we'll take it up along the side of the stairs. Let's go."

"What about MacDonald and Irving?"

"Rescue'll get them. Come on, we gotta get some water up there."

Three men from Rescue ran into the hall as Lazard and Schultz began to make their way up the stairs. One of the men, Haggerty, began to help Schultz jockey the line behind Lazard, while the others went to the injured firefighters.

More men had pushed through the front door, including Felsch and McQuire, who still held the line from Lazard's pumper and were waiting for water. Lazard called to them to follow him. As he edged his way up the side of the staircase, Lazard saw the men from Rescue begin to lift MacDonald, whose screams grew louder and more desperate.

But then Lazard saw flames at the top of the stairs and he pushed everything from his mind except the fire. "Give me more line," he called, as Schultz and Haggerty pulled the line behind him.

The air grew thick with smoke. As he neared the top of the stairs, Lazard kept coughing and gray mucus streamed from his nose. He paused to put on his face mask and open the regulator. The safety bell rang briefly to indicate that air had begun to flow.

12

"He moved the car three weeks ago," said Lazard. "Told me he hadn't been worried at first."

"You believe him?" asked Baxter.

"I neither believe nor disbelieve him."

"What about his being out in the boat fishing?" asked Quaid.

"That's probably true enough. I don't think he'd make his daughters lie."

The three men were in the arson office. It was 7:30 Friday morning. The windows were open and the sound of rush-hour traffic could be heard from Southampton. In the distance the Boston skyline stood out against a bright blue sky.

Lazard was at the desk nearest the window using a Yellow Pages to make up a list of Trieger's competition. During the day, he intended to call them. The desk was cluttered with books on fire codes, ashtrays, piles of blank report forms, photographs of fire scenes, a computer printout on vandalism fires, dirty coffee cups, a pair of reading glasses, a stapler, a black telephone with four lines, ballpoint pens, and note pads. Under the glass covering the desktop were the typed telephone numbers of police agencies and departments, the Bureau of Alcohol, Tobacco and Firearms, the

Governor's Committee on Violent Crime and Harassment, important city numbers, and a list of Fire Department extensions.

The two men going off duty, Jerry Phelps and Roy Hufnagel, were also in the office. They had to appear in court later that morning and were getting cleaned up and changing their clothes. Hufnagel was a small, sad man. He had recently returned to the squad after being out for several months recuperating from a heart attack. Phelps was the lieutenant. The curse of his life was a little heart-shaped mouth that any flapper would have given her pearls for. He kept it covered with a shaggy moustache and stoically accepted the teasing of the clean-shaven firemen, preferring to be teased about the moustache than about having a mouth like a perfect cupid's bow. Baxter generally called him "fag-lips."

At the moment, Baxter was making coffee in a tiny bathroom attached to the office near the front window. The shower stall was filled with boxes containing the files of old cases. More boxes were on the shelves above the coffee maker.

As Baxter made the coffee, inspectors from Fire Prevention kept checking to see if it was ready. Their questions ranged from "Don't you have that crap ready yet" to "What the fuck, Ruby, jacking off again?" To everyone Baxter replied, "Stuff your head."

As Lazard sat at the desk, Phelps kept coming over to retrieve a few things he had forgotten: keys, a pen. Lazard tried to ignore him. Both Hufnagel and Phelps turned in reports on more accidental fires than anyone else since O'Neill, their ex-captain, and Lazard was certain they often received money for this. He knew they would justify it by saying that some fire would get classified as being of undetermined origin anyway, so what was the difference between that and listing it as of accidental origin. Lazard guessed they earned an extra couple of thousand a year this way. He also knew they would complain about their financial burdens—medical bills or putting a kid through college. It made Lazard hate them and he could rarely see them without making some crack.

As Phelps reached over Lazard's shoulder to retrieve his notebook, Lazard pushed himself away from the desk and said, "Hey, Phelps, you run across any accidental Molotov cocktails last night?"

Phelps put his notebook in his pocket and looked at Lazard suspiciously. "What's that supposed to mean, Frank?"

"I mean your moonlighting for organized crime."

Even as he said it, Lazard knew he had gone too far. He also knew that his anger had something to do with Trieger and feelings which had been stirred up by going to Trieger's for dinner.

The several people in the office became quiet. Phelps took a step toward Lazard, who tried to push himself out of his chair and grab his cane at the same time with the result that he stumbled against the wall. Before he could even turn toward Phelps, Baxter had come between them.

"Jesus, Frank, what's gotten into you?"

Lazard wanted to say that Phelps was getting paid off by the same people who had burned the three-decker which had cost him his leg. Then he gave it up. He would only be earning the ill-will of the department. As Baxter was fond of repeating: They were still firemen, no matter what. Quaid had drawn Phelps to the other side of the office and was talking to him. Hufnagel had left, probably hoping to avoid a scene.

"Nothing," said Lazard. "Let's just forget it."

"You should apologize to him, Frank."

"I said let's forget it. It was a joke, the whole thing was a joke."

As he spoke, Lazard saw Phelps pull away from Quaid and leave the office. Lazard felt relieved. Despite his growing embarrassment, he would not have been able to apologize.

Quaid went back to his desk and sat down. "That's a bad way to let off steam, Frank."

Lazard shrugged. He realized he had been foolish and wanted to change the subject. Picking up his notebook, he looked at the names of the furniture leasing companies that he had copied down. Then, in exasperation, he turned to Baxter. "Come on, Ruby, finish with that coffee. We've got to get moving."

Shortly, Baxter would visit Trieger's office, where he would talk to employees, get the names of people who had been fired or quit, and inspect Trieger's books. He would also check the Registry of Deeds for mortgages on his home and on the warehouse. At the same time, Lazard would check the competition, visit Massachusetts Properties, which owned the warehouse, and visit Trieger's insurance agent. Although Lazard and Baxter were supposed to stay together, Lazard felt if they remained in radio and telephone contact, they could easily respond to any fire call.

Apart from the Trieger investigation, Lazard needed more information about the Bridal Boutique fire, and beyond that case were a dozen others in various stages of investigation which would require telephone calls and perhaps actual visits during the day.

Fatback Tucker wandered in a few minutes later carrying a bag of three dozen doughnuts. These he would sell for 20 cents each, which would more than pay for the four he ate himself. Seeing Quaid at the desk he thought of as his own, Tucker asked, "You going to be there long?" Fatback wore a sport coat with black and white checks, a peach-colored shirt, and a purple tie with a silver-dollar clip.

Since there were two desks to be shared by eleven men, Fatback's tone of injured ownership always irritated Quaid. "I'm going to be here until you promise to wash my car once a week for the rest of the year. Why'n't you just put a coupla chairs together." Quaid was compiling a list of the apartments he had missed or where no one had been home.

Fatback rolled his eyes and put the bag of doughnuts on the desk. By now the coffee was ready and the Fire Prevention inspectors began buying doughnuts.

"Where's Cassidy?" asked Lazard.

"In court," said Fatback.

"What's he got?"

Fatback looked at a list of pending and upcoming court cases attached to the green bulletin board above the desks. "That kid that was burning the apartment houses. Charlestown District Court."

"You know if he's learned anything about that extortion business?"

"He's seen a coupla guys," said Fatback. "That bomb fucked him up. Hey, Quaid, you going to make it to the funeral?"

Harris and Roberts were being buried at 2 P.M. out of Holy Name Cathedral. Other fire departments were sending representatives, coming from as far away as Washington, D.C., and Chicago.

"I'm going to try," said Quaid. "Depends if I get finished in the projects." He began to ask Lazard the same question, then stopped. Lazard was staring at a blank sheet of paper. There was no sign of the anger he had shown toward Phelps a few minutes before.

Pugliese arrived at 8 o'clock. There were nine other people in

94

the office, including Chief Flanagan, who had come to discuss the Plympton Street fire with Lazard and Quaid.

"Hey, Pugliese," said Baxter, "they're not bringing in a lieutenant-detective after all. They're all on the courthouse bombing."

"We never needed one," said Pugliese. "Anything that needs doing, I can do myself." Pugliese felt shy in the arson office and tried to hide it by appearing pompous. He found it hard to talk to firemen who answered monosyllabically. Among themselves he knew they could talk happily about nothing for hours. It was their second profession.

Leaning against a green locker, Pugliese watched the nine men in the office. He thought it was like being on a crowded bus. Only Lazard and Quaid were working. Whenever he was preoccupied, Quaid began whistling pseudo-musical phrases from popular songs of the '30s. At the moment he had fastened on a five-note sequence from "Smoke Gets in Your Eyes" and was repeating it with slight variation for the twentieth time. Lazard kept glancing at Quaid, but whether from irritation or what Pugliese couldn't tell. Lazard's face was always so blank that Pugliese never knew what he was thinking. He looked at Lazard's high forehead and uncombed fringe of short brown hair, the large blue eyes with circles under them. Pugliese thought he resembled one of the monks who'd sometimes visited his school when he was growing up in East Boston. Lazard's glance shifted briefly to Pugliese, who looked away.

"Hey, Pugliese," said Fatback, "whaddaya got in your pockets?"

Pugliese pressed back a little harder against the locker. He wore a blue blazer and in each of the side pockets were two large bulges. Pugliese dug into a pocket and took out a white lacrosse ball. "A ball. I got four."

"What the fuck you doing with four balls?" asked Baxter.

Pugliese tossed the ball into the air and caught it. "I've been reading about juggling and I thought I'd see what it's like. The principle's fairly simple . . ."

"For cryin' out loud, Pugliese," said Baxter, "whaddaya want to juggle a bunch of balls for?"

"Maybe he's having a hard time getting it up," said an inspector.

"Hey, Pugliese, they increase your potency?"

"Least I got six balls," said Pugliese, "you jakes only got two."

"Stuff your head," said Baxter.

It was too bad, thought Quaid, that Pugliese always insisted on putting his foot in his mouth. Firemen didn't like being called jakes by nonfiremen. Personally, Quaid had nothing against juggling. He knew if he could juggle, it would make his daughter very happy.

Nearly four hours later Lazard stood behind a two-story white frame house on Woodward off Dorchester Avenue. He wore his fire coat, helmet, and boots. The first-floor windows were smashed and burn marks surrounded the top parts of the frames, rising over each window like a ragged black arch. Littering the back yard were beer cans, broken glass, plastic containers, and bits of newspaper blown up against a wire fence. From inside the house came a constant crashing and sound of plaster falling on wood floors as firefighters pulled down ceilings to find any trace of flame. A few more minutes, Lazard thought, and the house would have been totally involved. As it was, damage was estimated at $5,000. Firefighters had discovered two separate fires downstairs and the chief of District 6 had called the Arson Squad.

When they'd got the call, Lazard had been at Massachusetts Properties and Baxter at Trieger's office. Lazard had already talked to the heads of the other furniture leasing companies on the phone. None was critical of Trieger or felt he was capturing too much of the market. If Lazard had more time, he might check if any had something to gain by the removal of Trieger's company. On the telephone, however, there was no hint of anything suspicious. Lazard knew that didn't mean anything, that it was just a bad excuse.

Baxter learned Trieger had a small mortgage on his home but no outstanding debts. He had spent most of the morning talking to Trieger's employees. All liked Trieger and had nothing bad to say about him. Baxter made a list of the employees who had left in the seven years the business had been in operation. There were eight and none had been fired, but Baxter hoped to talk to them anyway. So far there was no evidence that anyone had a grudge against Trieger. That afternoon Baxter meant to go through Trieger's books.

Lazard had talked to the president of Massachusetts Properties. Again, there were no outstanding debts and no angry people; nor did it seem the land would be more valuable without the warehouse. The suspicious suicide turned out to be a clerk who had died of cancer.

As he stood behind the burned house, however, Lazard was not thinking about this particular fire or even about Trieger. He was thinking about a fire some months before in which a storefront or house had been torched and the owner, whose name he didn't remember, had been Lebanese or Syrian or at least Moslem, he was sure of that. But he didn't know exactly when or where it was or the names of the people involved. This house was also owned by a Lebanese, and all Lazard knew for certain was that this Lebanese and the Moslem of several months before looked very much alike.

The owner of this house was Welid Shehab, a man in his late twenties who was in the United States on a student visa. He had taken some courses at Boston State College and was delaying his return to Lebanon because of the troubles, as he called them.

Shehab said he had left his house early in the morning and got back shortly after eleven to find it burning and surrounded by firemen. Asked why he thought the house might have been torched, he said the local residents were probably prejudiced against Lebanese or, being Christian, were anti-Moslem.

"Why'd you buy a house in South Boston?" Lazard had asked.

Shehab raised his hand, touching his chest. "I had to live somewhere. The house was inexpensive."

Lazard had talked to Shehab when he first arrived about a half hour earlier. Across the street approximately fifty people had silently watched the firemen put out the fire. Merrick, the photographer, took some crowd shots. Near the house Baxter was talking to the District 6 chief, getting details about where and how the fire had started.

"But why here? Why not someplace near Boston State?"

"I liked this house."

"Who's it insured with?"

Shehab was a slender man with thick black hair combed back over his head. Lazard thought the man he had spoken with months before had had a moustache. Neither man had any distinguishing features: a thin, nondescript face with a sharp nose. Suspended from a silver chain around Shehab's neck was a clear green stone which Baxter kept calling a heathen evil eye.

"FAIR Plan," said Shehab.

"How long have you lived here?"

"Two months."

"And you've been insured with FAIR Plan two months?"

"One month."

FAIR Plan stood for Fair Access to Insurance Requirements. It was a quasi-governmental organization that provided insurance in high-risk urban areas, which, when conceived in the mid-1960s, meant riot-prone areas. Although FAIR Plan inspected all property before issuing a policy, it was required by law to issue a policy to anyone who applied. Lazard recalled many cases where someone had bought a house cheaply from the Department of Housing and Urban Development, made a few cosmetic improvements, insured with FAIR Plan, and then burned it. Unfortunately, he could seldom prove it in criminal court. But the increasing arson rate and number of fraudulent claims had led FAIR Plan, along with other insurance companies, to begin hiring private arson investigators to supply them with evidence to withstand a civil suit if they refused to honor a claim. These had been so successful that private arson investigators now outnumbered public investigators in the state by three to one.

Leaving the back of the house, Lazard walked around to the front to talk to Shehab a second time. Although he hadn't recalled where he had seen the other Moslem, he thought it was in Dorchester about six months before. Lazard wondered where he had gotten the money for a down payment. Recently Lazard had read a report which claimed that members of the Palestine Liberation Organization in the United States were engaged in various types of insurance fraud to raise money for their struggle against Israel. This included burning buildings. Although it struck him as unlikely that Shehab was a member of the PLO, Lazard knew he would never be able to prove it one way or the other, would never have time to link Shehab to that earlier fire and bring the whole matter to court.

Shehab was standing by Engine 1. If he was disappointed at not having a more profitable fire, he gave no sign of it. He appeared relaxed and, to Lazard, even confident, as if he knew his guilt could never be proven. He wore a bright green shirt with the top three buttons unbuttoned. Lazard wanted to grab him by the front of his shirt and shake him until he admitted everything, even, Lazard found himself thinking, his responsibility for all the cases Lazard ever had to leave unsolved.

"We've met before, haven't we?" said Lazard.

"I don't believe so."

"You had a fire several months ago. We met then."

"I have had no other fires."

"You've changed your name, shaved, and burned another building. What're you going to do next time, grow a beard?"

Shehab tried to step around Lazard in order to move away from the fire engine. "You firemen, you are no different from those who burned my house. You say these Lebanese people, they all look the same. This other man, what was he? Egyptian? Turkish?"

"Why didn't you have much furniture in the house?"

"I was still decorating it."

"Where's the paint?"

"I had not bought it yet."

"Where was that other fire?"

As Lazard asked each question, he pushed Shehab back against the fire engine until at last Shehab could back up no farther. Then, without thinking, Lazard lifted his cane and pushed the tip against Shehab's chest. Lazard hardly became aware of his action until he saw the fear in Shehab's eyes, then pain.

Almost immediately, Baxter was beside him. "Come on, Frank, let up on him."

Lazard looked at Baxter in surprise, then lowered the cane. Glancing at Shehab, Lazard saw he was smiling. Furious, Lazard stepped forward and slapped him across the face. "You torched this place and you torched another and I'll put you in jail for it."

At 1 P.M. Quaid was looking for Pugliese along Harrison Avenue. He had finished talking to all the people he could find and none had supplied additional information about the fire. Quaid guessed he had spoken to several hundred suspicious and silent local residents.

One of the people he had talked to was Joseph Schacter. Quaid had found him in the first-floor hall of his apartment house. Although he didn't like Schacter, Quaid was one of those people who feel guilty because of their unfriendly feelings, and consequently was often more attentive to people he disliked than to his friends.

"You haven't seen those boys?" Quaid had asked.

"No, but they're out there someplace. Right now they're probably no more'n two blocks away planning to burn something."

Schacter had been bringing up some tires from the basement. As they talked, he kept wiping his neck with a yellow dish towel.

"What makes you think they started any fires?"

"What're they messing with hydrants for if they're not interested in fires? Stands to reason they burned the warehouse."

It was about an hour after seeing Schacter that Quaid finally found Pugliese standing in front of a boarded-up store. Pugliese was tossing a ball in the air over and over. He would have said he was popping it, meaning he was flexing his hand, spreading his fingers, and giving his wrist a quick snap while neither raising nor lowering the level of his palm. The point was to keep the ball from spinning, the hand from moving, and the distance the ball traveled the same each time. It was the basic throw in juggling. Pugliese was dying to tell this to someone.

Quaid watched for a moment, then said, "Ready to go back?"

Pugliese hadn't heard him approach. Turning, he dropped the ball, then retrieved it when it rolled to a stop among some garbage cans. "I just have a few places to recheck."

"Well, I've pretty much finished and want to get something to eat before the funeral. I guess I'll see you later. That's a good-looking toss you got there."

Pugliese assumed Quaid was joking. As he watched him walk away, Pugliese thought of the three years he had spent stopping speeders on the turnpike and told himself the marshal's office had to be better than that. Then he walked up Harrison toward Plympton. His feet hurt and 50 yards ahead was a bench where he hoped to rest. The day was sunny, warm, and Pugliese could just detect the smell of the sea.

The State Fire Marshal's Office belonged to the Division of Fire Prevention of the Department of Public Safety. It was supposed to investigate all suspicious fires, fires of undetermined origin, and explosions, along with enforcing state fire-prevention rules and regulations. It also had to approve plans for all self-service gas stations, tank trucks carrying inflammables, and storage facilities for inflammables; approve applications for public warehousemen's licenses; approve emergency lights, oil burners, heat reclaimers; approve applications to set off fireworks, revolutionary muskets, cannons, and the use of all explosives.

To do this were supposedly a captain of detectives, seventeen lieutenant-detectives, seven troopers on special assignment, two explosives technicians, a fire-prevention engineer, and clerical help. Actually there were six vacancies for lieutenant-detective, no fire-prevention engineer, and the captain had been out for eight months with an obscure kidney disease. There were only nine men in the state who investigated just fires, including Pugliese.

Sitting on the bench with his feet stuck out, Pugliese stared across the vacant lots at the wreckage of the warehouse. He knew he had to go back to the apartments where no one had been home and try again. But his feet hurt and it was more comfortable in the sun, and he enjoyed shutting his eyes and thinking how lucky he was not to be catching speeders on the turnpike and it didn't really matter having dozens of investigations where nothing was learned and nothing solved.

Pugliese grew aware of someone else sitting down on the bench. Opening his eyes, he saw a man in his mid-fifties staring at him expectantly. He was a small man with thinning brown hair, a pointy nose, and practically no chin. He wore a shabby brown pin-stripe suit. Pugliese looked away, then looked back again. The man was still staring.

"Are you a policeman or a fireman?" asked the man. He had a heavy accent which Pugliese didn't recognize. When he opened his mouth, Pugliese saw that his teeth bent slightly inward.

"A policeman."

"Good, I do not like firemen. They do a lot of damage, breaking things and getting them wet."

Pugliese took a ball out of his pocket and rolled it along his thigh. It was too nice a day to talk to crazy people. "They do that to put out the fire," he said.

"That's why they say they do it, but really they do it because they like it. It makes them glad to break things. My brother-in-law in Hungary, he was a fireman and he was a bad man. During the rising, he did nothing but sit in his basement."

Pugliese glanced again at the man, who began to talk faster, seemingly excited at having proved his point about firemen.

"You know, I am a mechanic and I fix diesel trucks good, but where I work I do not finish until one in the morning and sometimes I do not get home until two and then, you know, it is difficult to sleep after working so hard and sometimes I do not get to sleep before five or six in the morning."

Pugliese got to his feet. Over on Washington was a Mexican restaurant where he could stuff himself on tortillas. "Have you tried naming the fifty states?"

"Wait a moment, you know, in my country I was a great walker. I loved to walk for miles out into the country. Sometimes I would walk so far I would have to sleep at a farm or in the fields. But here everybody has an automobile, and someone who walks, they say he is crazy. But sometimes when I cannot sleep I go for walks and this often upsets people. For example, there is a night watchman on that next street and twice he has stopped me and called me names and threatened to hit me. You know the man I mean? He guards the warehouse that was burned and where I saw the car that all those firemen have been asking about."

Fifteen minutes later, Pugliese half dragged the Hungarian through the door of the arson office. "Where's Quaid?"

Fatback was alone, cleaning his nails with a brass letter opener. "Check the john."

Pugliese led the Hungarian, whose name was Basil Kaczka, to the men's room. Pushing open the door, he saw that one of the stall doors was shut. "Quaid, you in there?"

There was a rustling of newspaper. "What do you want?"

"I've got him."

"Got who?"

"The guy that saw the car."

"Where is he?"

"Right beside me. Three-thirty Monday morning. A dark maroon Cougar with a black vinyl roof; 1975. He's a fuckin' mechanic."

There was a silence, then the sound of water flushing.

At 3:30 Friday afternoon Lazard was sitting in the office of Trieger's insurance agent on the twelfth floor of a building in downtown Boston. From the window he could see across the harbor to Logan Airport and the control tower rising up more than twenty stories like a contemporary version of the Colossus of Rhodes.

The agent was Robert Barnes, a middleaged man with brown

102

hair turning gray at the temples. He wore a pair of tortoiseshell glasses which kept slipping down his nose so he looked at Lazard over the frames.

"He hasn't as yet submitted a claim, but he notified us of the fire and he's hired a public adjuster from a reputable firm. Both he and our own adjuster have been trying to determine the extent of the loss. Most likely it will be in the neighborhood of $100,000. Mr. Trieger has been perfectly helpful and has given our man complete access to his business."

"But he increased his insurance a month ago?"

"That's right. However, he hadn't increased his insurance in over a year and what with inflation and his expanded business, it seemed a perfectly sensible move." Barnes reached across his desk and handed Lazard a piece of paper. "Those are the dates Mr. Trieger has increased his insurance in the seven years he has been with us. Also the amounts. Each reflects the expansion of his business and inflation. I certainly don't think he was overinsured."

"Did he give any reason for increasing his insurance?"

"Just that he hadn't seen to it for a while."

"Had you contacted him about selling him additional insurance?"

"Not at all, I hadn't spoken to him for over a year."

"Has he had any other fires?" As he spoke, Lazard rubbed his bad leg, which had begun to ache. He felt dissatisfied with himself and vaguely irritated with Barnes for being so reasonable and proper.

"No, this is the first time he'll be submitting a claim."

"When you saw him, did he say anything that struck you as out of place?"

Barnes paused to light a cigarette. "No, I don't think so."

"What do you mean, 'think so'?"

"Well, as I say, he didn't mention the extortion threat, not that it would have made any difference. We talked a little about the insurance industry and I recall he asked if some companies challenged claims more than others. It seems a perfectly innocent question."

"Did he ask you for the names of these companies?"

"Oh, no, nothing like that. He just seemed mildly curious."

"You like him, don't you?"

Barnes stubbed out his cigarette in a square black ashtray.

"He's a very likable person. As you know, there are companies that never challenge a claim, no matter how strong their evidence against the insured. I mean, he could have changed his insurance but he just didn't seem that interested."

That afternoon someone poured a can of paint thinner over some rags in the stairwell of an apartment house in Dorchester and lit them. There was little available fuel other than a banister and two doors, and the fire was contained to the downstairs hall. The chief of District 7 called Baxter and Lazard, who questioned neighbors and occupants of the building. No one had seen anything.

Earlier they had driven by the Bridal Boutique. It had been closed, but Lazard managed to get the owner's widow on the telephone. She had answered some of his remaining questions about the financial state of the business. In any case, no one would go to jail and no one would get any money except the bank holding the mortgage. They hadn't been back to headquarters and still had to write up the reports on Welid Shehab's fire.

At 5:30 they were on their way to Trieger's office. Baxter had finished going over Trieger's books. There was nothing to show that the business was not healthy, expanding, and profitable. Only one item stood out: in 1971 Trieger had borrowed $15,000 from a bank. He had long since repaid the money and the only thing unusual about the loan was there seemed no reason for it: no immediate purchase of property or furniture, no sudden expansion of his business.

Baxter saw nothing curious about the loan. "Maybe I missed something. Maybe it was other debts. Who's to say? The guy's gotta good business. If I was the kinda fella to buy stock, maybe I'd pick up a few shares. Anyway, $15,000, it's nothing."

"Then why did he need it?" Lazard sat with his hands resting on the crook of his aluminum cane. They kept getting bogged down in rush-hour traffic and he looked out at the other cars with growing impatience.

"Maybe for that place up in New Hampshire."

"He already owned that. I just want to ask him, that's all."

Trieger's showroom looked like several immaculate houses without walls: living rooms, dining rooms, bedrooms separated by narrow aisles, and all on a thick red carpet. A gleaming brass bed was covered with an old-fashioned quilt decorated with red and yellow flowers. Trieger led the way back to his office. Seeing the bed made Baxter feel tired.

"You should get some mannequins and have 'em playing cards or something," Baxter said.

Trieger laughed. "That'd make it too spooky for me."

The office was furnished with a couch and two armchairs. "Now," said Trieger, sitting down at his desk, "what can I do for you?" On the desk was a white telephone, an ivory desk set, and an 8-by-10 photograph of Trieger's wife and two daughters.

Lazard and Baxter sat on the couch. The lower half of the walls was paneled with dark wood, the top half painted light green. Lazard leaned forward with his elbows on his knees. He kept thinking about Welid Shehab and the other Moslem who might have been the same man.

"I saw Barnes today. He said you increased your insurance on the warehouse four weeks ago."

"I increased all my insurance."

"How come?"

"It was about time. That extortion thing was beginning to get to me. I expected to hear from them and when I didn't I started to worry."

"Don't you think it's suspicious to raise your insurance and then have a fire?"

"What can I say? I'd been threatened so I increased my insurance to the actual worth of my business."

"Did you consider changing your insurance to another company?"

"No, why should I?"

"What about the warehouse itself, were you pretty crowded in there?"

"You mean did I burn it to get a bigger place? No, there was plenty of room." There was a little anger in Trieger's voice.

Lazard leaned back. He wanted a cigarette. He found himself thinking that he liked Trieger, then told himself it didn't matter. "You know the funeral was today?"

"The firemen?"

"Harris and Roberts. They were buried out of Holy Name. I take it you didn't go."

"No, I mean I didn't know. I feel terrible about that."

Lazard could sense Baxter looking at him. He leaned forward

again: elbows on his knees, hands folded together. He wondered if Trieger were guilty and, if so, what had driven him to burn his warehouse. "You should come over to Fire Headquarters sometime and I'll take you up to Memorial Hall. They got all the pictures there. Guys who died in fires or got thrown off the rigs or had something fall on them. Maybe 125 pictures with Harris and Roberts at the end of the row." Lazard watched how Trieger sat at his desk, how he folded his arms, then unfolded them.

"I'd like to see it. You don't have to tell me they're dead. You think I don't know? I've been wanting to ask, I know this sounds clumsy, is there some kind of fund or something? I mean, I realize it's nothing, it's an insult even to offer."

"There's a relief fund at Fire Headquarters," said Baxter, speaking more gently than Lazard. He gave Trieger the address.

Lazard found himself growing angry with Trieger. He disliked people who were so innocent about the world, so ignorant about the constant death and destruction that follows one through life. At least losing the use of his leg had taught him that.

"Why did you borrow $15,000 in 1971?"

Trieger didn't say anything, as if trying to remember. He unfolded his arms and touched his right cheek as if touching a sore place. "My brother needed the money and I lent it to him."

"You usually lend him so much money?"

"Of course not, but he lent me money to get started in business."

"Didn't you pay him back?"

"Sure, but when he needed the money, I couldn't really refuse."

"What did he need it for?"

"His motel had been losing money and he thought if he did some extensive remodeling, business might pick up."

"Did it?"

"To some degree, yes."

"Has he paid back the money?"

"Not all of it."

"How much?"

"About $5,000. He put a bar in the motel. He used to have one in Revere."

"He's in Miami?"

"North Miami, yes."

After they had left, Baxter said, "Well, what d'you think?"

"I don't think."

"Maybe you were a little hard on him."

"What are you, my mother? I want to solve this case. If he's guilty, then I'm going to break him."

"I thought you used to be friends?"

"So what?"

They were called to two fires that evening; the first at 6:30, a house in Allston. The district chief decided it was an electrical fire, but Lazard wasn't sure. Afterward they spent an hour in the office, where Lazard finished the follow-up report on the Bridal Boutique and began the report on Shehab's fire. He was unable to do much because of the presence of Pugliese's fiancée, Virginia Lufkin. Pugliese had arranged to pick her up at seven, but at eight she was still waiting. She had long brown hair and a good figure. Her mouth and nose were too large to let her be conventionally pretty, but she had big brown eyes and enough animation to give her a kind of beauty. Lazard found her very attractive and for that reason felt irritated with Pugliese for letting her hang around the office.

"Andy was going to give me a ride home. I'll just take a train."

"Where do you live?" Lazard's clothes reeked of smoke, but he felt uncomfortable about changing them with a woman in the office.

"Salem. I came in after school to do some shopping."

Virginia Lufkin walked to the window. She wore a green cotton shirtdress that showed off her figure. The sky was dark although some gray could still be seen in the west. The lights of the buildings downtown outlined their shapes against the night sky.

"I wish he'd left a note," she said.

"He could be here any minute," said Baxter, yawning.

But at 9 o'clock, when they got the call to go to the second fire, she was still waiting.

"Why don't you call a cab," said Lazard. "If we were going in that direction, we'd give you a ride to the station."

"That's okay." She smiled slightly. For the past forty-five minutes she had been grading papers. Four times she had called Pugliese's home but there was no answer. Standing by her, Lazard discovered himself looking at her breasts. Then he realized she was aware of this. He looked away and again felt angry with Pugliese.

The fire was an address in Mattapan. Baxter drove. As always, they knew nothing except that the district chief wanted them. Lazard watched their flashing dome light reflect off other cars and store windows.

"You talk to any of those ex-employees?" Lazard asked.

"Not yet. There's really only six. Two moved to California."

"If the fire was set by phone, maybe they called from California."

"Sure, they could call collect and let the operator set it off. Now we only gotta find the right operator."

Lazard went back to looking out the window. After a moment, he said, "If you can start a fire just by telephoning, why set it off at quarter to seven?"

"Why not?"

"But why that particular time?"

"Maybe it wasn't the arsonist who called. Maybe it was a legitimate business call."

"At 6:45 in the morning on a holiday?"

"Maybe it was a wrong number."

The burning building was a vacant three-story Victorian house broken into small apartments and rooms. Three separate fires had been started in the downstairs. The district chief said that when they arrived thick black smoke had been pushing through most of the upper-story windows.

Engine 53 had been first to get a line into the building, but just inside the door a gasoline bomb had gone off, burning three men. Similar bombs had exploded in the back. Officers then kept their men out of the building and two more alarms were struck.

"Fuckin' little bags of gasoline hanging from the doorknobs," said a lieutenant from Ladder 16. "I saw one when we busted the side windows. Also got 'em hanging from light fixtures in the ceiling. Those guys could be in the hospital for some time."

Occasionally arsonists used small bags of gasoline to dissuade firefighters from entering a building. Hung from the ceiling or door, they would explode when the room was opened and a fresh supply of oxygen raised the temperature.

Lazard and Baxter stayed at the fire scene until 11:30. They talked to neighbors and people on the street but learned little of value. The building was owned by a finance company in Hyde Park. A representative of the company came to see about boarding up what was left. He gave Lazard the names of his superiors, but Lazard would have to wait until Tuesday to talk to them.

It was midnight when they got back to the office. Lazard almost expected to find Virginia Lufkin, but the office was dark and the door shut. Lazard changed his clothes but the smell of smoke remained in his hair. Even though he wiped his head with wet paper towels, he was aware of the smell all night.

It was 2 o'clock before they finished their reports. Baxter rolled his bed into the inspectors' office across the hall, but Lazard wanted to find the name of the Moslem who had had the fire several months before. The files were arranged street by street. Lazard checked the city map for streets in Dorchester: Neponset, Adams, Bowdoin, Lonsdale.

The sun rose at 4:48 that Saturday morning. It was another cloudless day. Sitting on the floor, Lazard hardly noticed. He was reading a yellow arson report about a fire on Whitten Street in Dorchester on November 16. The house had been totally destroyed. Damage was estimated at $40,000. The owner of the house was Samir Shatilah, a Lebanese in the United States on a student visa.

Lazard wouldn't be able to look for Shatilah until Tuesday. Even if he left a note asking Quaid to do it on Monday, it would still mean a delay. Lazard tossed the file on his desk and stood up. His legs were stiff. The lower file drawer was open and Lazard pushed it shut: a noise like a small explosion.

13

Lazard didn't wake up until 4 o'clock Saturday afternoon. His bedroom window had no curtain and, around the edges of the closed green shade, angles of sunlight widened and narrowed as the shade moved in a breeze. Lazard lay on his back and looked at the ceiling. The walls were light yellow. From somewhere he could hear a child crying.

He got up and spent twenty minutes doing a series of Royal Canadian Air Force exercises. As always, his version of the stationary run hurt his leg. Then he showered, shaved, made coffee, fried some eggs. He felt restless, as if waiting for something to happen. He put a Bunny Berigan record on the stereo, then took it off. Going to the window, he spent ten minutes watching three boys playing with skateboards on Hancock.

For an hour he studied Spanish, speaking and repeating his lists of words. He had copied out fifty words to a sheet of paper and now had twenty-five of these sheets. Then he tried reading the translation of a South American novel he had bought during the week. The book confused him. The chapters could be read in any order and many pages were interchangeable. Lazard read for an hour, then went back to the window. The boys with their skateboards were gone. A young woman in a blue dress was pushing a baby carriage.

Sometimes on his days off, he would go to a movie, sometimes to a concert. He enjoyed the open rehearsals held by the Boston Symphony on Wednesday nights. He enjoyed it that the members of the orchestra didn't wear black, but dressed in street clothes and looked almost like anybody. But mostly he didn't like his days off and sometimes it seemed he spent those days off just waiting to go back to work, as if he were a kind of plant that bloomed only during fire and chaos.

That evening Lazard visited a number of singles bars on Boylston and Newbury streets. He did this about once a month, more out of duty than desire. He wore a bluish-gray double-knit suit, a dark blue shirt, and a dark blue tie with white stripes. His hair as always was a ragged brown fringe. Lazard would stay at a bar for half an hour, then try someplace else. At no place was he aware of any woman looking at him with any particular interest.

Around 11 he walked down to the harbor area. When he had joined the Fire Department in 1960, it felt strange being almost the only fireman not from Boston. Now after sixteen years he was as comfortable on these streets as anywhere, although he knew that to some firemen he didn't have a past. He ended up at a bar on Atlantic Avenue called The Wharf which extended over the water. He still felt restless and for the first time a kind of disappointment. He kept thinking of Virginia Lufkin as he had seen her the previous day silhouetted against the Boston skyline in her green dress.

Sitting at the bar, he looked out through the large windows at about forty sailboats moored along Lewis Wharf. They ranged from 20 to nearly 50 feet in length. Lazard asked himself which sailboat he would choose if he could have his choice. For half an hour he inspected the boats and thought about sailing to different parts of the world and what it would feel like to be alone on the ocean at night, then he felt foolish for playing such a game, and then he wondered if he was going to be a lieutenant in the Arson Squad forever.

He thought of himself as bound to the Fire Department as if by ropes, but as this idea passed through his mind the visual image was of himself dangling from ropes like a puppet: ropes which were manipulated by various chiefs urging him on to an impossible dance

111

without music or pleasure. No wonder Phelps and Hufnagel took money for cases they could never solve anyway. Lazard found himself thinking of Trieger and hoping he was innocent. As far as he could see there was still no motive. He wondered what would happen if he discovered one. The possibility frightened him.

The next day it rained. Lazard woke later than he intended because he had forgotten the switch to daylight savings time. After breakfast he decided to go to the office and get the addresses of the two Lebanese: Welid Shehab and Samir Shatilah. As he walked to his car he noticed an old woman standing by a telephone pole across the street. He had seen her before, wandering along Hancock in all weather talking to herself. Now she had a rope around the pole and kept pulling it. She was small, wizened, and although white reminded Lazard of the old woman who said she would pray for his leg.

When Lazard reached the office, it was empty. That was just as well because he hadn't wanted to explain himself. Working overtime was disapproved of, even if one wasn't paid.

He spent three hours driving around Dorchester, South Boston, and Roxbury looking for Shatilah and Shehab, but they weren't at the addresses they had given, nor had their neighbors seen them; in fact they couldn't remember ever having seen them.

At last Lazard gave it up and went home. A little later Quaid called to see if he wanted to come over and see the Bruins-Kings game on TV, but Lazard didn't feel like it.

On Saturday Quaid took Geraldine sailing. He was a member of Community Boating, a sailing club on the Boston side of the Charles. He signed out a 15-foot Mercury and spent two hours sailing up to Harvard Bridge, then back to Longfellow Bridge, then to Harvard Bridge again. The day was bright and sunny, and the temperature in the high 60s.

Geraldine sat up toward the bow. Wearing a yellow blouse, orange and red pants, and an orange life vest, she looked like a patchwork child. Whenever Quaid came about, she put her hands on her head and ducked. Geraldine liked sailing better than riding in the car or going to her special school. She liked looking at the water and the other boats and staring out at the ragged skyline. Quaid would sing and she would follow slightly behind, rocking back and forth and singing one drawn-out note that would last the entire song. Often other boats would draw near and their occupants would stare at the plump vacant child and the plump middleaged man singing "Yellow Rose of Texas" and "When Johnny Comes Marching Home."

Warren Cassidy didn't think of the Fire Department all weekend. If by any chance he had, he would have taken himself by the lapels, as it were, and given himself a shake. He had a small apartment on East 6th Street in South Boston just a few blocks from the house where he had lived with his parents until joining the army in 1947. He found his apartment comfortable enough and if someone had told him it resembled the officers' quarters in a firehouse, he would have been more pleased then otherwise.

Saturday night Cassidy went out with Violet Sheridan. They went out twice a week, on Tuesdays and Saturdays, and had done this since meeting six years before. Violet Sheridan was a forty-year-old legal secretary in Boston. She had uncontrollable red hair, wore thick glasses, and had what she described as a slight weight problem. Saturdays she and Cassidy ate an early dinner at a small Italian restaurant in the North End, then went to a movie. Usually they went to one of the three Cheri theaters because they were used to them. Then they'd return to Violet's apartment on Dartmouth in the Back Bay, play several hands of gin rummy, and make love. They did this every Saturday. By midnight Cassidy was always back in his own apartment.

Cassidy had been married eight years to a woman who nagged him unmercifully. In 1960 she died of breast cancer. After a suitable period of mourning, his aunts and uncles urged him to remarry. But by then Cassidy had grown accustomed to the silence. Life was too short to live it according to the wishes of one's relatives. In 1964, Cassidy had been trapped in an elevator during a fire and barely escaped through a door in the ceiling. After that his stubbornness and impatience with the world increased.

On Saturday Baxter and his wife Harriet and their friends the MacGillivrays, Neil and Ruth, drove up to Seabrook, New Hampshire, to the dog races. Baxter had never been to dog races before, although he often saw the horses at Rockingham and Suffolk Downs. He wasn't even sure he approved of dog racing. He'd never thought about it.

His wife bet several times and lost. Baxter watched six races without betting a dime. Then, before the seventh, he put $10 on a dog named Prairie Handle for no reason he could think of. He didn't particularly like greyhounds. At home he had a nice enough cocker spaniel named Babs. Prairie Handle won easily and paid $28. Ruby Baxter strolled back from the window with $140.

Harriet, who had criticized her husband for betting $10 on a dog with as stupid a name as Prairie Handle, said they could use the money to buy a dishwasher. But Baxter said no. He wanted a tape deck for his Dodge Dart so when he drove to work he could put on Glenn Miller and listen to Pennsylvania six five oh-oh-oh.

As a child Pugliese had collected model cars, primarily the kinds that had later become extinct: Stutz Bearcats and Cords. He even built some out of wood but after scarring his fingers with X-Acto knives, he turned purely to collecting.

When Pugliese entered Basil Kaczka's apartment Friday evening, the first thing he saw was a wall of shelves filled with model cars. Kaczka had built them all. Most were carved and ranged from several inches to a foot long: antique cars, modern cars, racing, sports, various foreign and futuristics cars of Kaczka's own design. There was even a model of the baseball-shaped car with a Red Sox cap that fetched pitchers from the bullpen at Fenway Park.

In another room was an elaborate track. Many of the cars could be driven by remote control. While it might have occurred to Lazard that such a device could set off a bomb in a warehouse, Pugliese didn't think of it and his pleasure was unmarred.

Saturday he spent the day apologizing to Virginia Lufkin. She, who had never owned a model car, was not sympathetic. Worse, Pugliese had been enjoying a closer than usual relationship with his fiancée, and she had been responding warmly enough to his talk about marriage to make him hope for a summer wedding. Now all was changed. And while by evening she claimed to have forgiven him, it was not a consoling sort of forgiveness.

Sunday night Pugliese had tickets for the Bruins-Kings game in Boston Garden. This was the seventh game of the quarter finals and while it seemed inconceivable that the Kings might bump the Bruins from their chances at the Stanley Cup, the Bruins had certainly not been playing well.

Although Virginia Lufkin was more interested in hockey than

model cars, she told Pugliese she couldn't go after all. She had schoolwork to prepare. Thinking he had been forgiven, Pugliese took this poorly and invited a woman he had known in high school, recently divorced, who had once been known as a hot number. She loved hockey. The Bruins won 3–0 before a crowd of 14,567.

Early Saturday morning Trieger, his wife, and two daughters drove up to their cottage on Lake Sunapee. All day he scraped and painted the outside, despite the blackflies that flew into the wet paint, into his mouth and eyes, crawled through his hair to his scalp, and bit him pitilessly. Because of the rain Sunday, he worked indoors, scraping windows, planing the edge of a sticky door, fixing a bed with two broken slats, and puttering around until his wife could stand no more and they drove home early.

Bobby Dodge spent the weekend hiding in his apartment. When the phone rang, he didn't answer it. When there was a knock at the door, he sat quietly. He was rude to his wife and at one point tried to hit her. Then he cried. She didn't know about the gambling debt and thought he was in trouble over another woman.

Monday morning he left his apartment at seven to go to work. As he turned the corner around the building, someone touched his arm. Dodge nearly fell down, he was so scared.

"Hey, man, where you been keepin' yourself?" said John Gaines.

"I been around."

"Hidin' behind that pretty wife?" Gaines was a muscular man a few inches taller than Dodge and at least twenty-five pounds heavier. He had on a leisure suit made up of patches of different shades of brown. He wore no shirt and the jacket was unbuttoned halfway down his chest. On his head was a brown leather cap and around his neck was a thin chain with a tiny silver spoon.

"Mr. Pierce, he's been pretty good to you, but he wants his money tonight."

"And if I don't have it?"

"Man, I get paid to scare people. I don't need to scare you, I mean, you're a friend." He formed a fist, then opened his index finger and thumb, pointing the finger at Bobby Dodge. He made a single clicking noise. "See you tonight, kid."

Dodge went to work because he wanted to talk to his boss,

Leonard Quick. All that day he painted cars and tried to strengthen his courage. At 5 o'clock he went into his boss's office.

Quick had a round, almost oriental black face that gave no indication what he was thinking. Sitting behind his desk, he leaned back, cradling his neck with his hands. He listened to Dodge's story about the gambling and Henry Pierce and at the end there was still no indication of what he was thinking and Dodge couldn't tell if that was a good sign or a bad sign. Then he leaned forward.

"You think I'm gonna lay out nine hundred bills to save your black ass?"

Dodge said nothing.

"You think you work good enough to deserve that kinda money? You think I can't go out on the street and get some half-dead junkie who won't work twice as hard? Man, it's late to be asking favors."

Dodge didn't see why Leonard Quick just couldn't say no and let it go at that. All his life people had been telling him how to act. And here was Leonard Quick making him feel bad when no good would come out of it and no use.

"You gotta nice wife, baby on the way. You gotta job. Shit, boy, I should never hired your ass outta jail."

Bobby Dodge turned to leave.

"Wait a minute, boy, I don't have $900, and a coupla hundred wouldn't help you unless you use it to get outta town."

Dodge looked at the floor. His hands had been closed and he opened them as if letting something fall. Then he turned and left the office.

At 8 o'clock Monday morning Joseph Schacter called Quaid to say he'd seen one of the boys who had put the rocks in the hydrant. It had been on the previous evening in a neighborhood grocery, and Schacter had heard the owner of the grocery call the boy Gary. Ten minutes later Quaid arrived at Schacter's apartment and the two men drove to the grocery on Washington. The owner wasn't there but he lived nearby and Quaid got his address. They woke him up and Schacter described the boy he had seen: tall, thin, fourteen, straggly afro, narrow face and chin.

"That's Gary Howard, he's not a bad kid."

Quaid then left Schacter, called the juvenile authorities, and arranged to have someone meet him at the junior high school. The person who met him was Joan Hendricks, a black police sergeant in her early thirties. Someone went to get Gary out of class. They took him back to the juvenile unit at District 4 headquarters on Warren Avenue. Sitting in the back seat, Gary Howard looked out the window. It was rainy, windy, and cold, colder than it had been for two weeks.

Gary Howard was put in a small room with green walls and after a while Quaid went in to talk to him. Joan Hendricks sat by the door. Quaid felt nervous with young people and it bothered him to think this boy was not much older than his daughter. Gary had slid down on his chair so he was sitting on the tip of his spine. His head was turned to the right and he seemed to be staring down at a spot where the baseboard joined the floor. Quaid looked but didn't see anything.

The room contained a desk, three straight chairs, and smelled of disinfectant. Quaid sat down on the edge of the desk. "Why'd you put those rocks in the hydrant?" He tried to keep his voice calm and conversational.

Gary didn't seem to have heard. He wore brown slacks, a close-fitting yellow and green striped shirt and sneakers.

"Why'd you put the rocks in the hydrant?"

Still no answer. Joan Hendricks started to speak but Quaid shook his head. Stepping away from the desk, Quaid crouched down near the spot on the baseboard at which Gary seemed to be staring, in order to catch his eye.

"You do it because your buddies were arrested?"

The boy turned away so he was facing the spot where Quaid had been sitting on the desk. "I didn't need no reason to do it. I just did it, that's all."

Quaid walked back to the desk and for a moment Gary Howard looked at him before turning back to the baseboard. There was a certain wariness in his glance. Maybe a little fear.

"Did someone pay you to do it?" asked Quaid gently.

There was a slight squeaking noise as the boy jiggled his sneaker on the green linoleum. "I already told you, I didn't need no reason. Man, I just did it because I wanted to do it."

"I bet someone paid you. I bet someone came and offered you twenty-five bucks. If you took any less than that, you got robbed."

"What the fuck I care what you think for?"

Quaid walked to the window which looked out across an alley

117

to a brick wall where two windows were covered with black paint. "Two men were killed in that fire."

"Honky firemen?"

"How much you get paid?"

"Man, how often do I gotta say it?"

"Who else was with you?"

"No one was with me."

"Witnesses saw other kids."

"You know that much, you go find them."

"How much you get paid to put the rocks in the hydrant?"

Actually Quaid didn't think anyone had paid him. He even doubted that Gary had done it because his friends were arrested. Maybe that had been the slightest of reasons. Quaid imagined several boys acting out of boredom, a vague hostility, and because it would be a good joke the next time the firemen used the hydrant and no water came out.

Monday afternoon Warren Cassidy went out to find the remaining three men on his active list of possible extortion suspects. Flanagan sent Pugliese with him. It was either go with Cassidy or go with Phelps and Hufnagel, and Phelps couldn't stand Pugliese.

Cassidy drove with his hands at the top of the wheel and seemed to think that all other cars existed merely to get in his way. Whenever another driver would do something he didn't like, Cassidy would roll down his window and spit.

"You see the Bruins game last night?" Pugliese asked Cassidy.

"Nope."

"Thirty-eight shots on goal."

"Hockey's a fuckin' waste of time."

Pugliese thought Cassidy was mad at him most of the day. As a matter of fact, Cassidy was in a good mood. When they left the office Pugliese noticed Cassidy tuck a .38 into his belt. He wanted to ask Cassidy if he expected to use it but didn't want Cassidy to think he was nervous.

The first person on their list was William MacNevin. The address was in Dorchester. When they arrived, Cassidy was told that MacNevin hadn't lived there in six months. He was given an address in Everett.

Pugliese found it impossible to ride in silence. "You know, this mechanic who saw the car at the warehouse, he has the most fuckin' amazing collection of model cars. Ever see a Bugatti?"

Cassidy gave no indication of having heard. On his head was a bamboo-colored Macora hat with a Madras band and a snap brim. He had bought the hat on Saturday, and the fact it was raining didn't matter because he took the hat off whenever he got out of the car.

William MacNevin had moved from Everett four months before. Cassidy was given an address in Quincy.

"What about baseball," said Pugliese, "you like the Red Sox?"

"Nah, I was a Braves fan."

"Braves?"

"Boston Braves. When they went to Milwaukee, it was all over. Used to see a lotta their games as a kid."

"When did they move?"

"Early fifties."

"Guess I was too young."

In Quincy they learned that William MacNevin had moved to Los Angeles around the middle of March. Cassidy shrugged and spat. Then he crossed out MacNevin's name and moved on to the next: Marvin Page and he lived in Somerville.

"You ever see Heinlein?" asked Cassidy. Heinlein was the State Fire Marshal.

"Sure, he's in there almost every day."

"What d'you think of him?"

"He's a good guy. Gotta lotta great stories."

"He's a pig's ass, a Republican candyman. Why don't he quit?"

Pugliese looked out at the traffic on Mass. Ave., which they were crossing for the fourth time that afternoon. A small boy in a yellow slicker was waving a baseball pennant around and around his head.

"He's not so bad," said Pugliese guiltily.

"He's single-handedly fucked up the marshal's office, that's all."

The position of State Fire Marshal was a six-year political appointment. Most appointees took their $15,900 salary and big car and never showed up at the office. Heinlein, although he had no fire experience, came to work regularly, sat on a lot of committees, and complained loudly about how his men were treated. Heinlein had been appointed by a Republican governor. When that governor was defeated, the new Democratic governor asked for Heinlein's resignation. Heinlein refused and many people dated the marshal's inability to get funds from that refusal.

The marshal's main power was to call a fire marshal's inquest at which anyone who might have knowledge of a fire could be summoned and examined under oath. These were often done with some degree of pomp. Several times Heinlein had called them in small Massachusetts towns, brought in realtors, town selectmen and city officials, local police and firemen and so increased the town's paranoia level that the criminal activity under investigation stopped for several months.

"You got many crooked dicks over there?" asked Cassidy.

"What's that supposed to mean?" Pugliese thought he was making some sexual reference.

"You know, guys that take bribes not to investigate fires."

Pugliese was scandalized. "Of course not."

Cassidy laughed. It was a sound like stones being dropped in an empty metal drum. "You're a baby, Pugsy. Every fuckin' fire chief in the state's got an adjuster in his back pocket."

"What do you mean?"

"I mean a public adjuster he gives business to and who gives him a little something back."

When they reached Marvin Page's house, a woman told them that Page was working at a garage off Somerville Avenue. The garage was a gray cinder-block building with the name "Frank's Garage" painted in white letters on a red board over the door. About eight cars were being worked on. In a farther room, a Corvette was being painted dark green.

Page was a small man in his early forties. He wore mechanic's overalls that seemed new. He appeared almost glad to see Cassidy. In 1971, Page had been sentenced to three years for an Arson II conviction—burning of a building other than a dwelling—after pleading guilty to avoid being tried for extortion.

"My whole life's been changed. Gotta good job here. Believe me, lieutenant, I ain't done nothin' I shouldn't."

"What about a week ago Sunday? Say between Sunday and Monday?"

Page appeared to think. They were in a small office off the garage with brown walls and a large calendar from Sim's Auto Parts with a picture of a girl in a bikini tossing a beach ball.

"Last Sunday night, I played cards with some guys, then went and saw this broad, she's an old friend but I don't want my wife to know." Page winked.

"Give me some names," said Cassidy.

Page wrote out five names. Pugliese was moved by Page's cheerfulness. He had a round red face and when he smiled his eyes wrinkled into friendly slits. It made Pugliese think that prison could improve a person after all.

As they drove away, Pugliese said, "He's a nice guy."

Cassidy raised his hands off the wheel, then lowered them again. The brim of his Macora hat was just level with his eyes. "You'd be friendly too if a cop came to check you out and there you are with a bunch of stolen cars."

"What makes you think they're stolen?"

Cassidy didn't answer. They crossed the Charles River Dam past the Museum of Science. "How come you want to do this stuff in the marshal's office?" asked Cassidy.

"It's interesting."

"You like fires, that your trouble?"

"I mean the work's interesting."

"You like to get down there and investigate dead bodies?"

"I don't know about that."

"Take someone who gets caught in a fire, a woman for example, what's the last thing to burn up?"

They were climbing the ramp of the Southeast Expressway. Cassidy gunned the Dodge, cutting off a green pick-up. Pugliese rolled down his window. The car filled with cold air. "I don't know," he said.

"The uterus, that's the last thing to go."

"You mean the womb?"

"That's right, a uterus is like a womb. Now what about a man, what's the last thing to go on a man?"

"I've no idea." Pugliese wondered if Cassidy tormented him on purpose.

"The prostate, that's the last bit. See, even with a tiny piece you can tell if it's a man or a woman."

"What about, you know, the penis?"

"One of the first things, phffft, a roman candle."

Pugliese didn't say anything for a while. Then: "We going to look for that last guy?"

"Too late. I'll do it myself some other time."

121

14

"There's a fire at 14 Emerald Court in the Castle Square apartments. People are screaming."

"Could I have your name, address, and phone number?"

"Pete Morgan. I live across the court at number 8. 555-8379. You gotta hurry, people are screaming."

"They're already on their way."

"Play it once more," said Lazard. He was straddling a chair in a small room in Fire Alarm Headquarters. Nearby Baxter leaned against a desk. His back hurt but he didn't want to sit down. The principal operator, John Lafferty, rewound the tape, pushed the start button, and put his hands in his pockets.

"There's a fire at 14 Emerald Court . . ." A man's voice, loud with a thick Boston accent: Day-ahs a fy-ah. It was 8 A.M. Tuesday morning. Ten minutes before, Lazard had called the phone number given by Pete Morgan. It belonged to a single woman in the South End. No Peter Morgan was listed in the phone book and the people at 8 Emerald Court were named Spears. In any case, it had been a false alarm. What made it important was it had been phoned in two minutes before Raymond Farkus noticed the flames on Plympton Street.

After listening to the tape again, Lazard said, "What's that stuff at the end? Like someone else talking."

Lafferty rewound the tape. He'd come on duty half an hour before and felt he had more serious work to do. Besides, he didn't much like the Arson Squad. They weren't firemen and they weren't cops. Neither fish nor fowl was how he described it to himself.

"If those rigs hadn't gone to Emerald Court," asked Lazard, "what difference would it have made on the Plympton Street fire?"

"Engine 3 and the aerial tower are right on Harrison," said Lafferty. "That fire was almost in their back yard."

"So how much did it slow them up?"

Lafferty looked at the incident card: 15,107. "The alarm was struck at 6:48. Harris arrived and called in a second alarm at 6:52. Maybe it took an extra three minutes. Engine 22 and Ladder 13 arrived at 6:54. What was it, kerosene? It'd been burning ten minutes before any water hit it."

"Play the tape again," said Lazard. "Louder this time."

"There's a fire . . ." The voice echoed off the stone walls of the office. Again, at the end, was a second voice.

Lazard limped over to the tape recorder. "Just do that last bit, where he says, 'They're already on their way.'"

They had to listen three more times before the second voice became clear: "Trans World Airlines announces the departure . . ."

"Fuckin' Logan," said Baxter, "he made the call from Logan Airport, for cryin' out loud."

However, just as they got in their car to drive out to the airport, Lazard and Baxter received a call to a fire on Columbus near Weston: Box 2221. It was a shoe store and had gone into a second alarm before being brought under control. More than ever Lazard felt the frustration of putting aside one investigation for another. Again he told himself that if it hadn't been for his divorce, if he had been present at the beginning of the investigation of the burned warehouse, then he wouldn't feel so off balance, so slightly out of step. But even if he'd been at the beginning he would still have to deal with these other investigations. Who knew how long the shoe store might tie them up? And after that there was Welid Shehab and Samir Shatilah, and the rooming house with the little bags of gasoline hanging from the doorknobs, and the three burned firemen.

Baxter had just turned the corner onto Mass. Ave. at Symphony Hall when Lazard said, "What's Quaid doing today?"

"He had to do something with that kid who put the rocks in the hydrant."

"Call in. If he's there, tell him to get out to that shoe store. If he's not, get Fatback."

"Fatback? You serious?"

"He's got two feet and a mouth, doesn't he? He can walk and ask questions."

"But we're the ones who got the call."

"So what. We still have to find that damned Arab and we have to talk to the owners of that rooming house. Then, if we're lucky, maybe we can get out to the airport, if nothing else happens. Flanagan said to give priority to the warehouse, so that's what I'm doing."

It was on the tip of Baxter's tongue to say, But that was last week. Instead, he picked up the microphone to call Teddy. Then he took a quick glance at Lazard to see if he looked in any way peculiar. But even after Quaid had agreed to take the shoe store and Baxter had turned toward South Boston in order to search for the Lebanese, he continued to feel upset at Lazard's departure from routine. Baxter didn't know how to talk about it, however, and, instead, he drove jerkily—too much gas, too much brake—to show Lazard he wasn't happy.

After spending an hour unsuccessfully searching for Shehab and Shatilah, Lazard at last gave it up and they turned south toward Hyde Park and Bay State Finance, which owned the rooming house in Mattapan. But again Lazard felt dissatisfied. The rooming house had been burned so deliberately that Lazard suspected someone of trying to unload it by selling it to the insurance company. That someone was probably Bay State Finance, but proving it could take weeks. As they drove south on Blue Hill Avenue, Lazard stared out at the run-down houses and gray sky. He kept thinking of the tape recording he had heard at Fire Alarm.

"Stop at Engine 52," said Lazard, "I want to call Cassidy."

"What for?"

"I'm going to give him Bay State Finance."

"But it's our collar."

"That can't be helped."

"First you dump that shoe store on Teddy and now this. We're going to have one helluva reputation."

"What can I say, Ruby, I'm lieutenant."

Baxter was silent. He wondered if Lazard was going off his rocker and if he, Baxter, would have to do anything about it. "Cassidy's not going to like that. He's still chasing those extortion people."

"That extortion thing's a lot of crap. Look, here's someone who wants to burn a warehouse that's practically next door to a fire station. So what's he do? He sets up the warehouse so he can blow it simply by telephoning. Then he calls in a false alarm to the fire station, waits a couple of minutes for the rigs to get out of the neighborhood, and, boom, there goes the warehouse. He does this with two phone calls from Logan and fifteen minutes later he's on a plane flying to god knows where."

"Is that what you expect to find out at Logan?"

"I expect nothing. I just want to go see."

No flights leave Logan between 1 A.M. and 6 A.M. Between 6 and 7 are half a dozen flights, but only one—a 6:50 Allegheny flight to Buffalo, Detroit, and Minneapolis—could be taken by someone making a call at 6:45.

However, at 7 o'clock five airlines have flights to sixty cities. Lazard calculated that as many as a thousand people might have flown out of Boston at 7 A.M. Monday, April 19. He considered how long it would take to check their alibis for the twelve hours before the flight. Possibly the man who made the call had flown out at 7:05 or 7:10. He considered the time it would take to record the voices of everyone who had flown from Boston between 7 and 7:30: just the men and each one saying, "There's a fire at 14 Emerald Court."

"Come on, Ruby, let's talk to the state police."

They'd been sitting across from the American Airlines ticket counter studying the timetables of eleven airlines. Baxter hadn't said much, still showing his disapproval for turning their cases over to Quaïd and Cassidy. Now he said, "You know, this guy could of had his own plane, maybe even hired one."

"That's true."

Troop F of the Massachusetts State Police was on the eighteenth floor of the Logan control tower. The walls were glass. In one direction lay all of Boston spread out against the gray sky; in the other direction was the ocean: black under heavy clouds. Careful not to get too close to the windows, Baxter could just discern the curve of the earth.

They were taken back and introduced to a Lieutenant Gillespie, a stocky man in his mid-thirties with black curly hair and a blue suit that managed to look like a uniform without being one. It was a small office, but the glass wall and view of the airport and ocean gave it infinite size. Baxter stood by the door. He had heard of windows breaking and secretaries being sucked into the sky.

Lazard sat down in a chair next to Gillespie's desk. He didn't appear to notice the ocean. "We're looking for a guy who flew out of here around seven last Monday morning. He'd been driving a 1975 dark maroon Cougar with a black vinyl roof. It might have been stolen. You turned up anything like that?"

Gillespie leaned back in his swivel chair and linked his hands behind his head. "We got a report on a '75 Cougar more'n a week ago. You know, we probably turn up ten cars a month, maybe lose a little more'n that. Guy drives in with a jalopy, takes a ticket from the spitter, drives out in a new 'Vette five minutes later. We get to keep the jalopy." Gillespie scratched his ear and looked at Baxter standing near the door. "This Cougar, it was stolen from Lynn on Good Friday. There's a lotta cars in these lots. We checked, but didn't pick up its number."

Lazard looked down at his shoes. Putting them side by side, he pushed them up so they touched a line in the gray tile. Then he tried to imagine a world where he could consistently get clear yes or no answers.

"We pick up a guy taking a 'Vette. Know what they get him on? 'Using without authority.' Can you beat that?"

"You find this Cougar or didn't you?" asked Lazard.

"Picked it up this morning. Had clean plates but the description said it had a dent in the rear right side. One of my men saw it and checked the engine number."

"Where's it now?"

"Towed it over to the garage at Central Plaza. Owner's supposed to pick it up."

"Let's take a look at it," said Lazard.

The dent in the rear right side of the Cougar looked as if

someone had punched it with a metal fist: a round area five inches across. The interior of the car was clean. Gillespie opened the trunk. It was empty but Lazard smelled kerosene. Leaving the car, he arranged to have it towed over to 1010 Commonwealth Avenue. Then he called Lakin to say it was coming.

"Owner's not going to like that," said Gillespie. "I told him he could have it today."

Lazard shrugged. He started to say "So what," then just shrugged again.

It was 2:30 by the time they drove back to Boston. Traffic was heavy in the Sumner Tunnel and slowed to five miles per hour. Lazard hated the tunnel, hated the taste of the air.

"I tell you I seen Maloney this morning?" asked Baxter. "Just got back from vacation. Drove out west. Anyway, he stopped in Tucson and saw O'Neill. Fuckin' O'Neill, he's bragging about having a mistress twenty-five years younger than himself, and his wife, she's takin' dancing lessons. Can you believe it? A mistress no less, and Maloney says he's lost weight and wears shirts with flowers and shit all over them. Who'da thought it?"

"What did you expect?" asked Lazard. "How many years yo ι think O'Neill took bribes?"

"What d'you mean?"

"Let's say he did it for teι years and tucked away about $4,000 a year. You can buy a lot of whores for $40,000."

"Jesus, Frank, I thought you liked O'Neill. He brought you onto the squad, didn't he? Anyway, those cases, he could never of got them to court. A few bucks, what's it matter?"

Lazard barely listened. Instead, he thought with growing dislike of Lieutenant Paul Harris, whose aggressiveness had caused him to lead his men too far into the warehouse. He was simply another young lieutenant trying to boost his reputation. Lazard saw him as being killed as much by ambition as by the falling ceiling. Beyond that, Harris's death had also been caused by the stones in the hydrant, by the anger and boredom of some fourteen-year-old boy. If the temperature hadn't hit 94 on Easter Sunday, then Harris wouldn't have been killed. If Harris were still alive, the investigation would have ended by now: filed away and marked "closed pending further information."

From Logan they were called to an apartment fire in Roxbury, apparently started by a man whose wife was sleeping with someone else. Baxter was aware of Lazard growing more and more irritable. He wouldn't talk, refused to stop for a sandwich, and stared sullenly from the side window. They didn't get back to Fire Headquarters until 5 o'clock.

Upon entering the office, Lazard immediately went to the farther desk and telephoned the lieutenant in charge of the firemen's relief fund. "Hey, Jack, you get a donation from a man named Trieger, Howard Page Trieger?" There was a pause. From the other desk, Baxter watched as Lazard kept jabbing at a pad of paper with a ballpoint pen. "How much?" Another pause. "Thanks." Lazard hung up.

"How much did he give?" asked Baxter.

"Five hundred dollars."

"That doesn't prove anything."

"That's true," said Lazard, and began dialing another number. "May I speak to Mr. Patterson?"

Patterson was a lawyer with FAIR Plan. Lazard told him about Welid Shehab and Samir Shatilah, and his suspicion they were the same man. Although members of the Arson Squad often talked with private investigators, it was ethically questionable for the Fire Department to call an insurance company and suggest it hire a private investigator to look into a case that the Fire Department didn't have time to investigate itself. But an investigator could devote weeks to Shehab, and while the Lebanese might not go to jail, neither would he collect his insurance money. It was far easier to prove insurance fraud in a civil court, where the company only had to show a preponderance of evidence, than in a criminal court, where Shehab would have to be found guilty beyond a reasonable doubt.

As Lazard talked on the phone, Baxter watched him with increasing disapproval, which he tried to communicate by breathing heavily.

"You got something caught in your throat, Ruby?" asked Lazard once he had hung up.

"That's the third case you dumped today," said Baxter. He had bought several jelly doughnuts from a machine downstairs and was now licking raspberry filling from his fingers.

"Feels good," said Lazard.

Shortly after talking to Patterson, Lazard got a call from David Bascomb, who was second in command of the investigations division of Jerome Bryant, Inc., a Boston security company. The investigations division consisted of about forty-five men and half were usually concerned with arson.

Bascomb and Lazard were fairly good friends and often exchanged information on cases. "What's on your mind?" asked Lazard.

"Meet me at Ho-Jo's at 6:30, will you?" The restaurant was next to Fire Headquarters at the junction of Mass. Ave. and Southampton.

"You don't want to come here?"

"Ruby'd glare at me. How about it?"

"If I'm not there by 6:35, it means we got a call."

Lazard spent the next forty-five minutes writing up his notes, plus the report on the fire that afternoon. He always signed his reports Francis Lazard, although he didn't think of himself as Francis and even forgot about it except when signing reports and getting his paycheck. In all official business, he was Francis, and while he didn't dislike the name, it felt like someone else's.

At 6:25 he told Baxter he was going next door to meet David Bascomb. Baxter was watching television with his feet on the desk. "Tell fag-locks from me to get his hair cut," he said.

Bascomb had light brown hair that partly covered his ears and curled down to his collar. He sat in a back booth. In front of him were two cups of coffee and two slices of apple pie with vanilla ice cream. As Lazard sat down, Bascomb pushed a cup of coffee and piece of pie across the table. "You look like you lost some weight."

"You buying me off with ice cream and pie? How you been?"

"Can't complain." Bascomb was a tall, muscular man of thirty-eight. He had a long, clean-shaven face and wore glasses with small rectangular black frames that made him look inoffensive. He had on a tan gabardine suit.

"Well?" asked Lazard, taking a bite of pie.

"The insurance agent Robert Barnes told his company you weren't happy that this Trieger guy increased his insurance before the fire. They gave us a little money. You mind talking?"

"I guess not." But even as he said it Lazard knew it wasn't true. He didn't want to tell Bascomb about Trieger, felt that he wouldn't be able to communicate his own sense of the man. He also felt as if he were betraying Trieger and this surprised him.

Then he told himself it didn't matter. There was no reason why Bascomb shouldn't know everything.

Bascomb listened without interrupting. A few years before, he had quit smoking and as a replacement chewed toothpicks. When he finished with a toothpick, he broke it into four ragged parts and left it in a small pile. He went through toothpicks quickly and before Lazard was done Bascomb had five small piles in a row beside his coffee cup. Whenever Bascomb visited Lazard's apartment, Lazard would find bits of toothpick for days afterward.

"Are you suspicious of Trieger?" asked Bascomb.

"Not necessarily, but everything's too neat."

"He's a friend of yours?"

"Years ago."

"What about now?"

"He's still a friendly guy. I can't see him burning down his own place, but that doesn't mean anything."

"You mean if the reason was big enough?"

"Sure." Again Lazard felt uncomfortable, as if he were intentionally doing Trieger a bad turn. And again he told himself that it didn't matter, that it was his job.

"Where do you think we should start looking?" asked Bascomb.

"I don't think there's any motive around here," said Lazard. He glanced out at the parking lot. For the past few minutes it had been raining heavily. He watched a young couple run from their car to the restaurant.

"Where'd that guy take a plane to?" asked Lazard. "Trieger's got a brother in North Miami who's got a motel. He's pretty close to him. The brother used to gamble a little. Maybe he's having some trouble. If I had the time, I'd look into the brother."

"All right, we'll start there."

That evening Lazard still wanted to talk to Trieger's employees, but at 8 o'clock they had to go to a fire in an office building on Boylston Street. By 9:30 Lazard decided it had been caused by a defective heater. On their way back to Fire Headquarters, they were called to a bar in Roxbury where someone had thrown a gasoline bomb through the back door. Four people had been slightly burned. Bricks had been thrown at the responding apparatus. Lazard and Baxter spent two hours at the scene but were unable to discover who threw the bomb or why.

Bobby Dodge was ducked down in an alley off Washington near Derby. It was quarter to eleven Tuesday night. Around the corner was a liquor store that would close in fifteen minutes. Dodge wasn't thinking about the liquor store. He was thinking back to December, 1971, when he had been waiting around the corner from a 24-hour grocery store trying to build up his nerve. It had taken half an hour and he had run right into an off-duty policeman buying a quart of orange juice. He was lucky he hadn't been shot.

Since Monday evening he'd been hiding. He hadn't gone home and he hadn't gone to work, except after midnight when he slipped into the garage through a second-story window and slept. Tuesday morning he had seen Dionne. She hadn't cared about his problems until she learned he had $300. She said she knew of a card game and maybe Bobby could win something. Dionne was a tall woman with great long legs. At one point he'd been up to $576. Then he'd been having a good time. When he left two hours later, he had $10. He kept telling himself he should be sick, but for some reason it barely fazed him. It was as if it'd been meant to happen, that someplace there was a record of what happened to Bobby Dodge on April 27, 1976, and in one part it said Dodge lost $290 to a man named Milton Patch who couldn't play seven-card without his dark glasses. And when it happened it was as if Bobby Dodge were saying to himself, yes, I remember this part, I've already read this part.

Dodge stood up and brushed off his jeans. It was pitch dark and cold. Tucked in his belt behind his back and under his brown jacket was a short bayonet he had brought home from Vietnam. He didn't have much faith in what he was doing. He was doing it because he couldn't stand the waiting and hiding.

It was a small liquor store. The black man behind the counter didn't look up as he came in. One other customer, an old man, was looking at cheap whiskey. Bobby went past him to the wine section. He picked up and put back down three or four bottles of sweet wine, waiting for the other man to leave. The liquor store seemed hot and stuffy after being outdoors.

The other customer paid for a pint of whiskey and left. Bobby

Dodge carried his bottle to the counter: California ruby port. It cost $1.79 and he put down $2.00. He still hadn't looked at the clerk, and saw only his hands and a silver ring in the shape of entwined snakes. When the clerk opened the cash register, Dodge pulled the bayonet from his belt and held it to the man's chest.

"Put the money on the counter." Glancing at the clerk, Dodge saw he was a young man with a round, pleasant face. "I won't hurt you, just do like I say."

The clerk tossed the money on the counter so it scattered slightly. There were a lot of small bills. Dodge moved to gather them up. As he looked away from the clerk, the man grabbed the bottle of port and swung it at the bayonet, hitting Bobby's right wrist. At the same time, he began searching for something below the counter and shouting: "Larry, where the fuck's the gun? Some guy's sticking us up! Where the fuck's the fuckin' gun, goddamn it, I told you to leave it on the goddamn shelf."

By the time the clerk began shouting, Bobby Dodge was halfway to the door. His hand was numb but he held onto the bayonet. He didn't have any money, however. Worse, he had left his $2.00 on the counter. He had always been a good runner and he sprinted down Washington, then turned on Newcomb. While he'd been in the store, it had started to drizzle. The streetlights reflected in the puddles and on the wet finish of the parked cars.

As he ran, it occurred to him the clerk had been lying: that there was no gun and probably no Larry. How dumb, he thought, what a dumb thing to do. He turned onto Harrison, walking quickly toward Boston City Hospital.

Crossing Mass. Ave., he continued past the hospital. He had no destination in mind, but walked and tried not to think. The bayonet was tucked in his belt behind his back.

A young nurse came out of a building in front of him and turned up Harrison, walking in the same direction. She was a white woman and carried a black purse in her left hand. Without thinking, Dodge sprinted forward and grabbed the purse. At first she wouldn't let go. He was surprised at the fear he saw in her face. He yanked the purse away and started running. The nurse yelled. There were more shouts and he was aware of people chasing him. He ran clutching the purse to his chest. He turned right on Newton and ran across Franklin Square to Washington. He felt good and was almost laughing.

Stopping by a streetlamp, he opened the purse and took out the wallet. It contained five dollars. He searched through the purse but found no more money except some loose change, maybe 50 cents.

He looked through the wallet again. There was a photograph of an older couple in front of a Christmas tree and another of a girl on a horse. Walking up Washington, he started to throw the purse away, then stopped. On the corner was a mailbox. He would drop the purse inside. As he approached it, he couldn't decide whether to put back the five dollars. At the last moment, he kept the money. He heard the purse fall into the box. What was he going to do with five dollars? He looked at the five-dollar bill and started to put it through the slot, then drew back. The mailman would steal it.

He walked up Washington holding the five-dollar bill. A train crossed on the elevated tracks and the sound rattled against the buildings. Ahead, Bobby Dodge saw a police car coming toward him. He crumpled up the five-dollar bill and dropped it in the gutter. The police car passed, and he kept walking. Couldn't do much with five dollars anyway. He'd spend the night at the garage, then in the morning he'd pick up a few things at home and head south. If he got a job, he could send for Cecilia. Bobby Dodge noticed the drizzle had stopped. He felt good about throwing away the five dollars.

15

Wednesday morning the sky began to clear and the sun could be seen out over the ocean when Warren Cassidy left his apartment at 7 o'clock. But it was chilly, barely 50 degrees, and he chided himself and called himself stupid for not wearing a raincoat over his jacket. He carried his Macora hat and when he saw the sun he put it on.

Instead of going directly to Fire Headquarters, he drove to Tremont Street in Roxbury. He was looking for a number on Hammond which was the address of the last name on his list of extortion suspects. If he didn't go early, he might not be able to go at all since he'd be caught up in the Bay State Finance investigation.

His car was a dark green Camaro and he rode with his right arm stretched out along the top of the seat and his left holding the wheel. Slouched in the corner, he could just see his face in the side mirror: long, angular, and faded gray from the dirt on the window. His hat was tilted back on his head. The heat was turned on and he felt warmer, although not happier.

Cassidy was furious at Lazard for giving him Bay State Finance. Such cases were nearly impossible to bring to court. Moreover, a company like Bay State would hire lawyers to so confuse the issue that no assistant district attorney would want to touch the case. Cassidy had spoken to the company's president the previous afternoon and the man had been as confident as St. Peter out of a job.

Fatback had urged Cassidy to complain to Flanagan, saying that Lazard was clearly getting out of hand. But Cassidy couldn't imagine it. If he had a gripe, then he'd tell Lazard himself. Why go whining to some chief?

The last name on Cassidy's list was Robert Dodge. Cassidy vaguely remembered the case. Dodge had been a handyman for a North Shore realtor mixed up with some fraud fires. For a while nothing had been proved, although an insurance company had once successfully withheld payment of a claim. Then the realtor ignited himself while torching a house and died. Robert Dodge had been with him and suffered minor burns. Afterward he had gone to jail, although not for long. Less than a year, Cassidy remembered.

The State Fire Marshal's Office had handled the case, and one of the lieutenant-detectives since transferred to a Crime Prevention and Control Team had told Cassidy about it. Anyway, Robert Dodge was a name he had gotten from the marshal's office. He'd then checked the address with the police. If the bomb hadn't exploded at the Probation Department, Cassidy would have used their files for verification.

On the right side of Hammond was a row of decrepit three-story brownstones. On the left was a cluster of low-cost housing. Although a hundred years newer than the brownstones, the low-cost housing looked older. Robert Dodge lived in the middle of the block. Cassidy parked and locked his Camero. Looking at his expensive digital watch, he saw it was exactly 7:15.

Cassidy found the street door open and went up. Dodge's apartment was on the third floor. The walls were mustard yellow and a black rubber runner covered the stairs and landings. Cassidy knocked, but there was no answer. He knocked again, using the soft part of his fist.

A woman's voice called from the other side of the door: "He's not here."

"Fire Department. Open up."

The door opened a crack, then wider. A young black woman stood in the doorway wearing a man's brown bathrobe. She had apparently just woken up and kept opening her eyes wide to clear them of sleep. Although she was small and the robe much too big for her, it was obvious she was pregnant. There was a thought at the back of Cassidy's mind that he couldn't put a finger to.

"I'm looking for Robert Dodge."

"He's not here. He hasn't been here since Monday."

"But he lives here?"

"Yes, I'm his wife. I'm . . . I don't know where he is."

She was a foot shorter than Cassidy and had a very dark oval face. He guessed she was about eighteen. She seemed frightened.

"Is he in trouble?"

"He won't talk to me. Some other men been lookin' for him. I'd call the cops but I don't want to make it worse."

Cassidy gave her his card. "If he comes in, call me. I just want to ask some questions." Again there was something nagging his memory.

As Cassidy began descending the stairs, a young black man turned the corner of the landing beneath him. Both men stopped and looked at one another. The young man wore jeans, sneakers, and a dirty brown jacket. As he looked at Cassidy, his eyes widened slightly.

Cassidy thought he looked definitely frightened and couldn't imagine why. He decided to frighten him a little more.

"Hey!" Cassidy shouted.

The man turned and bolted down the stairs. Cassidy went after him, jumped from the landing, and hit the man's shoulder, throwing him into the first-floor hall. As Cassidy started to get up, the other man ran toward him, kicking out and hitting Cassidy's left thigh, knocking him back against the wall. Cassidy reached for his gun, but before he could touch it, the young man yanked out a short bayonet and put the point to Cassidy's chest.

They stood breathing heavily. Cassidy felt the pressure of the point against his shirt, increasing and decreasing with the rise and fall of his chest. The young man no longer seemed so much frightened as angry.

"Why the fuck can't you leave me alone?"

He reached forward and snatched Cassidy's gun from the clip at his belt: a Smith & Wesson .38 Chief's Special.

"You're just making worse trouble for yourself." Cassidy made himself talk slowly so he wouldn't appear frightened. "Give me the gun and you can go."

"I need it, man, I couldn't be in worse trouble. Lie down on the floor. I'll kill you I see you again."

Cassidy knelt down on the floor. The black rubber runner dug into his knees. Bobby Dodge shoved Cassidy forward onto his face, then ran out the door. Slowly getting to his feet, Cassidy brushed off his gray slacks. He realized what had been troubling him. The Robert Dodge he was looking for was white.

Lazard also woke early on Wednesday, at least for him. He had gone to sleep about 8:30 that morning, then got up when the alarm went off at 1. He showered, shaved, and dressed as if going to work. In fact, he was going to work, although he would keep it a secret from the department. He had decided that all his time had to go into the warehouse fire, that he simply couldn't wait until Saturday to continue his investigation. To hell with Baxter and his sighs.

He made coffee and took two doughnuts from the refrigerator. As he finished his coffee, he looked over a list of Trieger's employees. There were seven. He settled on Allen Kanelos, who repaired furniture at Trieger's warehouse and had been responsible for the building.

Lazard called Trieger's office and asked where he could find Kanelos. The secretary, Mrs. Lydon, told him that Trieger had rented space at a warehouse in East Cambridge, down from Lechmere Sales. He could find Kanelos there.

Shortly before 2 o'clock, Lazard parked his Ford in front of the warehouse on First Street: a one-story cinder-block building with sliding gray doors. He carried a plain wooden cane and irrationally he regretted not having the aluminum cane which he kept in the office and always used when he was working. Going through a door near the corner, Lazard entered an area about 40 by 60 feet lit by banks of neon lights. Along the left wall were fifteen pieces of new furniture wrapped in clear plastic. Opposite them were a similar number of older pieces. The furniture filled a fraction of the room, making the room feel even larger and emptier than it was.

By itself in the middle of the room was a chair stripped down to bare boards and webbing. A middle-aged man wearing green work clothes stood over it holding a square of foam rubber.

"No salesmen in here."

"I'm with the Fire Department." Lazard showed his identification. "You're Kanelos?"

The man nodded. "You sure did one helluva job putting out that warehouse. I lost some good tools."

"I want to talk to you. Mind if we sit down?"

"You sit. I gotta work."

Kanelos turned back to the chair and began fitting the piece of foam rubber on top of some wide mesh webbing. From next door came the whine of a circular saw.

Lazard pulled over a blue armchair, sat down, and watched Kanelos for a minute. The lines on the man's forehead and between his mouth and chin were so deep and dark that they appeared dirty. Lazard began to wonder what he should ask. All week he had felt the presence of important information which he hadn't been able to reach, hadn't known what questions would lead him there.

"How long you worked for Trieger?"

"Seven years."

"Like him?"

"He's a good guy, a good man to work for."

"Before the fire, were you aware of anyone watching the warehouse or hanging around?"

"Nah, weren't any windows to see outta." As he talked, Kanelos kept working without looking at Lazard.

"Weren't you pretty much by yourself?"

"Not really. Fred and Sal'd be in and out, you know, movin' stuff. Then Trieger'd come over."

"A lot?"

"Yeah, he'd come over almost every day. In the summer, other times too, he'd bring me a beer, you know, that Australian beer in dem big oil cans? He'd bring me one of those. Around there, the nearest liquor store was halfa mile. So, a hot day, Trieger'd keep me supplied. I'd offer to pay him, those oil cans cost a good buck, but he said keep it, it came with the job." Kanelos was a man of average height and weight with receding gray hair. As he worked, he kept wrinkling his nose at the chair, pushing it and poking it crossly as if it were being willful.

"Did he work on his car when he came over?"

"The MG? Ain't that a beaut? Not much, he'd work on it weekends. Once he said, Hey, Kanelos, let's go for a spin. I got in, sort of a tight fit, you know, and I said, hey boss, none of these speed races. A car like that, I figured he'd really rip. No way. You'd think he was drivin' his grandmother. If the top hadn't been down, I'd of gone to sleep for sure. We get back, I can tell he's relieved. Like he's just finished givin' the car its exercise or something. Now he don't have to take it out for a while."

"Did he say why he was moving it?"

"Said he wanted to keep it at home."

"Did he give a reason?"

"Maybe he said something about takin' it up nort'. You know, he's got this place on a lake." Kanelos had attached more foam rubber to the back and arms of the chair. Taking a piece of green material, he began to tack it to the frame. The circular saw had stopped and the room was quiet except for the tap of the hammer.

Lazard leaned back and looked around the large room. There was a scurrying noise off in a far corner and Lazard saw a rat dragging a piece of white bread. He wondered what to ask next and found himself thinking of Trieger's brother in Miami. Was there a motive there? Lazard, who had never had a brother, tried to imagine what Trieger might do to help his own.

"You say Trieger comes in nearly every day, didn't he take a trip for a couple of days, sometime before the beginning of March?"

"You asking or telling?"

"Asking."

"Lemme see, like I say sometimes he don't come in, but one day he come in, you know how the weather was, one day he come in and he's gotta tan and I said to him, hey, you been hangin' out under a sunlight or somethin' and he said, nah, I been down south."

"When was this?"

"I don't know, February or March, leastways after Christmas. Maybe February 'cause it was really cold."

Lazard slowly got to his feet and leaned on his cane. He could feel himself smiling stupidly.

From the warehouse, Lazard drove to Trieger's office. Trieger's secretary walked over to meet him as he came in.

"Trieger around?"

"He went out for a bit, but he should be back anytime." Mrs. Lydon was a matronly dark-haired woman, and wore a yellow skirt and light green blouse. Around her neck was a string of amber beads.

"Business pretty slow?" asked Lazard as they walked back toward Mrs. Lydon's desk.

"More furniture will be coming in this week. There's not much to do until then."

"The waiting must get boring," said Lazard. "Too bad you can't take a vacation." Mrs. Lydon had sat back down and Lazard was leaning against the corner of her desk. He imagined their conversation unwinding like a film and it seemed he knew her answers even before she spoke them. Near him on the desk was a photograph of twin little boys in blue overalls wrestling over a large yellow ball.

"Well, there's still furniture coming back and we had to write our customers about the fire. I could certainly use a vacation from that if it weren't the wrong time of year."

"Where do you usually go?"

"I go to Bermuda for two weeks in January."

"I never been south," said Lazard. "Didn't Trieger go south for a vacation in February?"

She shook her head. "Two days. I don't call that a vacation."

"Where'd he go?"

"Miami." Mrs. Lydon paused, took a tissue from her purse, and wiped something from her eye. Then she looked past Lazard and said, "Here's Mr. Trieger now."

Lazard had seen the office door open, watched Trieger come in and hesitate, looking from Lazard to his secretary.

"Hello, Frank, good to see you. How you been?"

"Not bad. I wanted to ask a couple more questions."

"Let's go into my office." Trieger held the door as Lazard limped past him. It seemed to Lazard that Trieger was wary and slightly nervous.

"Tell me," said Lazard, "any of your employees mention seeing someone hanging around the warehouse before the fire?"

Instead of going to his desk, Trieger sat down on the couch. It had a floral pattern of lilacs and chrysanthemums. Lazard took the armchair, stretching his bad leg in front of him and lowering himself slowly.

"No one mentioned seeing anyone," said Trieger, "although the warehouse didn't really have any windows to see out of. How's the investigation coming?"

140

"A little slow. We've got a list of extortion suspects and a couple of guys are visiting them one by one. Takes time."

"I guess so. I probably been thinking too much about that insurance money, although the bank's been good about that. I'm the kind of guy that can't sit still, you know, compulsive-worker type."

Trieger had a tanned, square face with a wide mouth. It was a generous, animated face; the face of a man who believed too readily what he was told, the face of someone who wasn't paranoid enough. Despite himself, Lazard felt drawn to it. He decided to stop maneuvering and get to the point. "By the way," he asked, "why'd you go to Miami in February?"

Trieger took a cigarette from a box on the coffee table. "See my brother, he had some business problems he wanted help with. Anything that gets me outta the cold weather's good enough for me."

"You were there two days?"

"That's right."

"When?"

"End of February. The twenty-third, I think."

"What kind of problems was he having?"

"Well, I wouldn't call them actually problems. He wanted to buy about twenty double beds for the motel and about the same number of armchairs. I've a lot of contacts in the field and was able to save him some money." Trieger sat in the middle of the couch with his arms stretched along the top. As he talked, he kept lifting and dropping his hands.

"It must have cost you something to go down there."

"He's my brother, I owe him a lot. He thought I could help so I flew down. Got some sun, even did a little fishing."

"Did you help him?"

"I think so."

"Did he buy the furniture?"

"Not yet."

Lazard leaned back, putting his hands behind his neck. Again he had the sense that he knew exactly where the conversation was going and for the hundredth time he wished he had never known Trieger. "How's Norma?"

"Fine as always. She really liked that evening you came over."

"Been up north?"

"Went last weekend. Tried to do some painting but it rained. You should come up some time. The sun'd do you good."

"Sun?"

"Both Norma and I thought you looked tired, you know, too pale."

"You take the MG up north?"

"No, not yet."

Lazard leaned forward. His hands were restless and he wanted a cigarette. He pressed his fingertips together so they made a small cage. He imagined the tension from one hand passing into the fingers of the other, then he thought, no, they were just fingers.

"I'd like you to take a polygraph test. I think I can set one up for next week, maybe Tuesday."

"You mean a lie-detector test?"

"That's right, do you mind?"

"Not at all, I'd be glad to do it."

Theodore Quaid tilted back in his swivel chair and noticed a spot of mud on his left shoe. Taking a white handkerchief from his breast pocket, he shook it open, dipped the tip in a cup of cold coffee, and wiped the shoe clean.

He had hoped not to go to any fire scenes that day, but in the morning he had visited the burned shoe store for the third time, just to look at it. The day before he had talked to the owner, whose name was Palumbo. Along with the shoe store that Lazard had dumped on him, Quaid was also involved in about two dozen other investigations and although he would have preferred not to deal with the shoe store he at least understood Lazard's need for more time to investigate the warehouse fire. In any case, the shoe store wouldn't take much work. The arson was obvious and the only person who stood to gain by it was Palumbo himself.

Quaid relit his pipe, then blew gently through the stem. It was late Wednesday afternoon and he could see the sunlight reflecting off the distant buildings downtown. Across the office, Fatback was going through a card file of arson suspects, searching for the name of a Puerto Rican whom Phelps had just called about. The Puerto Rican had supposedly burned a garage, while the man Fatback was looking for also liked to burn garages.

"If it's the same fuckin' Rican," said Fatback, "and he gets

Judge Carpenter, then he's goin' to get his ass shipped back to San Juan with no shoes."

Carpenter was a district judge who believed that nothing humiliated Puerto Ricans as much as being sent back to Puerto Rico without shoes. Consequently he had returned about twenty shoeless Puerto Ricans to San Juan. If ever they tried to appeal, their cases automatically went to Superior Court, where they received jail sentences.

"It's him all right. Phelps is goin' to love this."

"Cassidy been in today?" asked Quaid.

"He was in around eleven. Didn't say anything, just in and out. What's he workin' on?"

"Bay State Finance."

"That the one Lazard dropped on him?"

"Yes."

"Nah, he didn't say anything. You think Lazard's okay?"

"What do you mean?"

"The way he's dumpin' these cases." Fatback shut the file and returned to his desk.

"He's still working on the warehouse fire."

"Lakin turn up anything on the car?"

"Kerosene in the trunk, that's all. Pugliese's up in Lynn talking to the owner."

"Fucking waste of time," said Fatback.

Although he wouldn't have said anything to Fatback, Quaid felt concerned about Lazard. He knew his friend was working on his days off and he worried that Lazard might get in trouble for it.

"Say, did I tell you that Phelps threw that private dick outta the office?" asked Fatback. "Served his ass right, you ask me."

"Who do you mean?"

"That hippie-looking guy that works for Bryant, you know, Bascomb."

"What happened?" Quaid began filling his pipe.

"Beats me. They were just talkin' and all of a sudden Phelps gets all huffy and tells Bascomb to get out."

"What'd Bascomb do?"

"Just left without a word. No wisecrack, no nothin'. What do you think happened?"

Quaid shook his head. "Who knows?" Actually, he guessed that Bascomb had been asking too many questions about some fire

143

that Phelps had called accidental but clearly wasn't. For years Phelps had been taking his additional source of income for granted and it had made him greedy. Not long before, most private insurance investigators tended to be ex-firemen who accepted what the Arson Squad told them. But now there were a growing number of young and eager investigators with FBI or state police experience whose only allegiance was to the insurance company that employed them. Not only did they outnumber the public investigators, they could also spend far longer on a particular case. Quaid knew that if a company like FAIR Plan or any other big insurance company complained about the quality of public arson investigation and Jerry Bryant assigned twenty men to look into it, then Phelps could be in real trouble.

16

Five firefighters dug into a mound of debris with shovels and long pikes. In front of them rose the wreckage of fallen beams, tilting walls, and dark piles of burned furniture. Nearby waited a group of photographers and newsmen. Above the newsmen, a pigeon hung suspended in mid-flight.

Lazard tossed the photograph back on the desk and picked up another taken from the rear of the warehouse. It showed the collapsed back wall, piles of bricks, and more charred beams protruding at different angles. Twenty photographs were spread out on the desk: 8-by-10 black-and-white photos taken of the warehouse during the fire.

Lazard had hoped the photographs would give him a greater sense of what had happened, but no feeling came from these pictures, not even the one showing the mound of debris covering the bodies of Harris and Roberts. His awareness that this was the warehouse was intellectual: the grayness, the black fire coats, the smoke, the dark piles of wreckage—these could be from anywhere.

It was 5 o'clock Thursday afternoon. Fatback was putting away his reports and preparing to leave. In a chair by the file cabinets, Virginia Lufkin graded papers piled on a clipboard in her lap.

When Lazard had arrived at 4:30, Fatback had been alone. "Whaddaya doing aroun' here?" Fatback asked accusingly.

"I want to look at some pictures."

"Why'n't you go to a movie?"

Virginia Lufkin had appeared fifteen minutes later. Although Fatback often complained about her waiting for Pugliese, he always went out of his way to give her the best chair.

"Gotta big date?"

"Just dinner. I haven't gone out to dinner for ages."

She wore very little makeup, just a small amount of eye-liner. She saw Lazard looking at her and smiled. Taking some papers from a brown vinyl attaché case, she began to read. In her mouth she held a felt-tip pen which she occasionally removed to make some mark or comment.

Shortly after five, Fatback put on his coat. "You gonna see the game tonight?" he asked Lazard. The Flyers were playing the Bruins in the second game of their series.

"I don't know," said Lazard. Although he'd agreed to go to Quaid's to see the game on television, he didn't want to and had promised only in order to please his friend.

"Cassidy in today?" asked Lazard.

"Once this morning, then he stopped by twice, no, once this afternoon. Seemed sorta funny." Fatback inserted the eraser end of a yellow pencil in his ear and wiggled it.

"Funny?" Lazard couldn't imagine Cassidy being funny.

"Preoccupied. You sure he's working on that finance company?"

"Supposed to be. Why?"

"Didn't mention it, that's all. He also called about six times to see if anyone had left any messages."

After Fatback left, Lazard returned to looking at the photographs. The pictures of wreckage and desolation remained just pictures. He kept thinking that while they were being taken, he'd been with his lawyer dealing with the remnants of his marriage. The only emotions stirred up by the photographs concerned Elizabeth. In his mind he saw her wearing a blue dress he didn't remember and with her hair cut short. In his hand was a photograph of firefighters standing in a street criss-crossed with hose, white streaks of water coming from the pumpers and motionless black smoke like mountains at dusk.

Apart from the steady crackle of the radio over the desk, the only noises came from Virginia Lufkin rustling her papers or moving in her chair. It was nearly 5:30.

"Where's Pugliese?" asked Lazard, although he knew. Pugliese was still in Lynn trying to discover if there had been any witnesses to the theft of the Mercury Cougar.

She raised her head. Her brown hair was in one braid down her back. "He didn't tell me. He only said he'd be back by five."

"Ever find out where he was last Friday?"

Setting her papers on the floor, Virginia stood up and stretched, putting her hands on her hips and arching her back. Lazard looked at her, then looked away. "He'd found someone who had a collection of model cars," she said. "I guess it was a large collection. What are those pictures?"

"A fire."

"Can I see?"

Lazard didn't want her to but couldn't think why so he said, "Sure."

She stood behind him staring down at the photographs on the desk. Lazard moved his chair to the left. She wore a white cotton polo shirt with red and green stripes and a green skirt with slash pockets. She was perspiring slightly and Lazard could just detect a bitter smell.

"What fire is this?"

"The warehouse about two weeks ago."

"Is that where two firemen were killed?"

"Yes."

"Andy told me about it. It sounded terrible."

Reaching for a picture, she brushed Lazard's arm. He moved his chair farther toward the wall. "What're those men digging into?"

"The ceiling fell on Harris and Roberts. They're under that pile."

She put the picture back on the desk. "That's awful."

Lazard stood up and moved around her to the file cabinet. He watched her leaning over the desk and felt very conscious of the curve of her breasts and waist, her long legs against the green fabric of her skirt. He began to imagine making love to her, of coming up behind her and pushing her against the desk.

Pugliese telephoned at 5:45. He was excited and spoke quickly. "Who's this? Lazard? I got some fantastic news. You know that

147

car? I found a guy who saw it stolen. He works in a hardware. Said a kid took it. Skinny kid with blond hair. Would you believe it, fuckin' Lynn cops had a good idea who it was and this clerk, this hardware guy, he recognized the mugshot. Says he's positive. Kid by the name of Georgie Connors." Pugliese pronounced it Jaw-gee.

"You arrest him?"

"Just made the I.D. I'm going after him now."

"You know Virginia's here?"

"Ginny? Fuck, it completely went out of my head. Let me talk to her, will you?"

Lazard handed her the phone. "It's Pugliese."

"Hello, Andy? Where are you?" Her voice was expectant but with a bit of anger. She stood by Lazard's desk looking out at the Boston skyline. Lazard went back to sorting through the pictures, but found it impossible not to be aware of Virginia Lufkin.

"So we won't be going out after all? No, I'm glad you found him. I'll just take the train back . . . Of course I'm angry, why wouldn't I be angry." She hung up the phone, then noticed Lazard looking at her. "Sometimes he makes me furious," she said.

She stood still for a moment, then went to collect her books and put her papers in her attaché case. The snaps on the case clicked shut. Lazard watched her. She took a yellow raincoat from the coat rack behind the door, started to put it on, then draped it over her arm and picked up the attaché case. Seeing Lazard, she returned his stare until he grew uncomfortable.

"What are you going to do?" he asked.

"Take a train back to Salem." She stood in the doorway.

"I'm through here, let me drive you."

"I couldn't do that, it's too far."

Lazard got up and reached for his brown cane. "My car's out-side. Come on, let's go." He left the pictures on the desk.

There was still a lot of traffic on the expressway. They crossed Tobin Bridge, heading north on Route 95. Neither of them spoke much. He said something about how the traffic was always bad through here; and she said the sky was clearing and it was sup-posed to be nice tomorrow. Lazard didn't look at her, but could see her from the corner of his eye, looking out at the traffic and sometimes looking at him. He was very aware of her body and could see the line of her thigh beside him. Sometimes he let his hand fall near it. He hadn't made love to a woman for a long time,

148

hadn't thought he wanted to. He imagined letting everything go, becoming a person for whom life was easier. For a moment, he found himself thinking of Trieger, then he thought of Virginia again, of parking in some desolate place and making love violently in the back seat, of tearing her clothes. He found himself getting an erection and moved his hand to his lap so she wouldn't notice.

They drove north on Route 1 through Malden and Saugus, the road bordered by a mercantile slum of shopping centers, liquor stores, motels, gas stations, bargain stores offering carpet for $4 per square yard, and leisure suits for $19 each.

"You hungry?" asked Lazard.

"Starving."

"Let's stop."

They had Reuben sandwiches and cheesecake at Godfried's, a suburban delicatessen. Lazard wasn't hungry and had to force himself to finish the sandwich and left half his cheesecake uneaten. From the restaurant, he called Quaid and said he wouldn't be coming.

As they drank their coffee, Lazard asked, "What do you teach?"

"American history and geography, seventh and eighth grades. You know, what they used to call social studies."

"You like it?"

"Pretty much. You live in Boston?"

"Cambridge. I moved there last January."

"There's such a lot going on. It must be exciting."

"It's okay."

Her single braid hung over her left shoulder, and she held onto it with her left hand as if hanging onto a strap. He wanted to tell her she was beautiful, make some personal comment to show how he felt, but all the words he could think of seemed clumsy.

It was nearly dark when they left. As he held the car door, she momentarily took hold of his arm above the elbow and squeezed it. A feeling of relief swept through him.

Traffic had thinned out on Route 1. It was only several miles to Route 128, where he would turn off for Salem. Although Lazard knew what he wanted, he was again unsure of the words. The top two buttons of Virginia's polo shirt were undone and Lazard was aware of a triangle of white skin.

As they approached Route 128, Lazard said, "Do you want to stop at a motel?"

She was silent a moment. "Yes," she answered.

Lazard turned into the first motel they came to. It had a marquee advertising special weekday rates. Virginia Lufkin waited in the car as Lazard paid for the room. It was $15 and he had to promise not to mess up the other bed.

The room had green walls, blond furniture, and a blue table lamp with black velvet poodles raised on the white shade. Lazard touched Virginia's elbow as they entered the room. It was stuffy and there was a sweet smell of disinfectant. A heater clicked on.

They took the farther bed and at first they were clumsy. Lazard got a knot in his shoelace. The sheets were clammy, almost damp, and stiff as if starched. She made love violently, scratching his back and pinning his legs with hers, holding him to her. Lazard was afraid someone might hear. He buried his face in the nape of her neck and felt swept away, even though it seemed she wasn't responding particularly to him, as if he were almost incidental to her pleasure. It was over very quickly. Afterward she got up and went to the bathroom.

The room became hot. A blond dressing table and mirror faced the bed. Lazard stretched so he could see himself, then was startled that he looked so much older than he had anticipated. His short brown hair stood up on end. He moved so he could no longer see himself. A television was bolted to a platform bolted to the wall near the front window. The only light came from a standing lamp by the door which had more poodles on the shade. The toilet flushed and Virginia Lufkin returned to the room.

Her skin was tanned and Lazard saw the outline of whiter skin which had been covered by a bikini. She got a cigarette from her purse, lit it, then offered it to Lazard. He took it and she lit another for herself. She was restless or unsure. Walking to the TV, she turned it on, turned it off, then turned it on again. She had long thin legs, a high waist. Her breasts were slightly pointed and turned outward. The television came on, but no sound. In black and white, it showed a new car by itself on a huge stage.

Virginia Lufkin lay down beside Lazard. She was naked except for her earrings—two yellow half moons—and a watch with a narrow black strap. She began to say something, then saw his leg. Lazard heard her take a quick breath.

"What happened to it?"

"It got burned in a fire."

"How?"

Lazard regretted he hadn't covered it. Parts of the skin were mottled in different shades of pink, parts were dead white and seamed and puckered from skin grafts.

"I was too eager."

"What do you mean?"

"I went someplace I shouldn't and got caught, that's all."

"Does it hurt?"

"No."

She reached out and touched it gently, drawing one finger along the leg from the foot to just past the knee. "Why's it worse here?"

"The rubber of the boot melted and stuck to the skin."

Virginia Lufkin withdrew her hand, but slowly. She glanced into Lazard's face. "Are you sure it doesn't hurt?"

"Yes."

"Are you married?"

"Not anymore."

"Do you like Andy?"

"He's all right. Are you going to marry him?"

"I can't decide."

They made love again. It was equally violent and again she scratched his back, but this time Lazard felt she was reacting to him, to who he was. He held onto her buttocks, pressing her to him as they rocked back and forth. He couldn't imagine her being violent with Pugliese.

Afterward she went to sleep on his arm. Lazard lay on his back. The television was still on and showed the hockey game, but the set was too far away to see more than black figures skating across the ice, moving back and forth like bees before a hive. It was impossible to tell which were Bruins and which Flyers. The horizontal hold needed adjusting and every few seconds the picture slowly moved up the screen.

The other double bed was identical to the one in which they lay. Lazard could see it in the mirror and together the two beds formed a sort of before and after picture. He stared at the reflection of the other bed and it was as if they had never made love, as if they had just entered the room. He felt a disappointment he couldn't verbalize. He wished his whole life were different but he didn't know what to do about it. He felt angry at Pugliese for telling Virginia to meet him in the arson office, as if it were Pugliese's fault that Lazard had made love to his fiancée. Then he shook his head at his own foolishness.

Virginia Lufkin slept without a sound, her body curled toward him. The weight of her head on his arm cut off the circulation and it began to fall asleep. Then it began to hurt, but Lazard didn't move. He was afraid of waking her. He didn't know how to talk or what to say.

When Lazard got home at midnight, the phone was ringing.

"Lazard?" It was Cassidy.

"Yes."

"I've been trying to get you."

Lazard waited.

"I'm in trouble."

"How do you mean?"

"Lazard, this is outside the department. Nothing goes back, all right?"

"What's wrong?"

Lazard stood in the middle of his living room. He could see through his front window out to Hancock. In the boardinghouse across the street, he noticed a man or the silhouette of a man staring down from an attic window. As he watched, he faintly detected the smell of Virginia's body from the hand holding the telephone.

"Someone stole my gun."

"What?"

"I said, someone stole my gun."

"How did it happen?"

"What the fuck's it matter how it happened. He's already used it to knock over a liquor store. If he's picked up and that gun's traced back to me . . ." His voice rose and he stopped. When he spoke again, his voice was flat and matter of fact.

"Some kid took it. I'll explain tomorrow. I been talking to his wife. He's about to leave town. I think we can grab him in the morning. You'll help me?"

"I guess so."

"Meet me at eight at Herald and Washington. Baxter's coming, Pugliese also."

"Pugliese?"

"He's the only one can make a fuckin' arrest. You got a gun?"

"No."

"I guess it doesn't matter."

They hung up. The man had moved from the window across the street and the light was off. Lazard's apartment was stuffy and he went to open a window. The only sound came from the water pipes in the bathroom, a constant dripping and gurgling that sounded like a voice: urgent and meaningless.

Later in the hospital with his destroyed leg, Lazard had realized he should have paid more attention to the booby-trapped stairs since they gave further evidence of arson. Fires burn according to specific rules, but when arson is involved none of those rules hold.

Lazard knew this, but his ambition, plus his pleasure at manning the tip of the lead hose going into the burning three-decker, pushed that concern aside. Indeed, his only worry had been that the blow from the nozzle had cracked a rib, which might keep him from playing basketball the next night. He was star forward of the District 7 team and the main reason his team was first in Division 2.

As Lazard had neared the top of the stairs to the second floor, almost crawling on his belly with the line running beneath him, he pushed one foot against the banister, the other against the wall. Then, when he felt sufficiently braced, he eased open the nozzle and water smashed off the walls and spattered into the upstairs hall.

"Give me three more feet," he shouted.

Schultz and Haggerty jockeyed the line behind him and Lazard pushed his way up the stairs, testing each board before he gave it his full weight. As the water hit the fire there was a great hissing. Smoke billowed back down the stairs along with hot steam which burned Lazard's neck and face. He lowered his head and went up another step.

"More line!"

The flame at the top of the stairs had gone dark as the fire retreated down the hall. By now Ladders 7 and 23 had vented the building, breaking the windows and putting holes in the roof to draw off the heat and smoke. Glancing back down the stairs, Lazard saw Felsch, McQuire, and a third man edging their way around the hole in the stairs with their 2½-inch line. Just ahead of them was Captain Lovell from Engine 24 with a lamp. Constantly Lazard was jostled by Schultz and Haggerty, who kept heaving at the line, trying to give him a few more feet while attempting to control its bucking so Lazard could aim the nozzle.

At the top of the stairs, Lazard pushed forward on his knees into the second-floor hall. The fire was about 15 feet down the hall and Lazard pointed the nozzle up toward the ceiling. Felsch and McQuire with the second line appeared through the smoke at the top of the stairs. Captain Lovell directed them to attack the fire in the front rooms. He too was wearing an air pack and his orders, shouted through the face mask, were muffled and nearly overwhelmed by the roaring of the fire and water. Getting to his feet, Lazard heaved the line another yard forward, then rotated the nozzle so the water spattered off the walls and ceiling.

Captain Lovell leaned forward and shouted toward Lazard's ear. "Good job. Take a breather, Lazard. Go on back." Lovell was called Durante by other firefighters, although not to his face. Some years before, the inside of his throat had been severely scorched during a fire, giving him the raspy voice of the comedian.

Although Lazard's arms and shoulders ached, he wanted to stay on the tip as long as possible. "Just a little longer," he shouted.

Before Lovell could reply there was a tremendous whoosh and dark red flame came rushing at them along the ceiling and walls, a red wave that sent them running back toward the stairs. Lazard could feel the uncovered skin on his face and neck blister. He yanked up the nozzle so the water hit the ceiling almost directly above them. Schultz dove into the stairway, letting go of the line, and Lazard had to wrap himself around the nozzle to keep it from breaking loose. Captain Lovell was also halfway down the stairs. Haggerty heaved at the line behind Lazard, trying to give him greater freedom. Layers of paint on the walls and ceiling kept melting and igniting, sending flying gobs of flame down on top of them. Lazard felt a burning on his left hand and saw that a dollop of molten paint had fallen under the gauntlet of his glove and onto the back of his hand.

The fire was almost above their heads as they crouched down by the stairway. Hot steam from the water burned Lazard's face. He guessed that some kind of accelerant had been ignited, probably gasoline. As Lazard kept the water moving across the flame, it began to grow dark and back down the hall. He lay on his belly by a door that presumably led to the third floor and as the fire retreated down the hall and the noise diminished, he began to hear a faint banging on the other side.

Lovell crawled up to Lazard and tugged at his arm. "Beat it. Engine 52 will take over. Good job."

"There's someone on the other side of that door," shouted Lazard. "Turn your light on it."

Lazard gave the nozzle to a man from Engine 52, then jumped up and grabbed the doorknob. It was locked. He stepped back and kicked the lower panel of the door. The temperature, when he stood up, seemed to increase by a hundred degrees. He kicked the door again.

"Get a halligan bar," shouted Lovell.

But Lazard doubted there would be time and he kept kicking. Haggerty, Schultz, and the new man had moved farther down the hall, leaving Lazard and Captain Lovell alone by the door.

"I thought Ladder 7 had cleared the building," shouted Lazard.

Lovell began kicking at the door. "The third floor was supposed to be vacant."

At last they made a hole, then they made it wider. A woman in a light-colored dress half crawled, half tumbled through it. She was terrified and nearly overcome by smoke.

"Is anyone else up there?" asked Lazard, taking her by the shoulders.

The woman looked at him as if she hadn't heard. She kept coughing. She was about forty and strands of gray hair fell across her face. Lazard struck her across the cheek. "Come on, who else is up there?"

"My niece's baby. He's crippled. I couldn't get to him. The smoke . . ."

"Where is he?"

"The bedroom."

"What's wrong with him?"

"His leg, he lost a leg."

Lazard turned and began crawling through the hole in the door. Lovell grabbed him. "You can't go up there. It's right above the fire. You don't even have a light."

Reaching out, Lazard took the light from Lovell's hand. "Now I do," he said.

155

17

The boy on the bicycle held a bottle of orange pop in one hand and a small bag of groceries in the other. Both hands were raised above his head. It was a cheap yellow 10-speed which he balanced by shifting his weight, but he did it so gracefully that he scarcely seemed to move. He was black and about fourteen. He wore blue gym shorts and a green tank top with blue trim. A red baseball cap was turned backwards on his head.

Without slowing, the boy merged with the traffic on Shawmut, weaving in front of a cab and taking a drink from the bottle. As he sped up, the bike rocked back and forth.

It was 8:30 Friday morning. The air was warm and the sky free of clouds. The boy cut across Berkeley on a yellow light, then made gentle S-shapes as he passed the Castle Square apartment complex. He took a last drink, tilting his head back to get the remaining drops. The bike turned onto Herald. There were no cars and the boy made a series of wide S's, rocking his body back and forth with his arms outstretched: one hand holding an empty bottle, the other a small bag of groceries.

Halfway up the block toward Tremont, he passed four men

getting out of a tan Ford. Baxter climbed out first and watched the boy glide by. He stopped and Cassidy bumped into him.

"What the fuck you doing?"

Pugliese got out the other side. Lazard rolled up the windows and locked the car. Glancing up, he saw a black kid on a yellow bike make a gliding no-hands turn onto Tremont.

"I never could do that," said Baxter. "Those balloon tire jobs, they were too heavy."

"What the hell you jabbering about?" said Cassidy. "Let's get going."

The four men walked toward Tremont. Lazard was aware of Pugliese directly behind him and wished he would walk someplace else. He kept thinking of Virginia Lufkin, how she had wrapped her legs around his, pressing him to her. He felt guilty about this, but didn't, he thought, sufficiently regret it.

Pugliese was depressed and kept sighing. He had spent the entire evening looking for Georgie Connors, the possible car thief. Connors had been raised in Lynn and Pugliese had talked to his parents, brothers and sisters, uncles and cousins, various friends. No one had seen him all week. Pugliese felt some of them were lying, but there was nothing he could do about it except grow indignant. Connors had been jailed several times in the past for car theft and if he were convicted again it could mean a substantial sentence. In any case, Pugliese felt honored that Cassidy had asked for his help. He imagined a growing intimacy with Cassidy; imagined the two of them feared and respected as a crime-fighting team.

Cassidy had explained how he'd confused the two Robert Dodges and lost his revolver. Bobby Dodge's wife had told him that her husband was in other trouble, and by hunting down his friends he had learned about the gambling and Henry Pierce. Cassidy had spent two days searching for Dodge but discovered only where he had been. The previous evening Dodge had held up a liquor store in Roxbury, got $800, and now he intended to escape south. Before leaving, however, he meant to see his girlfriend, Dionne Rogers, who was a whore, according to Bobby Dodge's wife, and who had been hiding him for nearly a week.

"How do you know that's true?" Lazard had asked.

"His wife told me. I talked to her again this morning and she said she'd been in touch with this Dionne and Dionne told her that Dodge would be visiting her between ten and eleven."

"Why should she tell her that?" Lazard felt skeptical and had no faith in Cassidy's plans.

"She wants him outta her apartment. She's a hooker and the guy's messing up her business."

They had discussed this sitting in Lazard's car parked behind the offices of the *Herald American* a few blocks away. Cassidy didn't want to use his car because he thought Dodge might recognize it.

"Ruby and I'll wait in her apartment. Lazard, you stay out in the hall around the corner. Pugliese stays on the street. I'll be watching from the window. Anyone goes into her building looking like this Robert Dodge, you give a wave, understand me, Pugliese?"

"Sure."

"I don't want to get myself shot 'cause you been stupid."

Cassidy, Baxter, and Pugliese had guns. Lazard was unarmed. He carried his brown wooden cane and kept thinking he ought to be using his aluminum one.

The apartment complex was made up of two- and three-story units with two or four apartments on each floor. Dionne Rogers lived on the third floor of a unit facing Herald Street. Across Herald was the great ditch formed by the Massachusetts Turnpike.

Pugliese kept walking up the street. "Take care, you guys."

No one answered him.

Cassidy pushed a button in the lobby. The lock buzzed and he opened the door. He wore a blue seersucker suit and highly polished black shoes. His Macora hat was tilted far back on his head.

"She knows we're coming?" asked Baxter, surprised.

"Sure, how else could we do this?"

It didn't occur to Lazard to worry that he didn't have a gun. He didn't think of it. Mostly he was glad at having gotten away from Pugliese. If he let his mind relax, he could see the mirror in the motel and the reflection of the undisturbed bed.

The apartment building was well cared for. It was much nicer than Lazard's building and, as he followed Cassidy and Baxter up the stairs, he decided it was cleaner as well. The halls and stairs were covered with brown carpeting that dampened their footsteps.

At the third-floor landing Cassidy and Baxter turned right toward the open door of Dionne Rogers's apartment. Lazard turned left. From somewhere came the hum of a vacuum cleaner. The sunlight coming through the window at the end of the hall made the white walls shimmer.

Despite the carpeting, Bobby Dodge heard them coming. He had arrived half an hour earlier only to find Dionne with a syringe preparing to shoot up. At first his presence terrified her, but now she was half asleep, rocking back and forth in a black rocking chair. She wore a white dress that looked like a lacy Victorian nightshirt. On her head was an auburn wig with masses of curls and ringlets that cascaded over her shoulders.

Bobby thought it was Henry Pierce coming up the stairs. He waited in a short hallway leading to the kitchen. In his hand was the .38 stolen from Cassidy. Yesterday, when he had robbed the liquor store, the gun had made everything easy. He only had to show it and everybody had quietly laid down on the floor. No fuss, no muss. He hoped it was Henry Pierce and he meant to kill him.

Instead, it was the tall white man from whom he had stolen the revolver. Behind him was a fat, pasty-faced man who looked frightened. It was he who saw Dodge first. He pointed and shouted, stumbling back and trying to drag something from his pocket.

Bobby Dodge stepped into the room raising his revolver. "You fuck, you want your fuckin' gun, I'll give it to you."

Cassidy had drawn his revolver. Baxter was still struggling to get his out of his back pocket. Dodge fired once, hitting Cassidy in his shoulder, spinning him sideways. His hat flew off and Baxter, in his excitement, stepped on it. Dionne screamed, a single abrupt noise, but kept rocking back and forth, her auburn curls flickering in the sunlight. Dodge fired again, shattering a pottery lamp. Cassidy fired and missed. The bullet ricocheted off the wall with a high whine. Bobby Dodge fired three more times, hitting Cassidy again so that his legs seemed to fold up beneath him and he fell forward onto the rug. The fat man already lay motionless. Dodge ran forward, scooped up Cassidy's second gun, and ran out of the room.

The hall was empty. He ran down the stairs and as he ran he heard the glass smash in the front door below and the door slam open. He raised his gun and when he reached the second-floor landing he nearly charged into another white man who was just pulling a revolver from the holster at his waist.

"Drop it, man," said Bobby Dodge. "Drop it 'fore I kill you."

When Lazard heard the shots, he stepped around the corner out of sight. Then there was the sound of someone running, and from downstairs came the sound of breaking glass, which he knew was Pugliese. Lazard limped to the stairs and was about to go on to the apartment when he heard shouting from below. Slowly Lazard descended the stairs. Dodge was still shouting.

"You fuck, why can't you leave me alone? What the fuck I ever done to you?"

And Pugliese: "I never seen you, I never seen you in my life."

Lazard stopped just before the landing. Ten feet away, a young black man was pointing two revolvers at Pugliese. Another lay on the carpet between them. Pugliese had his hands outstretched, blocking his chest as if he meant to catch the bullet. His face was all squinched up. Each time he stepped back, the black man took another step toward him. Lazard was struck by Pugliese's face, which looked as if he were already in great pain.

"I'm gonna kill you, you fuck, just like those honkies upstairs." Dodge was so angry that the words became jumbled in his mouth.

Pugliese bumped against the white wall. His bright yellow sport coat seemed to glitter in the light from the window.

Without much thought, Lazard limped forward, running, almost hopping on his good leg, swinging himself forward on his cane. Dodge must have seen something in Pugliese's eyes because he began to turn. Lazard lifted his cane, gripping it by the end with both hands, and as Dodge turned he threw himself forward and swung. The crook of the cane hit the black man just below the base of his skull. Then Lazard toppled against him, knocking him back toward Pugliese, who scrambled out of the way. Letting go of his cane, Lazard grabbed at the two revolvers, wrenching them free as the two men hit the floor. Dodge tried to twist away, but Lazard smashed the butt of the revolver against Bobby Dodge's skull. Then he hit him again, cutting his skin so blood got on his hand. When he saw the blood, Lazard dropped both revolvers and pushed himself away. In any case, Dodge was unconscious.

Pugliese reached out and took Lazard's arm to help him up. Lazard shook him loose. Then he rolled over, grabbed his cane, and pushed himself to his feet. They stood there looking down at Bobby Dodge half curled with his knees drawn up on the brown carpet. A trickle of blood ran from his hair down to his chin. The building was silent apart from the sound of Pugliese's heavy breathing. Pugliese stepped around the man on the floor and put his hand on Lazard's arm.

"Jesus, Frank, he was going to kill me . . ."

Lazard pulled away. "Forget it. You got handcuffs? Put them on him." It embarrassed Lazard to have saved Pugliese's life. It immensely complicated their relationship just at the point when Lazard wanted no relationship whatsoever. He also realized that no matter how much he desired Virginia Lufkin this act of saving her fiancé's life made any meeting with her impossible.

He picked up Cassidy's guns and limped back upstairs, almost looking forward to any awfulness that might distract him from thinking about Pugliese. Dionne Rogers's door stood open. Entering, Lazard saw Baxter lying on his back, staring at the ceiling and blinking. He seemed unhurt. At least there was no blood.

From Cassidy there was a lot of blood. He lay on a round yellow and pink shag rug and blood oozed over it onto the squares of white tile. Beyond him a beautiful black woman rocked back and forth in an antique rocker, not looking at anyone. The air smelled of gunpowder. Above the woman in a pagoda-shaped cage, two small gray birds with red beaks hurled themselves at the bars.

Lazard crouched down next to Cassidy and put his middle and ring fingers on the carotid artery in his neck. It was beating strongly. Sunlight streamed through the front windows. A lamp with a yellow pottery base lay smashed on the floor.

"You all right, Ruby?"

"Nothin', the guy didn't hit me or nothin'." Sitting up, Baxter began touching himself, but gently as if expecting to find damage. "God knows why."

Pugliese rushed into the room, then stopped when he saw Cassidy. "Oh, shit, I knew I should of gone up first. Cassidy's dead. Oh, Christ, no." He looked ready to burst into tears.

Cassidy groaned, tried to push himself up, then fell back onto the rug. "I'm not dead, you ass." He was bleeding from his shoulder and some other place on his body, staining his blue seersucker suit. He glared at the woman rocking back and forth and not seeing any of them. Cassidy's crushed Macora hat lay within a few feet of her chair.

In the distance, they heard sirens. They were getting closer and Lazard, Baxter, and Cassidy knew they weren't fire sirens.

Lazard took a pillow covered with white rabbit fur from a long blue couch. Then he came back and stuck it under Cassidy's head. "You're really going to get yelled at," he said.

18

"And if he picks up a germ in the hospital and dies," asked Lazard, "you going to stick his picture in Memorial Hall?"

Fire Commissioner McGorty leaned back, his hands on his desk. "What do you mean?"

"As having died in the line of duty."

"That's uncalled for, Lazard," said Flanagan.

McGorty looked from Lazard to the City Fire Marshal. It was early Friday afternoon and they were in McGorty's office. The door was closed and the secretary had been told not to disturb them. It was a large office with a lot of dark wood, leather, and fire souvenirs such as brass bells, a chrome-plated fire ax, and photographs of dignitaries shaking each other's hands. McGorty continued to stare at Lazard and Flanagan, who sat opposite him.

There'd been a confusion in McGorty's mind as to what had happened. That was Flanagan's fault. Although an intelligent man, he felt bullied by the politics of his job and a commissioner who had recently stripped him of four aides whom Flanagan had used as his personal chauffeurs. Although Flanagan earned $28,000, he had always felt poor.

The way Flanagan had described the events of the morning,

it sounded as if an unarmed investigator had been shot while attempting to question a suspect. Although the news was upsetting, McGorty saw in it the chance to publicize the conditions under which the Arson Squad labored. Next spring Cassidy might get a medal. Given this interpretation, Flanagan had been forced to be more precise.

He explained that Cassidy and Baxter had both been armed and that Bobby Dodge was not an arson suspect. He explained they wanted Dodge because he had stolen a gun from Cassidy which Cassidy ought not to have had in the first place.

McGorty then decided to alter the story. The public information officer would tell the press that an unarmed firefighter had been shot by a bandit who thought he was a policeman. They would minimize Cassidy's wounds, making them seem no worse than scratches. Actually one bullet had perforated Cassidy's left lung and the other had passed through the fleshy part of his left shoulder.

It had been at this point that Lazard had asked what would happen if Cassidy died in the hospital.

"He won't die," said McGorty. He was tall and muscular with a farmer's tan from playing golf.

"I don't see what you were doing there, Lazard," said Flanagan. "You're not supposed to be working today."

Lazard didn't answer. He had earlier spent two hours answering similar questions at police headquarters.

"Did you have a gun too?" asked the commissioner. "Christ, firemen carrying guns."

"I don't own a gun," said Lazard. He didn't think they believed him. He disliked McGorty's implication that he was surprised some men carried guns. He knew McGorty was aware Cassidy was armed, that others were armed also.

"It seems to me," said Flanagan, "that you're spending too much time on this warehouse fire."

"You told me to give it priority."

"I meant a coupla days. You going to keep at it forever? The way I see it, this's obviously an extortion fire and the investigation's reached a dead end." Flanagan paused. There were three gold stars on each wing of the collar of his shirt. He picked at one thoughtfully. "Don't get me wrong, I think you fellas did a great job tracing that car and turning it up at Logan. But what can we learn from that? Most likely the extortionist comes from some other city. Say, New York. He flies in to collect his money or burn a building, then flies out again. That's why Cassidy couldn't find anything. Okay, why burn the building? Because now and then he's got to show some muscle. But these guys, they get too greedy. Next week, next month, he'll go too far. What I say is we take this warehouse fire and close the case pending new information so the insurance company can start paying off. Then we call in the FBI. After all, crossing state lines to commit a crime, that makes it more or less their baby."

As Flanagan talked, Lazard stared down at his hands. He counted nine small scars and tried to think how he had gotten them. Then he realized he could simply say yes, agree with Flanagan, and Trieger would be let off the hook. Who'd care? Bascomb, of course, but he didn't have the power to do anything. Glancing up, Lazard saw the commissioner looking at him.

"What do you think, Lazard?" asked McGorty.

"There are inconsistencies in Trieger's story. He's agreed to take a polygraph test on Tuesday. I say wait until then."

McGorty pushed back his chair. "All right, we'll wait. But don't let this business interfere with your other work. And if you can't find the evidence, don't crucify the guy."

Lazard and Baxter worked again on Saturday, May 1. Baxter hoped for a quiet day, but at 8:30 they were called to a fire on Linden just off Dorchester Avenue. They found the arsonists within half an hour: all three were sitting at the top of a maple tree watching the firemen.

Two of the boys were eight, one was nine. They had taken a can of spot remover and sprayed it on the back of a three-decker. One of them said they hadn't expected it would burn so fast. Although by law anyone over the age of seven can be arrested, Lazard talked to their parents instead.

As they drove back to Fire Headquarters, Baxter said, "What'd you do if a kid of yours started a fire like that?"

"I don't have any kids." Lazard disliked hypothetical questions.

"Know what I'd do?"

"What?"

"Maybe I'd burn 'em, you know, just burn their hands a little to see what it felt like. Nah, I can't see that. My youngest kid, he's twenty-three. I catch him starting a fire, I'll bust his fuckin' jaw."

Baxter became silent again. He kept thinking how Bobby Dodge had fired five bullets in his direction and missed. Gently he touched his large stomach and felt amazed it didn't look like a chunk of Swiss cheese. It made him want to think of something else.

"You know," said Baxter, "I don't care they keep us running all day so long as we got nothing to do between five and six."

"Why's that?" asked Lazard.

"The Derby. Jesus, Frank, least you could be interested in the Kentucky Derby."

Lazard thought for a moment. They were driving through an area of run-down one- and two-story houses, many covered with cheap asbestos siding. Over the years quite a few had burned, and as he considered the Derby the faces of the people who had lived in these houses passed through Lazard's mind.

"One time when I was a kid," said Lazard, "me and my family, we were driving someplace and the Kentucky Derby came on the car radio. You know, there's a lot of talk before the race and they discussed all the horses and when they had finished I said to my Dad, 'Jet Pilot's going to win.' And he laughed, but then, so help me, Jet Pilot won the race."

"Who you think's gonna win this race?" asked Baxter.

"I don't know who's running."

"Well, to my way of thinking, Honest Pleasure is the horse to beat. That Baeza, he's hot."

They had been in the office about ten minutes when Lazard got a telephone call from David Bascomb.

"My man got back from Florida last night. Want to hear about it?"

"What'd he say?"

"I think I better come over."

David Bascomb stood leaning against the window ledge with his elbow on the portable TV. Also on the TV was a box of toothpicks. The lights were off and Bascomb's face was dark against the cloudy sky behind him.

"So what do you have for us?" asked Lazard. He again thought how a simple agreement with Flanagan would have ended the case.

Bascomb scratched his chin. "It's a little complicated."

"That's all right," said Lazard, "except for a few fires we don't have anything to do until the Kentucky Derby late this afternoon."

"There's a guy," said Bascomb, "a pilot, who worked around Miami for some of these small charter companies, you know, tourist flights up and down the coast or out to the Keys. The pilot's name was Larry Morgan. The police said he might have been involved in a little smuggling. Morgan would work at a place for a while, then there'd be a blow-up and he'd go someplace else. He never had his own plane or could put enough money together for a down payment."

Lazard sat at the nearer desk. Baxter sat with his feet up on the other desk in order to show Bascomb that whatever he said, Baxter wouldn't take it very seriously. Baxter thought Bascomb's hair was even longer than the last time he'd seen it: light brown and curling just past the collar.

"At the beginning of last September, Morgan bought a plane: a two-engine Beechcraft 2400. It's not new but it's not cheap. About two days later the police get a tip that a large amount of marijuana is to be flown in to a small airport southwest of Miami. They're told some guy's flying it up from Jamaica.

"The police get out there. After a while they see Morgan's Beechcraft preparing to land. It comes in lower and lower and just as the plane is touching down Morgan must have caught a glimpse of the police cars because he guns the engines, swoops up, banks, and that was that. He hit some power lines and the plane exploded. Morgan's killed right off. In the wreckage, the cops find about seven or eight bales of marijuana.

"Although Morgan's listed as sole owner of the plane, the police don't think he's big enough to get into smuggling by himself. They figure Morgan and somebody else borrowed the money, then hoped to pay it back with what they made from the marijuana."

"Where could they borrow the money?" asked Baxter. He didn't really care and was only being polite in order to humor Lazard. Bascomb had on a very wide tie with brightly colored shapes and squiggles, and Baxter kept trying to decide which he disliked most, the wideness or the squiggles.

"Loan sharks. They could borrow a lot of money, say between $30,000 and $40,000, then pay it back right away. They could probably get a long-term rate, paying 1½ to 2 percent vig per week, maybe $1,500 to $5,000 a month.

"The police figure the tip came from the loan shark himself.

167

Not only would he be sure of getting the vig, but the smuggling channels are pretty tight down there and they don't like new competition. A lot of the tips police get come from guys already into smuggling."

"How could Morgan pay interest if he was dead?" asked Baxter.

"It was the other one," said Lazard. His bad leg had begun to ache and he was massaging the calf. Almost unconsciously, he began feeling sorry for Trieger, as if someone were sick in his family or as if he had been seriously injured in a car crash.

Bascomb moved away from the television. "That's right. All the police had to do was wait. They knew pretty soon it'd become clear that somebody owed a lot of money. The police might not be able to touch him, but they still wanted to know what was going on."

"And it was Trieger?" asked Lazard.

"Yes."

"What d'you mean?" said Baxter.

Lazard sat up. "James Trieger, the brother, he's got a motel in North Miami."

"The police knew him anyway," said Bascomb. "He'd been involved in minor fencing. The sort of guy who could get you a television cheap, maybe a new rug. He also did some gambling. He'd set up a game in one of his rooms, then supply drinks and entertainment."

"How'd the police decide it was him?" asked Baxter.

"He started having a lot of poker games." Bascomb removed a toothpick from his mouth, broke it in four pieces, and took a fresh one. "Trouble is you can do that sort of thing too often. Trieger has this game in September, then he has another a few weeks later, then another. And he still has to pay off between $1,500 and $5,000 a month. These poker games, he's barely paying the vig.

"It becomes known he owes a lot of money and that he can do nothing but pay the interest. And it becomes generally known he'd been partners with Larry Morgan. This Trieger, he's got mortgages on everything. In January he starts missing some payments. When the police next see him, it looks like he's been roughed up a little."

Bascomb moved back to the window. The sky was darker and when he looked into the room, Baxter could hardly see his face, just a pale area like a small patch of cloud. "Trieger's the kind of person, all his life he's been looking for the big chance and this makes him stick his neck out. Used to be he did a lot of gambling. Mostly he lost and some debts piled up. This guy I sent down there, his name's Jerry York and he used to be a Boston cop. Anyway, in Miami York was digging out a lot of stuff primarily because Trieger talks too much. He found out that by 1971, Trieger owed $15,000. Then one day some guys showed up and broke both his arms. The bill was paid a week later. Want to know how?"

"His brother paid it," said Lazard, getting up. "We found it in his books." He walked into the small bathroom, filled a coffee cup with water, came back, and leaned against a file cabinet.

"That's right, his brother paid it." Bascomb looked at Lazard for a moment. "Anyway, in February Trieger's scrambling. He's borrowing money from whoever'll lend it. He's hiding out half the time. It turns out some guys've been hanging around his house. He's got two kids: a young son and a daughter about seventeen who Jerry York says is really something. Then for no apparent reason Trieger just stops. No one comes after him for money. He's not running. What happened? Has the vig been paid? York couldn't find anything."

Lazard glanced at Baxter, who was folding a sheet of paper into narrow strips. "It was his brother again," said Lazard. He walked to the window. To his left he could see the modern medical complex around Boston City Hospital. Beyond that was the area where the warehouse had stood.

"Trieger flew down to Miami on February twenty-third," said Lazard. "He stayed two days and came back on the twenty-fifth."

"You sure of that?"

"He told me."

"That doesn't prove he burned his own place," said Baxter.

"No." Lazard continued to look toward the warehouse.

"Why'd he say he went down to Florida?" asked Bascomb.

"Business with his brother, getting him some furniture cheap."

"Damn Jerry York." Bascomb sat down on the edge of the desk and began chewing another toothpick. "All right, so Howard Trieger goes down to bail out his brother. The loan shark probably suggested the fire. He'd get back his money plus ten percent of the insurance. Even so, Trieger makes about $50,000. Then they have him all set for blackmail. Sucker. They send someone up from

Miami and that's that, except two firemen get killed because some kids put stones in a hydrant."

"What about the Boston part of it?" asked Lazard.

"How d'you mean?"

"The extortion letter was mailed from Boston and the car stolen in Lynn. Trieger might have mailed the letter, but I doubt it. Also I don't think the torch stole the car. From what Pugliese has found out, someone stole it for him." Lazard went on to describe what Pugliese had learned from the Lynn police.

"That's not my problem," said Bascomb. "Most likely, once the fire was agreed on, the whole thing was taken out of Trieger's hands. After all, he's no professional. What are you going to do now?"

"I'll wait for the polygraph test on Tuesday."

"Think he'll take it?"

"I don't know."

"It'd be helpful," said Bascomb, "if you talked to the State Fire Marshal's Office. If you got Heinlein to call a marshal's inquest and put some of these questions to Trieger under oath, he'd have to perjure himself. I mean, there's no way he could tell the truth without incriminating himself and his brother. That would support the insurance company if they decide not to pay the claim."

"You're going to recommend nonpayment?" asked Lazard.

"I'm going to talk to them this afternoon, but I think so, yes. Trieger's trip to Florida pretty much settles it."

Baxter stood up and looked at Lazard and Bascomb critically. "You figure, considering the criminal types these brothers are mixed up with, if no money comes out of it, well, it could get kinda hairy."

Around noon, Lazard and Baxter were called to a fire in an empty house in Allston. Apparently it had been set by a derelict who was trying to heat up a can of soup with a small fire in one of the upstairs rooms. Lazard turned the man over to the police. When he and Baxter got back to the office at 2:30, they found Pugliese with his feet up on a desk cutting his nails. Seeing Lazard, he quickly put down his feet and looked embarrassed.

Lazard barely glanced at him. "What're you doing here?"

"Waiting for a phone call. The Lynn police were going to telephone about that kid."

"Why here?" Lazard had no wish to see Pugliese. The previous night he had called Virginia Lufkin in what he kept telling himself was a moment of weakness. In any case, Pugliese had answered the phone. Lazard had listened to him say, "Hello, hello," several times, then hung up.

"I was looking for you." Pugliese had on a gunmetal-gray leisure suit with a silver medallion around his neck.

"Why?"

"Cassidy wanted you to call him."

"I thought he was in the hospital." Lazard realized he was speaking abruptly but couldn't help it. Walking to the farther desk he sat down and then noticed Baxter staring at him with a kind of concern. Baxter looked away and made a show of taking off his green and white checked sport coat and carefully hanging it on the rack behind the door.

"That's right," said Pugliese, "he wanted you to call him there. I saw him a little while ago."

"So he sent you here and now you're waiting for a phone call?"

"Sort of. Look, I didn't get a chance but, well, I wanted to thank you for yesterday."

Lazard rolled a yellow arson report into his typewriter. "What do you mean?"

Pugliese's face began turning red. "For saving my life."

Lazard started to say something, then glanced at Baxter, who was watching him again. "That's okay, Pugliese. We'd have gotten into a lot of trouble with the state if you'd been shot." Taking his note pad from his side pocket, he turned back a couple of pages. He had no wish to talk about saving Pugliese's life. "Why're these Lynn cops calling about this guy anyway?"

Relieved, Pugliese launched into a story about how Georgie Connors, who might have stolen the car that was found at Logan, worked as an errand boy for a North Shore realtor by the name of DiTullio. Now Connors couldn't be found and DiTullio said he hadn't seen him. In fact no one had seen him. The general consensus was that someone had given Connors some money to leave town.

Instead of listening, Lazard tried to rid himself of his feelings of irritation. His clothes smelled of smoke from the fire in the empty house and he wanted to change them but felt he couldn't because of the scratches which Virginia Lufkin had left on his back. These were small but noticeable, and Lazard believed that Pugliese would immediately recognize them as having been caused by his fiancée. He knew this was foolish, that even if Pugliese saw the scratches there was nothing to say what had made them. But even so, Lazard didn't want Pugliese to notice his back, so he sat at his typewriter, enduring the smell of his smoky clothes, and pretended to listen.

Pugliese kept talking about the Lynn police until Lazard could stand no more. "Look, I better call Cassidy before it gets too late. Write up that stuff on the stolen car and let me see a copy. And one other thing, why don't you dig up a picture of DiTullio and see if he has a record of any fires." Lazard didn't expect this to lead to anything but at least it would keep Pugliese out of the office.

It took ten minutes for Lazard to get Cassidy on the phone. Cassidy's voice was more subdued than Lazard had ever known it. What he wanted was for Lazard to see Violet Sheridan and tell her he wouldn't be able to keep their date that evening.

"Why can't you call her?"

"She'd be upset."

"She'll be more upset if she thinks you can't talk on the phone."

"Then don't tell her what happened."

"She's got to be told something."

"I don't give a shit what you tell her, just handle it, that's all. I'm asking you a favor, will you do it?"

Violet Sheridan lived in a studio apartment on Dartmouth near Marlborough with a large marmalade cat named Brinsley. When Lazard and Baxter arrived, she was preparing to take a shower in expectation of Cassidy's visit. She had never heard of Lazard and Baxter—Cassidy never spoke of his colleagues—and Lazard had to explain what had happened through a crack in the door. Once she understood that Cassidy had been shot, she let them in right away.

Violet was a tall woman, nearly six feet, and wore an orange terry-cloth robe several sizes too large. She had red hair, freckles, and a pink complexion that became blotched when she cried. Her feet were bare and Baxter thought they were too big. Lazard didn't notice her feet. He thought she had a kind face and regretted bringing the news about Cassidy. She seemed about forty.

"Is he in much pain?"

"I don't think so," said Lazard. "They'd give him pills."

"Why didn't he call me?"

"He didn't want you to worry. Anyway, they'll be sending him home in a couple of days."

Lazard and Baxter sat side by side on a studio couch as the cat Brinsley rubbed back and forth against Lazard's aluminum cane. Violet stood in front of them and Lazard wished she would sit down but didn't want to make her uncomfortable by asking. On the walls were several pictures of Cassidy, all in uniform: one as a young MP in Germany, one as a firefighter. None of the pictures showed Cassidy smiling. What did he know about Cassidy? Most likely Cassidy and the woman before him had made love on the very spot where he was sitting.

"He and Baxter here went into the room together," said Lazard. "Cassidy went first. The man was waiting for them."

"Guy shot five times," said Baxter. "It's a wonder I wasn't hit too."

"Cassidy was protecting him," said Lazard. "He was hit twice but it's not so bad."

"Was he really protecting you?" asked Violet Sheridan.

Baxter reached down to stroke the cat. "I guess so," he said.

"You going to visit him?" asked Lazard.

"I don't think so, I might telephone."

"They wouldn't care," said Baxter. "I mean, you can go right into the hospital like anyone."

Violet Sheridan had begun to cry slightly, tears running down her cheeks. "No, it would embarrass him. I'll just wait until he gets better. Will you be seeing him today?"

"I'm not sure," said Lazard. "Soon anyway."

"Just tell him everything's all right," said Violet.

When they got back to the office, they found Pugliese still waiting. Baxter turned on the TV to Channel 5 to watch the Derby. Lazard didn't want to be around Pugliese so he went next door for a sandwich. When he returned at six, Pugliese was gone. Honest Pleasure had lost the Derby to Bold Forbes and Baxter had lost $10 to Pugliese.

"If you'd been here," said Baxter accusingly, "you coulda told me who was going to win."

That evening they were called to three fires in Dorchester and Roxbury, all in old Irish neighborhoods now populated by poor blacks. Many of the Irish firemen had known these neighborhoods as children and as they rolled up and repacked their lines they kept blaming the blacks for the destruction of their ancestral homes. Lazard had heard this sort of complaint many times, but as an outsider he had found it narrow-minded and almost comical. Tonight, however, he felt bored by the stupidity of it.

Two of the fires were in abandoned buildings; the third was in an apartment house. It had apparently started in a couch in a first-floor apartment, then spread to the hall. The district chief blamed it on careless disposal of smoking materials. Lazard knew he was wrong. It was rare for a cigarette to generate enough heat to char the wood frame and collapse the springs, which required a temperature of at least 1,150 degrees before they collapsed under their own weight, but he didn't have the energy to argue.

By midnight they were back in the office and by 2:30 Lazard was finishing his reports. Baxter, at the other desk, was reading through his own reports while glancing occasionally at Lazard to see if he was doing anything odd. They hadn't talked much since getting back.

When he had finished reading, Baxter got up and patted his stomach. "I'm off to bed."

Lazard didn't look up. "Okay, good night."

"You feel all right?"

"Sure."

"Nothin' been bothering you, I mean anything you want to talk about?" Baxter stood with his hands in his pockets. He looked embarrassed and half expected Lazard to shout at him.

Lazard glanced up from his typewriter. "Like what?"

"Well, we could talk about Trieger."

After staring at Baxter for a few seconds, Lazard started typing again. "There's nothing to talk about," he said.

Half an hour later Lazard had set up his own cot in the arson office. The radio was just loud enough to hear constant reports of vehicle and vandalism fires. The squad never went to vehicle fires unless someone was caught at the scene. From across the hall, Lazard could hear Baxter snoring. Lazard lay on his back and stared up at the two banks of darkened neon lights that showed dim gray in the light from the street. He smoked a cigarette and watched the smoke rise toward the ceiling.

He was thinking of a time about twelve years before when he and Trieger and their wives had gone out to Cape Cod for a weekend, spending the night in a motel in Provincetown. He remembered walking out on the beach late at night with Trieger. The air had been warm and lights were flickering out on the ocean. They had talked, but Lazard couldn't remember what they talked about. He recalled, however, the warm sand between his toes, the smell of fish and salt water, and the sound of waves against the shore like a slow pulse. After a while, the moon had come up: at first just a sliver of light, then more until the full moon balanced on the water, red and shimmering.

The next day was Sunday. The wind was gusty and it rained. Lazard didn't go out. He was supposed to go to Quaid's that evening to see the Bruins-Flyers game, but he didn't feel like it.

Shortly after four he received a telephone call from Elizabeth, his ex-wife. Her voice was cool, nearly toneless, and he almost didn't recognize it.

"Where are you?"

"Just down the street. Can I come over and talk a little?"

"Sure." Unable to help himself, Lazard felt an increasing excitement.

In the few minutes before she arrived, he carried the dirty dishes to the kitchen, picked up the newspapers around his chair, and pulled the blue blanket up over the bed so it looked more or less made.

"You look good. How've you been?" Lazard held the door and watched her enter. She wore a yellow sweater and a brown and yellow striped skirt. Over her arm she carried a wet trench coat.

"Pretty good. Is there someplace I can put this?"

Lazard hung her coat up in the bathroom, then proceeded to make coffee. Elizabeth wandered restlessly around the living room, glancing from the window, picking up a book, then putting it down. At last she sat down on one of the folding chairs and waited. Lazard brought her a cup of coffee. He found himself thinking if they ever got back together again, they would need more furniture. Sitting down in the armchair, he saw he was about a foot beneath her. He wanted to change his seat, but didn't want to appear nervous.

"I was surprised to hear your voice," said Lazard.

She didn't answer, but looked past him out the window to the tops of trees blowing back and forth in the wind. She sipped her coffee, then put it down on the floor. He remembered she took her coffee with sugar and that he had forgotten to give her any.

"You want sugar?"

"No, thanks. There's something I want to say. I didn't really want to come over, but I thought it would be cowardly if I just called or wrote a letter."

Lazard waited.

"I'm going to get married. He's a lawyer where I work. We've been friends for about two years." As she said this, she looked away. She had a narrow face with large brown eyes, a sharp angular chin. Although thirty-eight, she looked younger, Lazard thought.

"Why tell me?"

"I thought you should know."

"Do you love him?"

"Yes. What I also wanted to say was that until our divorce was settled, I didn't sleep with him. I know I could have and I know it probably wouldn't have mattered to you, but I never did."

"Why tell me?"

"I didn't want you to think I was concealing anything." She sat straight in the chair with her legs crossed and her hands folded in her lap.

"What's he like?"

"He's very kind."

"I hope you'll be happy."

She tried to smile. "How have you been?"

"Fine. You know, pretty busy."

"Have you been seeing anyone?"

"No, not really. You know that cousin of mine? Norma Trieger? We used to see her and her husband. I've seen them."

Elizabeth unclasped her hands. Her eyes moved across Lazard as if just noticing him. "How are they?"

"Pretty good." Then he wondered why he had said that, and he stopped and shook his head.

19

About 2:30 Monday morning a fire broke out on the third floor of an apartment house on Westland Avenue, a block from Fire Alarm Headquarters. Before being brought under control three hours later, it had gone into a fifth alarm and thirty fire companies had been called. The flames spread up through the fourth floor and the roof partly collapsed. A building on the next street, Symphony Road, seemed endangered and 150 persons were evacuated. Damage was estimated at over $100,000. The cause of the fire was undetermined.

Michael Neary and Robert Flaherty covered the fire for the Arson Squad. By 8 o'clock they were back in the office beginning their reports. Both were exhausted.

Jerry Phelps and Roy Hufnagel, who had that day's shift, had come in around seven and were drinking coffee and chatting with Fatback and Quaid. Phelps and Hufnagel were unusually cheerful, thinking themselves fortunate not to be stuck with a five-alarm fire.

"What about it, Flaherty," said Phelps, "why can't you get a cause on that fire? Jesus, you guys have a lousy average."

Flaherty was a tall man with an Irish face. He wore a tan

porkpie hat as if wearing it in the office would help him leave sooner. Generally, he saw life as a matter of good luck and bad luck. Recently, there'd been a lot of bad luck.

"No tellin', some junkie most likely." Flaherty spoke without looking up from the typewriter. Actually, he guessed the building had been torched so it could be remodeled and turned into expensive condominiums. It irritated him that he could never prove this, that he would have to spend several days on the fire and then leave it labeled as being of undetermined origin. He knew if the fire had occurred while Phelps and Hufnagel were working, they would call it accidental and might even get paid for their lie.

"Anyone killed in the fire?"

"A cat."

Phelps winked at Fatback, who had his mouth full of sugar doughnut. "Maybe the cat started the fire."

Flaherty didn't answer. Joking was also a form of bad luck. Hufnagel got himself some coffee. "Remember that fire in the North End," he said, "where the guy tied his cocker spaniel to the heater? Damn dog didn't stay put, chased the guy halfway down the street."

The office was sunlit and crowded. Pugliese arrived, took off his yellow sport coat, and hung it behind the door. Ever since he had begun investigating the stolen car, he had grown more businesslike. Fires he didn't know much about, but car theft was car theft. Today he would begin finding out about DiTullio for Lazard. He hoped it would make Lazard like him better. He saw their friendship increasing until at last he would take Baxter's place and he and Lazard would work together as a close-knit arson fighting team.

"What about the guy with the mice," said Phelps. "You'd like that, Pugliese. You're from East Boston, same as the guy with the mice."

"Is that the guy that made the mouse holes?" asked Fatback.

"That's right, he bored a hole in the wall and shoved the mice through. First, though, he wrapped their tails in cotton, dunked 'em in gasoline, and stuck a match to 'em. Mice scurried up five-six floors. You know those old buildings, rats' nests in the walls. Had himself one helluva fire."

"Rabbits," said Hufnagel, "that's what they use in the country. You wanna burn some fields, you soak some rabbits in gasoline, light 'em, and let 'em go. Some rabbits been known to run three miles."

That morning Lazard went out and bought an unfinished, three-shelf bookcase; then he bought paint and a disposable brush. The paint was supposed to be forest green, but when he opened it, he saw it was much lighter. He didn't like the color, but told himself he could grow used to it. After all, much of the space would be covered by books.

He meant to put the bookcase next to his armchair and tried to think of moving his books from rug to bookcase as a step forward. Putting papers down on the living room floor, he painted quickly but not neatly. David Bascomb had called saying he wanted to stop by at noon, and Lazard hoped to be finished by then. The windows were open and pigeons sat on the ledge where he had earlier put out crumbs. Apart from their cooing and the slap of the wet brush, the apartment was quiet.

When the doorbell buzzed at 12:10, Lazard had a single shelf to go. He wiped his hands on a blue rag, the tail from one of the dark blue shirts he had worn before making lieutenant, and pressed the button opening the door downstairs.

Bascomb was carefully dressed in a rust-colored linen sport coat. He nodded to Lazard, then pushed his glasses up his nose with one finger. "Getting pretty domestic, aren't you? Why don't you buy one that's already painted?"

"It's cheaper this way. Want coffee?"

"No, thanks." Bascomb sat down on a metal folding chair and leaned back so the chair balanced on two legs. The room smelled of paint. In another apartment, someone began practicing the piano.

"What's on your mind?" asked Lazard. He continued painting the last shelf.

"The insurance company has decided not to pay." Bascomb paused to take out a box of toothpicks. "But what they want first is a fire marshal's inquest so Trieger can be asked about his brother's debts."

"So why don't you ask for an inquest?"

"I'm not as chummy over there as you are. We've been making the state cops subpoena our files if they want anything."

"What makes you think they'd do it for me?"

"Don't give me that." Bascomb grinned.

"I'm still waiting for the polygraph test."

"When is it?"

"Tomorrow morning."

"You just going to show up and figure he'll be there?"

"I was going to call and confirm it."

"When?"

Lazard put the last strokes of green paint on the shelf. He disliked being pressured. "This afternoon. You going to put those toothpicks in an ashtray or will I have to crawl around after them?"

"You'll have to crawl around." Getting to his feet, Bascomb walked over to the books on the floor. He picked up a book on war strategy by Liddell Hart, leafed through it, then dropped it back on the pile. At last he took an ashtray from the card table and returned to his chair.

"If Trieger can be questioned about his brother under oath, he'll have to perjure himself. Either that or refuse to answer. Then we can use the transcript of the inquest in civil court. The way I see it, the moment he decided to have the fire, he gave up control. There's no way he can get it back. Even if he's never taken to court and the insurance company pays, he's still stuck with the same twerpy brother and some shylock who's now got a whole set of screws."

Lazard didn't say anything. He got up and looked at the bookcase, then limped around it and looked at it again. After a moment Lazard found himself thinking that he felt sorry for Trieger, that he didn't want to hurt him. He began to wish he had let Flanagan end the investigation. Now it was too late. If Bascomb thought he was dragging his feet, he would guess Lazard had taken a bribe.

"What do you think about Trieger?" asked Bascomb.

"Most people like him," said Lazard almost guiltily.

"What about you?"

"I try not to feel anything for him."

"Call him now."

Lazard stood facing Bascomb. Flecks of light green paint dotted Lazard's white shirt. He went to the telephone.

He was startled by how quickly he got through. When Trieger answered, Lazard was barely ready to speak.

"Frank, good to hear from you. How you been?"

"Not bad. Yourself?" He tried to imagine Trieger at his desk.

"Suffering from a dose of Red Sox fever. How those guys can win the pennant last year and now be in last place is the sort of thing that keeps me awake at night."

"You been to any games?" As Lazard said this, he noticed Bascomb turn toward him and raise his eyebrows.

"Couple. Taking my girls to see Kansas City tomorrow night. You feel like going sometime?"

"Maybe so." Lazard felt Bascomb watching him. "Howard, the reason I called, I wanted to confirm that time for tomorrow morning."

Trieger didn't answer at first. "Look, Frank, I was going to call you about that."

Lazard waited.

"I talked to my lawyer. He said he thought it was a bad idea, that these things aren't one hundred percent certain. If it was just me, I'd say sure. I mean, I don't care one way or the other. But the lawyer, well, I guess if I'm going to have one, I'd better go along with him."

Lieutenant-detective Hoffness was a tall, thick-chested man with shoulders that sloped so much that he almost seemed without them. He had bushy gray hair and a flat nose. His lower lip was fat and puffy, probably from years of tugging at it. He was tugging at it now.

"You really want to nail this guy, don't you?"

"It's not a matter of wanting to nail him."

They were in Hoffness's office, actually the captain's office, attached to the several rooms belonging to the State Fire Marshal. Hoffness sat at his desk fiddling with a transparent paperweight that contained a dandelion clock. He was wondering for the hundredth time how they got the damn thing in there. Lazard sat across the desk and looked at his fingers.

"Hey, we call an inquest, that's a lotta beans. Fuckin' staff lawyer wants $100 an hour. Then all those witnesses. Jesus, you gotta be sure."

"I'm sure." All of Lazard's muscles felt tight.

"Bascomb send you here?"

"I would have come anyway."

"Operations like Jerry Bryant's, it's a fuckin' one-way street. They expect us to help 'em anytime they want. So maybe we want a little something in return, like it's clam city. You know what they're workin' on now? They think some people have been taking bribes, I mean, both people here and over in the Fire Department. You're fuckin' lucky Charlie O'Neill quit and went to Arizona."

"Who told you about this?"

Hoffness shrugged and looked away. "No tellin' how much they know. We'll just have to wait for the grand jury. Christ, they'll probably yank back O'Neill and start him singing. So now they want an inquest?"

"You'll have complete access to their files on this. Their investigator, York, has agreed to testify. He's got statements from the Miami police about the plane crash and marijuana, plus tapes about Trieger. It's not just hearsay."

"Who else gets called?" Hoffness picked up a yellow pencil.

"The man who discovered the fire, Raymond Farkus."

"Why?"

"He can testify as to the explosion and where the fire started."

"Who else?" Hoffness was smiling slightly, and Lazard couldn't tell if it was mocking or what. He guessed, however, that Hoffness thought he was pushing for the inquest because he was afraid of Bascomb and Jerry Bryant.

"District Chief Foster and a firefighter, Eric McCarthy."

"Who's he?"

"He was jockeying line behind Roberts and Harris."

"Anyone else?"

"Quaid. He can talk about the rocks and stuff, also the car."

"Anyone else?"

"Just Trieger."

Hoffness leaned back in his chair. Covering his desk were plans for self-service gas stations which needed his approval. "I'll talk to Heinlein this afternoon. When do you want it?"

"This week. Friday."

"You're outta your fuckin' mind. Two weeks is the best I can do."

Lazard pushed himself to his feet with his cane. "I'm getting flak about this. Let's just get it over with. You can manage it."

"You guys over there must really have a grudge. That insurance company's gonna bust Trieger's ass in so many ways there won't be any point in his sitting down anymore."

Lazard started to say there was nothing personal, that once the investigation begins, it proceeds almost mechanically as long as new information is fed into it. But Hoffness was also an investigator. Supposedly he knew these things.

"If you can have the summons ready tomorrow morning," said Lazard, "I'll go with you when you deliver it."

Monday evening Lazard visited Cassidy in his semi-private room in Mass. General. Cassidy was bored, rude, and itched under his bandages. His roommate was an ex-shoe salesman being fitted with a plastic knee. Cassidy had him so cowed that he apologized for the disturbance each time he spoke to his doctor or nurse.

"Whaddaya doing here, Lazard? Nothin' good on TV?"

"Thought I'd see how you were. Want some mints?" He had brought a box of green mint wafers. Cassidy stared at them with disgust.

"What're those, suppositories?"

"I saw Violet Sheridan."

"So she said." Cassidy wore his own pajamas, which had been brought by his brother the parish priest. They were dark blue cotton and decorated with yellow ships' anchors.

"Has she been to visit you?"

"Course not. Why the hell you tell her I saved Ruby's life?"

Lazard stared down at Cassidy from the foot of the bed. It had begun to rain outside and Lazard wore a tan raincoat. He didn't want to sit down, even though his leg hurt him and he was tired of leaning on his cane. Over the years, he had visited many firemen in hospitals. In the next bed, the ex-shoe salesman looked at Lazard apprehensively, thinking he was angry or about to lose his temper, but Lazard was now thinking about his own time in the hospital, enduring skin graft after skin graft as the doctors worked on his leg.

"Why'd I tell her? No reason. How long are you here for?"

"I told 'em I was going home tomorrow. There's nobody in this hospital but assholes. You still working on that Trieger case?"

"Getting a marshal's inquest set up for next week."

"You're really dragging that one out, for crissake."

Lazard shifted his weight on his cane. He couldn't think of anything to say. The room smelled of disinfectant and made him feel closed in. "Tell me," he said at last, "when you were trapped in that burning elevator, what'd you think?"

Cassidy looked up, surprised. "You kiddin' me? I thought, I gotta get outta here, that's what I thought."

"Were you afraid?"

"Wasn't fuckin' time."

Lazard had a sudden desire to talk to Cassidy about the office but he wasn't sure how to begin. "Hoffness told me this afternoon that Jerry Bryant was investigating bribery in the department."

"What d'you mean?"

"You know, taking money for saying a fire was accidental."

"Only assholes take bribes."

"O'Neill took them. Others do too."

"O'Neill was an asshole. What'd he do, move to Tucson? Tucson's an asshole town."

"You ever been approached?"

Cassidy glanced at the ex-shoe salesman who had put on a headset and was watching a cowboy movie on the television. "Some guy came to my place a coupla years ago."

"What happened?"

"Threw his fuckin' ass down the stairs."

Lazard stood a bit longer. "Want me to see Violet again?"

"No reason. We're talking on the phone, but, you know, thanks for going over there."

"That's okay, we both wanted to, both Ruby and I."

Hoffness saw Trieger at his showroom at 11:30 Tuesday morning. Lazard went too, but apart from making the original introductions he said little.

Trieger tried to appear at ease. Hoffness didn't give him the summons right away, just told him to appear in a conference room at 1010 Commonwealth Avenue at 10 A.M. a week from Friday.

"I don't understand what this is," said Trieger. He was sitting at his desk. Hoffness stood in front of him with his hands behind his back. He wore a brick-red sport coat and gray trousers.

"Chapter 148, Section 3, of the General Laws says the marshal may investigate the circumstances of any fire occurring anywhere in the Commonwealth, and for such purposes may summon and examine under oath any person supposed to know or have means of knowing any material facts touching the subject of the investigation."

Trieger glanced at Lazard, who was looking at the floor. In front of the desk was a small red, yellow, and blue oriental rug. Its central design was a maze of red pomegranates and yellow leaves.

"What sort of material facts am I supposed to know?"

"That will come out at the inquest."

"Who else is being called?"

"The man who discovered the fire, four firemen, and a private detective."

"Who's the private detective?"

"His name's York. I don't know him personally. He works for your insurance company."

Lazard looked up briefly. Trieger had a red pencil which he was rolling back and forth under his palm, seemingly concentrating on that and not listening to Hoffness. He looked handsome and respectable.

"What if I can't make it?" asked Trieger.

"If the reason's good enough, the inquest could be rescheduled."

"What if it weren't good enough?"

Hoffness took the summons from his pocket and tossed it on the desk. "If you don't respond to this summons, I'll obtain a subpoena from the Suffolk County Superior Court. If you fail to respond to the subpoena, you'll be in contempt of court. Not only that, but your insurance company will drop you so fuckin' fast you'll feel like a prom queen with a dose of clap."

Lazard kept looking at the floor. The maze of pomegranates and leaves was enclosed by red and blue stripes. He knew Trieger was staring at him, but he didn't want to be friendly with this man and felt powerless to help him.

20

In his dream, the sound became a fire alarm, and the smell and rush of the firehouse came back to him. Waking, Lazard realized it was the telephone. He was in his own bed and the only smell was the smell of paint.

"Frank? This is Norma. Howard went out at 10:30 and he's not back. I'm worried."

Lazard stood in his underwear in the dark living room holding the phone. A cold breeze blew through the window. "What time is it?"

"Just past two. I'm sorry I woke you. He took a gun with him. I didn't know who else . . ."

Briefly, he imagined Trieger pursuing him with a gun. "That's all right, maybe I better come over."

As he dressed, Lazard tried to think what Trieger might be doing, but his mind felt sluggish and unresponsive. Mostly he was surprised to have thought that Trieger might shoot him. He told himself he had done nothing Trieger could blame him for. It took him fifteen minutes to reach Trieger's house in Brookline. Norma was waiting on the steps.

"He and the girls went to the ball game. They said he was quiet. Usually he gets excited and they have a good time. When they got back, he went out again right away. He keeps the gun in his bureau in the bedroom. When I went upstairs, I noticed the drawer was open and the gun was gone."

They had gone inside and were sitting at the kitchen table drinking coffee. Norma's brown shoulder-length hair was uncombed and she kept pushing it from her face. She had on a red and blue plaid bathrobe.

"Maybe he went to talk to some friend. The gun could have been gone before or he could have taken it for some other reason."

"But who would he go see?"

"Who're his friends?"

"He's got a lot of acquaintances but no one really close. I suppose you're one of the closest."

"Me? We're not friends."

The surface of the kitchen table was yellow Formica and the coffee cups were bright blue pottery. Lazard poured milk into his coffee from a cardboard carton. He wished he had a cigarette. In the middle of the table was a tall blue vase containing half a dozen yellow narcissus.

"Has he been depressed?" he asked.

"Tense, somehow. I thought he might be worrying about his business. He never talks about it much."

"Has he mentioned his brother?"

"James? Why should he?" She was silent a moment. When she spoke again, her voice was higher. "I think something's going on, but I don't know what it is. Why should he take a gun? He's never even shot it."

Lazard didn't answer and regretted coming. It was a large kitchen. The wallpaper had pictures of horses and buggies, men with top hats. Lazard couldn't get over Trieger thinking of him as a friend.

"Frank, what's bothering him?"

"He's probably still worried about the fire."

"I thought that was all settled."

"No."

"Tell me what's going on." She pushed her hand through her hair, smoothing the wrinkles on her forehead.

"The insurance company's still investigating the claim." He tried to make what he said sound unimportant, that Trieger was foolish to worry.

"What are they investigating?"

"Hasn't he said anything?"

"No, never."

Lazard pushed away his cup. "They think Howard might have needed the money to help out his brother."

"James." As she said the name, her face became passive. Getting up, she went to the stove and poured herself some more coffee. When she returned, Lazard couldn't tell what she was thinking. He wanted to ask, but didn't want her to know the extent of his involvement. The house was silent except for a clock ticking in the living room.

After several minutes, Norma walked to the window and looked out at the dark back yard. "Do you ever think of Michigan?"

Lazard glanced at her. "Sometimes."

"Do you remember when you used to have a crush on me?"

"What about it?" He was startled by the question.

She turned from the window and looked at him. "I remember one summer a whole bunch of us went out to the quarry in Grand Ledge. I guess I was seventeen. There was a cliff over the water. It must have been, oh, at least forty or fifty feet. It was on the far side from where we used to swim. You all kept daring each other to jump off the cliff into the water. No one wanted to. Someone had been hurt there once. At last you said you'd do it. The rest were too frightened, I don't blame them. I remember seeing you across the quarry on top of the cliff. Then you ran. For some reason, I thought you'd shout. You just fell with your hands above your head. I was never so frightened. You pretended it was nothing. Do you remember?"

All Lazard could remember was a terrifying fall through the air. He couldn't remember jumping or hitting the water or why he had done it, only the long feeling of weightlessness. "Yes, I remember," he said.

By four Trieger still hadn't returned. Lazard kept thinking he had to be at work at seven. Then he began to wonder what he would feel if it turned out that Trieger had shot himself or thrown himself in the river. He had just decided to call the hospitals and police when they heard a car in the driveway. Norma ran to the front door. Lazard stayed in the kitchen. He heard Norma making concerned noises in the hall but couldn't make out the words.

Then Trieger came into the kitchen. There was blood on his

lower lip and his left eye was swollen and bruised. He glanced at Lazard but didn't speak. Walking to the refrigerator, he opened the freezer and took out an ice cube tray. Norma followed him.

"Where have you been?" Her voice was soft.

Trieger didn't answer. He knocked the ice cubes into a red bowl, wrapped several in a paper towel, and pressed them to his cheek and eye. He wore a tan golfing jacket and brown slacks. The shoulder of the jacket was ripped and there was blood on the front.

"Howard, where did you go?" asked Norma. "What happened?"

"I don't want to talk about it." He stood with his back to Lazard, looking out the window.

"Howard."

"Please."

Norma turned away. Lazard sat at the table, looking at his hands in his lap. He thought they looked like the hands of an old man.

After a moment, Trieger turned around so that he faced Lazard across the table. The strong kitchen light heightened the reds and purples of his bruises. Lazard returned his stare, trying to defined what he saw in Trieger's expression: a mixture of anger and fear, but the eyes looked sad, almost seemed to grieve.

Trieger turned toward his wife. "Why'd you call Frank?"

"I was worried. When I saw the gun was gone, I thought . . . He's been very kind."

"He's trying to destroy our life." As Trieger said this, he swung out, hitting the vase of narcissus. It spun across the table, arced, and smashed against the wall, scattering water, yellow flowers, and bits of blue pottery.

Lazard got to his feet and took his raincoat from the chair. "I better go," he said.

"Why don't you say it," shouted Trieger, "you won't be happy till you see me dead."

Lazard fumbled with his raincoat, trying to hold himself up with his cane. He told himself that it wasn't true, that he had no wish to see Trieger hurt.

Trieger watched his wife picking up the flowers and fragments of vase. Then he stepped around the table and put his hand on Lazard's shoulder. "I'm sorry, Frank, I shouldn't have said those things."

At noon Wednesday, Lazard was at his desk typing follow-up reports on several fires from the past weeks. He was disgruntled because he had spent so much time on the warehouse fire that many of his other cases had gone stale. For much of the morning, he had been calling one person after another, but either the people he wanted couldn't be found or they didn't have the information he required.

Quaid, on the other hand, was fairly cheerful. His investigation of the shoe store fire which Lazard had dumped on him had turned up a witness who had seen the owner leaving his store about six in the morning, two hours before the fire broke out. He had talked to an assistant district attorney and was now preparing to file a complaint. As he made telephone calls and fussed over his papers, he kept whistling the first phrase of "I Get a Kick Out of You." Lazard stared at him but didn't say anything. He blamed his irritability on a lack of sleep.

Fatback, Baxter, and Flanagan stood in a small circle between the desks and file cabinets. Fatback held a box of candy sent from Tucson by their ex-captain, Charlie O'Neill. Taking a piece, he passed the box to Baxter, who took a piece and passed it to Flanagan. It was a round red box with red foil and ribbon and looked like a small fire around which they were warming themselves. As they ate the candy, they discussed the Bruins' defeat by the Flyers the night before. The Flyers now led the series 3–1.

Lazard got up to return some files. He was used to the crowded office and limped around the men as if they weren't there. The windows were open and a warm breeze and the smell of traffic drifted in from Southampton. Lazard kept feeling or imagining he felt the pressure on his shoulder where Trieger had squeezed it.

As he sat back down at his desk, he wondered for the hundredth time who had beaten up Trieger and why. He assumed it was connected with the fire but didn't see what Trieger had done to provoke it unless he had waved his gun at someone. Despite Trieger's breaking of the vase, Lazard couldn't imagine him being violent.

Possibly he could be made to talk at the inquest, although Lazard doubted it. No matter who Trieger implicated it would amount to little more than circumstantial evidence. What would happen was that the insurance company would refuse to pay and Trieger and his brother would be finished.

Lazard thought again how he had been worried the previous night that Trieger might kill himself. The irony was that if Trieger committed suicide, the insurance company would probably pay up just to avoid being accused of hounding Trieger to death.

Lazard wondered how long it would be before Trieger realized any of this, before he fully understood he was lost. Trieger had had an easy life with lots of success. He was like a child. Nothing sufficiently awful, like being trapped in a burning building, had ever happened to him, and it was hard for Trieger to imagine that it ever would.

Lazard rolled another sheet into his typewriter and began typing up some notes on a restaurant fire which had occurred several weeks before.

"Hey, Frank," said Baxter, "Flanagan says we're getting a new captain soon."

"Who's that?" asked Lazard.

"Captain from Ladder 11, Dempsey."

"What's he know about arson investigation?"

"He's been a fireman twenty-five years," said Flanagan.

"So what?" said Lazard. He began to say more, then decided against it. He remembered Dempsey as a smiling, pink-cheeked Irishman who had never seemed very bright.

"Whatever he needs to learn," said Flanagan, "we'll all help him learn it."

The sight of the three men stuffing themselves on O'Neill's candy made Lazard angry. "Like O'Neill, right? You know what people say about O'Neill in this town?"

Lazard saw Baxter looking embarrassed, as if Lazard had just said something particularly rude, like telling a filthy joke to the nuns. He knew they would say that despite O'Neill's faults they were all firemen and should stick together. They would blame Lazard's rudeness not on some idea of duty, but that he was working too hard or that he was not from Boston or that his leg must be hurting him.

Flanagan walked over and sat on the edge of Lazard's desk. "Now, Frank, you don't want to talk like that."

Lazard regretted losing his temper. "That's okay, chief, I'm sure Dempsey will be fine."

"You bet he will," said Flanagan. "I hear you got that inquest set up for next week. That's great, Frank. How much longer you think you'll need on the case?"

Lazard started typing again. "Just as long as it takes to get it right," he said.

Pugliese came in around one to check on several fires he had listed on a scrap of paper. Some of the files were in liquor cases on top of the lockers. Pugliese climbed on a chair and began shifting the boxes, disturbing layers of dust that floated down to where Fatback was sitting.

"What the fuck you doin', Pugliese?" demanded Fatback, waving his hands in front of him.

"I need to find some files." He tried to sound businesslike. When he had collected six folders, he went over to the window to read them. He had said hello to Lazard when he came in, now he said hello again. Lazard glanced up from his typing and nodded.

"What're you working on?" asked Lazard.

"I'm checking on DiTullio, like you said."

Lazard had almost forgotten. "Finding anything?"

Pugliese looked pleased, as if he had just learned how to spell some complicated word. "He's had a lot of fires. Six in the city"—Pugliese held up the files—"and about a dozen on the North Shore. He's got a lot of property up there. You know Lieutenant Berger in the marshal's office? He said a couple of them were pretty suspicious, although they couldn't bring him to court."

"Does he have a record?" asked Lazard.

"An assault conviction fifteen years ago. Got a suspended sentence. Berger says he's been mixed up in a lot of stuff but none of it's ever provable."

"Like now," said Lazard. "You got his picture?"

Pugliese dug into his briefcase, took out a large envelope, and tossed it on Lazard's desk. "Here's one," he said.

The picture showed a heavy-set middle-aged man seated in a booth of a restaurant with his arm around the shoulder of a heavy-set middle-aged woman. Neither was smiling.

"That's about two years old," said Pugliese. "They were investigating DiTullio for fencing stolen cars."

Lazard continued to look at the picture. The man had thick bushy eyebrows and thick brown hair which was brushed back over his head. He assumed the woman was DiTullio's wife, although she looked enough like him to be DiTullio in drag.

"Cute couple, don't you think? They're separated now."

"Let me keep this for a while," said Lazard, putting the picture back in the envelope. "Why don't you make a list of his fires, their causes, and who, if anyone, investigated them. You might also make a list of what property he owns." Lazard knew he could never bring DiTullio to court, but at least he could keep a file on him.

Pugliese went back to reading one of the reports. He was leaning against the windowsill and after about five minutes he turned to Lazard again. The sunlight glistened through his curly brown hair, forming an aura around the outline of his head. "Say, Frank."

Lazard looked up. "What?"

"What d'you think about marriage?"

Lazard studied Pugliese somewhat guiltily. He hadn't called Virginia Lufkin since that one time and tried not to think about her. Pugliese was smiling. He had round cheeks, straight teeth, and brown eyes that exuded sincerity. He wore a tie with a pattern of yellow daffodils, and a tie tack in the shape of a tiny Browning automatic.

"I guess marriage is okay for some people," said Lazard.

Pugliese nodded his head. "Yeah, I guess that's what I think too."

Half an hour later Lazard and Baxter were called to a three-alarm fire on Newbury Street. A women's clothing store had burned and the cause was either electrical or someone had sprayed some wires with inflammable hair spray. In any case, it kept Lazard and Baxter busy all afternoon.

The next day at 5 o'clock Trieger called Lazard at home and asked him to come over to his office at 6:30. Lazard had been asleep. He hadn't been able to leave the office until 9 that morning. Then he had spent most of the day appearing before a grand jury which was trying to determine probable cause on an apartment house fire that Lazard had investigated in September. He hadn't gotten home until 3:30.

"All right, I'll be there."

Lazard tried to sleep for another hour, but wasn't able to. Again he thought Trieger might try to hurt him and again he put it out of his mind. At last he got up and showered. Although he wasn't hungry, he made himself a bologna sandwich, then put half of it back in the refrigerator. The new bookcase with the books arranged in it was in place next to his chair. The books didn't disguise enough of the light green color to hide what Lazard thought of as its ugliness. Taking his tan raincoat from the closet, Lazard left his apartment. It was a clear warm day but windy and a bank of clouds was drifting in from the ocean.

Trieger was waiting for Lazard at the front door of his showroom. There seemed to be no one else around. "Thanks for coming," he said.

"Sure." Lazard thought Trieger seemed tense, as if he were trying to build up his nerve.

Trieger led the way to a couch covered with a beige material decorated with prints of butter churns and spinning wheels. He wore a blue suit. His cheek and left eye were a dark purple, and a small bandage covered part of his lower lip. In front of them was a coffee table designed to look like a shoemaker's bench.

Trieger sat at one end of the couch, leaning forward with his elbows on his knees. "What do you know about the fire?" he asked.

"Your brother's into a loan shark. You're trying to bail him out."

"You know about the marijuana and the plane crash?"

"Yes." Lazard was aware of saying the word almost too eagerly.

Trieger stood up. "I guess I don't feel like being in here. Let's go for a walk."

They left the showroom. Trieger locked the door. Turning right up School Street, they passed Old City Hall. In front were statues of Josiah Quincy and Benjamin Franklin. Even though it was past rush hour the sidewalks were still filled with people. Lazard's cane and bad leg had always made it hard for him to negotiate through a crowd.

"You know," said Trieger, "I couldn't refuse to help him. The last time they broke his arms. Can you imagine that? This time they threatened his family." Trieger paused to look at Lazard, then hurried on so it was difficult for Lazard to keep up. They passed Kings Chapel, then crossed over to the Parker House. Several times Trieger seemed about to speak, then changed his mind.

Stopping for the light at Tremont, Trieger said, "I don't know why I'm telling you this stuff. If you repeat it, I'll have to deny it." Then, as they crossed the street, "I been thinking about that inquest. It doesn't matter what they know, it's still only circumstantial evidence."

"It might not hold up in a criminal case, but it's enough for a civil court."

"What d'you mean?" They were approaching the Granary Burying Ground. Trieger was still hurrying, then he noticed Lazard limping behind him. "Sorry, I forgot."

"At the inquest you will be asked about your knowledge of certain events. You can lie, tell the truth, or refuse to talk. If they can prove the lie, then you face a perjury charge. In any case, testimony as to those events will be presented. On the grounds of that testimony, your insurance company will refuse to give you a dime. The only way for you to get it will be to sue them. The case will be heard in civil court. Your insurance company will present on their behalf the transcript of the inquest, plus the testimony of their investigators. The preponderance of evidence will be on the side of the insurance company and you will lose."

"Then Jimmy and I will be screwed."

"That's right."

Trieger was silent for a moment. He was again a few steps ahead of Lazard and he stopped to let Lazard catch up. "It seemed so easy for Jimmy. I mean, he had this pilot and a supplier in Jamaica. I don't know shit about that stuff. Christ, first he asked me. He needed $40,000. He said he'd double it in two weeks. The bastard, he was planning to make ten times that. He didn't say he was going to smuggle marijuana. Well, he's had a lot of schemes."

About twenty-five young people were clustered around Park Street Station. A man with long blond hair was playing the guitar and singing some country song. His guitar case was open on the sidewalk.

"I've let Jimmy have a lot of money, but never anything like that. How could I just give him $40,000? So he got it somewhere else. We never know, do we? That $40,000, it seems cheap now. The stuff he's done for me, that money would of been only a fraction. From September first to the end of February, he was paying $500 a week. Five months. They wanted to keep him for the rest of his life. How could he do that? I mean, he's got nothing."

They began walking up the hill in the Common. Remembering Lazard's leg, Trieger slowed down again. Two boys on skateboards shot by them.

Lazard had the sense of the case being solved, of winning. Soon everything would be in the hands of the lawyers and he could move on to something else. But despite this he kept asking himself about Trieger. What would happen to him? They reached the top of the hill by the war memorial. Looking out, they were surrounded by trees which seemed to rise above the buildings of the city. The air smelled of green, of luxuriant spring. Beneath all his thoughts, Lazard was aware of a sadness he didn't know what to do with.

"This guy in Miami," said Trieger, "he made it sound so easy. All I had to do was not be around when he said. Dammit, I love my work, but I thought, even if I only keep half the insurance, I can still build up again, and Jimmy, he'll be safe or at least they won't be breaking his arms and threatening his family. So I thought, no one lives down there. It's not like it's somebody's home or anything. It's just a warehouse. Jesus, when I heard those firemen got killed, I knew right then it was over."

They descended the hill toward Charles Street. The setting sun hung just above the trees in front of them.

"You know, at one point, I told this guy in Miami I'd changed my mind, that I couldn't go through with it. Know what he said? We don't need your permission. Can you believe it? I mean, I thought I'd have some kind of say. Forget it. The moment I met that guy that was that. They were going to burn me no matter what I said."

As they entered the Public Gardens, two young women passed in the other direction wheeling white wicker baby carriages. Lazard saw them glance at Trieger, and guessed it was because he was handsome and clearly unhappy; not because of the bruises.

"Who's the guy in Miami?" asked Lazard.

"I can't tell you."

"Why not?"

"Jesus, Frank, can't you see, they don't care. If I tell you, my house, my family, it's nothing."

"They beat you up."

"So what, I been beat up before. Think that's anything compared to what they can do to my girls? This guy in Miami, he wasn't any young man, he had a dog, one of those little white poodles, you know, they got pink eyes. He was so fuckin' kind and patient with that dog. It was tearing all over the place yapping. I could of killed it. But I thought, this guy's not so bad, look at how nice he treats that lousy dog. Well, this same old guy, the stuff he could do to my family, I don't want to think about it."

They crossed the bridge over the duck pond. The swan boats were tied up to their left beneath the bridge. The air smelled of lilac.

"What're you going to do about the inquest?" asked Lazard.

"I haven't decided. I talked to my lawyer, he'll come along. What's this detective know?"

"Everything."

Trieger put his hands in his pockets. "I'll have to deny it."

"First your brother's paying the vig, now he's not. Where'd he get the money?"

"Maybe there's another way. I mean, I could just disappear."

"If you don't show up, they'll have you for certain. Your brother's still going to be paying $500 a week, and you, you'll have no money. But if you confess, just tell the whole story, there'll be a chance of arresting those guys." Even as he said it, Lazard knew it was a lie, that he was just trying to make Trieger think he had another way out.

"I don't even know their names. This guy in Miami, he gave me a number to call in Boston if I had trouble. That's who I saw the other night. I mean, he just said all I had to do was open my mouth. You know what they can do? And they're in no hurry. Next week, next month, what does it matter? I mean, if it was just me."

They were walking up Arlington along the edge of the gardens. Across the street, a dark blue Bentley was parked in front of the Ritz-Carlton Hotel. A chauffeur opened the door and an old woman got out wearing a long white dress and white fur coat.

For a moment, Lazard considered letting Trieger go and calling off the inquest. Then he told himself he had no choice. The investigation was like some vehicle that was carrying him someplace: a plane, for instance, and he couldn't get off until it landed. But then he thought maybe that wasn't true, maybe he was simply afraid of Bascomb. Beds of tulips were planted along the border of the park, and in the decreasing light they seemed colorless and shadowy.

"You seen Elizabeth lately?" asked Trieger.

Lazard was surprised by the question. "Saw her last week. She's getting married."

197

"How does that make you feel?"

"I'm happy for her."

"Think you'll get married again?"

"I don't know." Lazard didn't want to talk about himself.

They crossed Boylston Street and headed toward Park Square. "Let's get a drink," said Trieger.

They went into a bar on the square. It was long, narrow, and dimly lit. At one end was a television with a seven-foot screen showing the Bruins-Flyers game being played in Philadelphia. Lazard and Trieger sat down in a booth and ordered a couple of drafts. They tried not to look at the television but it was so large and the movement so constant that they couldn't help themselves. There were about twenty people in the bar all watching the game and talking loudly.

"Did you tell Norma about the inquest?" asked Lazard.

"No, I couldn't stand that."

"What does she know?"

"Nothing really. She doesn't even realize there's an investigation. It's not fair, but I don't want her to know. She's been worrying a lot since the other night. Actually, I sent her and the kids up to the cottage. They left this afternoon."

"I tried not to tell her anything."

"I know, it was good of you to come over."

They watched the game for a while. At the end of the period, the Flyers were winning. On the huge screen, the puck looked like a black melon.

"What about the guy that actually burned the place," asked Lazard, "you know anything about him?"

"No, like I say, there was this guy in Miami and this guy the other night. I didn't go to his house or anything. He told me to meet him in the parking lot of some shopping center in Saugus. He came with another guy. I probably couldn't even recognize them. It was the other guy that showed the muscle."

"What happened to your gun?"

"They took it."

"Couldn't you do anything?"

"What am I, a hero? No, they had their own guns. Look, Frank, I'm a guy that rents furniture. What do I know about hoods with guns and that kind of life?"

Again Lazard considered letting Trieger go. He could tell

Hoffness there was nothing directly implicating Trieger, that he had decided extortionists had set the fire after all. Hoffness wouldn't believe him but what could he do? The idea frightened Lazard to the extent that he grew angry at Trieger for being friendly, as if the friendliness were an attempt to weaken his determination. They ordered two more beers. Through a combination of a lack of sleep and too little food, Lazard found himself getting drunk. They didn't say much during the rest of the game. Lazard got a couple of bags of potato chips and they shared them. As it became increasingly obvious that the Bruins were going to lose, the bar became quieter. The Flyers won six to three, knocking the Bruins out of the finals and their chance for the Stanley Cup.

Without the distraction of the television, the prospect of the inquest became more threatening. "I don't see what you're going to do," said Lazard. "They'll be asking these questions, you'll have to answer them."

"What if I'm not there?"

"You heard what Hoffness said. You'll end up with a contempt charge. That would suit your insurance company just fine."

Trieger didn't say anything. Several dimes and nickels were on the table by his glass and he kept moving them around, forming patterns.

"If you'd just kept your mouth shut," said Lazard, "you could have gotten away with it. Why'd you have to invite me over for dinner and be friendly and shit?"

Trieger finished his beer. In the dark booth it was difficult to see his face. "What can I say?"

"Christ, Howard, if you'd just left well enough alone. What'd I know? I knew nothing."

Lazard sat on the edge of his bed with his elbows resting on his knees. He was naked except for a pair of white Jockey shorts. The only light in the room came from around the edges of the drawn shade. Lazard was smoking a cigarette and slowly he exhaled the smoke from his lungs. For an hour he had tried to sleep, then he gave it up as a lost cause. The apartment was quiet but for the gurgling of pipes in the bathroom.

Lazard was brooding about Trieger, whom he had left in Park Square around 11, two hours before. He kept wondering why Trieger had invited him to dinner, had tried to reestablish a friendship even though Lazard was in charge of an investigation that could put Trieger in jail. Maybe Trieger had been trying to win him over, but that seemed improbable. Most likely, Trieger hadn't seen Lazard as enough of a threat. After all, Trieger had had nothing directly to do with the fire, so what could Lazard learn?

But Lazard also realized that Trieger had been struck by the change in him. How had Trieger seen him? Lonely, silent, damaged by his divorce or bad leg, the cause didn't matter. Almost shamefully, Lazard asked himself if Trieger had been trying to help him. He pushed the thought aside. No, Trieger was only being friendly. Then it occurred to him that in the same way Trieger had given up control of his life to help his brother, so had he made himself vulnerable by being nice to Lazard. He had opened himself up and Lazard, aspiring to be a precise machine, had moved in and destroyed him with no thought of consequences or responsibility.

What responsibility? Trieger had involved himself in a crime and Lazard had exposed him. That was his job. But Lazard knew that beyond any matter of criminality part of him also envied Trieger, envied his happiness and comfortable life; and he wondered how much of his drive to destroy Trieger had been inspired by that envy. What would Trieger have now? He would be lucky to stay out of jail.

Lazard stubbed out his cigarette, then lit another. He asked himself what he would do in Trieger's position. Without a doubt, he knew he would kill himself. It would make the insurance company pay, get his brother off the hook, and leave money for his family. It would also spare him the shame of being found guilty. Immediately, and again without a doubt, Lazard realized that was Trieger's own intention. It was why he had asked what would happen if he didn't show up at the inquest and why he had sent his wife and daughters up north, leaving him alone in the house.

As he thought this, Lazard experienced a small feeling of vindication. The feeling startled him even more than the idea that Trieger might commit suicide. Was he so damaged that he could take pleasure from Trieger's death? But how could he be so sure he would kill himself? Lazard imagined racing over to Trieger's house only to find him fast asleep or watching a late movie. He would feel like a fool. But then what if he didn't? What if he just went to sleep and woke in the morning to learn that Trieger had killed himself after all.

Lazard got to his feet, limped to his foot locker, and took his pants which were folded neatly on top. He told himself that if Trieger died, it would be the same as if he had shot him. And if Lazard allowed it to happen, he would be no better than Trieger's brother or Gary Howard. James Trieger had borrowed money, which began the chain of events leading to the warehouse fire. The brother was guilty in the same way Gary Howard was guilty of killing two firemen by putting rocks in the hydrant: each had refused to be responsible for the consequences of his actions.

Hurriedly Lazard finished dressing, then left his apartment and limped to the elevator. His car was parked out on Hancock. He imagined getting to Trieger's house and finding him dead in the living room. Although he would grieve, Lazard also knew that his guilt would finish any chance he had of climbing out of the morass of his own life. How could he build a normal life if he thought he had driven Trieger to suicide?

It was nearly quarter to two when he reached Trieger's house. The rain that had been threatening all night had begun to fall as Lazard left his apartment building: a heavy rain that swept across his windshield. As Lazard looked through his wipers, Trieger's white Victorian house seemed like some oversized toy at the bottom of a fish tank. Lights were on up- and downstairs and Lazard didn't know if this was a good sign or bad.

Lazard opened the door, grabbed his cane off the seat, and limped up the driveway. He was totally wet by the time he reached the front porch. Wiping the water from his eyes, he rang the bell, then rang it again. He could hear the two notes of the chimes ringing mutedly inside the house. After a moment, he rang the bell a third time. Then he tried the door. It was unlocked. Lazard opened it slowly and stepped into the hall. The house was silent except for the sound of rain drumming on the roof.

"Howard," Lazard called. There was no answer.

Lazard went into the living room, then the dining room and kitchen. He was aware of walking almost on tip-toe. His shoes were wet and left footprints on the rug. In the kitchen, Lazard took some paper towels and dried his face and hair. "Howard," he called. In each room he expected to find Trieger lying in some awful position. He went back to the hall.

"Trieger!"

Lazard began to climb the stairs to the second floor. He imagined Trieger dead in his bed or collapsed in the bathroom. The antique clock in the living room chimed the hour and at the first note, Lazard felt his heart leap.

The sound of rain was louder upstairs. There was no sign of Trieger. At first Lazard thought he might have packed a suitcase and left, but the closets and bureau drawers were all shut. He knew that didn't mean anything. Catching a glance of himself in the bedroom mirror, he was struck by how foolish he looked with his wet clothes and his short dark hair standing straight up on his head. He decided to check the garage to see if a car was missing. Norma had presumably driven the station wagon up north, so that would leave the Pontiac and the MG. Lazard hurried back downstairs.

The door to the garage was just past the kitchen. Lazard yanked it open so it slammed against the doorstop. In the light from the kitchen, he saw two cars parked side by side. The rain hammered on the roof. Then, in the dim light, Lazard saw someone sitting in the MG.

"Trieger!"

Almost fearfully, Lazard searched for the light switch next to the door. He found it and flicked it on. The light glistened on the bright red surface of the MG. Trieger was sitting behind the steering wheel. Slowly, he turned toward Lazard.

"Jesus, Howard, you scared the shit out of me. You all right?"

Trieger looked at Lazard without speaking. He wore a yellow and green plaid shirt. "Get out of here, Frank, just leave me alone."

"Look, Howard, I've had an idea. There's something I want to show you. Maybe we can work things out."

"What the hell can you do?"

"Just come with me."

"Where?"

"Do as I say. Believe me, I think I can fix it." Lazard wondered if that were true or if he would only make matters worse. On the other hand, what would be worse than Trieger's death?

Trieger got out of the MG and followed Lazard back into the house. Lazard's wet shoes made a squeaking noise on the kitchen floor. "Better get your raincoat," said Lazard.

"Where are we going?"

"Just lock up the house and come on."

Trieger turned off the lights and locked the front door. Then they hurried to Lazard's car.

"I don't see what you can do," said Trieger.

Lazard didn't answer, just held open the door for Trieger, then limped around to the other side. Rain was running down his neck. He opened his mouth to catch a few drops before getting into the car.

There was hardly any traffic. As they passed the Brookline Reservoir on Boylston, Lazard asked, "How do you think your wife would feel, finding you in the garage?"

Trieger shrugged. "I thought maybe you'd find me."

Ten minutes later Lazard drew to a stop in front of Fire Headquarters. Looking up at the arson office, he saw the lights were on. Hopefully, whoever was working was out on a call, although the way Lazard felt it wouldn't matter if the whole squad were there.

Trieger followed him into the building. "This where you work?"

Lazard nodded. They took the elevator to the third floor, then turned left down the hall. Trieger appeared curious but didn't say anything. Lazard felt almost embarrassed by the ugliness of the building.

The arson office was empty. Trieger stood in the doorway and looked around. Limping to his desk, Lazard found the envelope that Pugliese had given him the previous day. He took out the picture of DiTullio and handed it to Trieger.

"Is that the guy who beat you up?"

Trieger looked at the picture for a long time. "It was the guy with him," he said at last.

21

"So what if he burned a hundred buildings?" said Quaid. "You know as well as I do you'll never get him into court."

"We could get him charged," said Lazard.

"You kidding? There's no assistant D.A. who'd touch the case. DiTullio's no beginner. All you'd be doing is making things worse for Trieger."

It was 10 o'clock Saturday morning and Lazard and Quaid were sitting at Quaid's kitchen table drinking coffee and eating French toast. Quaid's daughter Geraldine stood nearby looking expectantly at Lazard, who held a multicolored ball in his lap. After a moment, he tossed it to her.

"The only way you can get out of this mess," said Quaid, "is to turn the case over to someone else."

"That's not true, I can cancel the inquest."

Quaid looked at his friend, then looked away. Nearby his wife was making more French toast. Lazard drank some coffee. He'd had four hours' sleep and felt stupid. After showing Trieger DiTullio's picture, he had driven him home and made him swear not to do anything foolish. Then Lazard had called Trieger around 9 that morning to see how he felt. Trieger had sounded almost cheerful, as if fully confident that Lazard could save him. It now seemed to Lazard that he had no choice but to save him.

"If you cancel the inquest," said Quaid, "that's not simply fraud. It makes you an accessory after the fact."

"I told him I could fix it," said Lazard.

"Are you so scared of him killing himself?" Quaid thought he had spoken too bluntly. "People make all kinds of threats."

"I don't know if he'd kill himself. It was just that I'd pushed him to it. I mean, I pushed and pushed and then that's all he had left to do. Part of me even wanted him to do it. You know that? Part of me was just waiting. I mean I was sitting in my room and saying to myself I'd beaten him and he was going to kill himself and that was just great. What kind of way is that to live? So we have a bunch of guys involved in a crime. Well, Trieger's the least guilty and he's the one getting nailed."

Quaid buttered a piece of French toast, then poured syrup over it. It was sunny that morning and Quaid loved how the warm spring air blew through the open window. In the back yard he saw the thin branches of a willow tree whipping around in the wind.

"If there's no inquest," said Quaid, "and the insurance company pays, then DiTullio and his buddies get their money. Know where that puts you? Right in the same club with O'Neill and Phelps."

"That's still not as bad as wrecking Trieger."

"Are you sure of that? Anyway, you've put lots of guys in jail."

"Trieger's a baby. He's no crook. He was just stupid. And that's not even the point. I mean, when I was after him, I didn't even care how guilty he was, I just wanted to break him."

Quaid's wife put another plate of French toast on the table. Buttering a slice, Quaid handed it to his daughter, who stuffed it into her mouth without swallowing.

"What trouble you think I'd have canceling the inquest?" asked Lazard.

Quaid pushed back his chair and stood up. Then he took his pipe and tobacco pouch from the right-hand pocket of his brown cardigan. "Flanagan's worried about you. He wants you off the case." Pausing to fill the pipe, he took some matches from another pocket, struck one and held it to the tobacco. "If you tell Flanagan that the extortion theory makes the most sense to you, he'll go along with it."

"Will he believe me?"

Quaid looked furious. "You're really asking for a lot, aren't you." Then he took hold of himself and drew on his pipe. "Flanagan wants as few problems as possible. With Cassidy on sick leave, we're even more shorthanded than usual. If you cancel the inquest, that'll free you up for other stuff."

"Is Cassidy out of the hospital?"

"He went home on Tuesday. I guess he wanted to come back to work, but Flanagan said he had to stay out at least two weeks. He's already called twice trying to get Flanagan to change his mind."

"You think I could talk to Flanagan, then try Hoffness?"

"Sure, I mean it's clear to both of them that it's Bascomb and the insurance company who're pushing for the inquest. Bascomb's not very popular around there. If you kick his feet out from underneath him, well, nobody's going to care too much. You're the only one who'll suffer."

"How d'you mean?"

"People are going to think you took some money."

"Let them." Lazard pushed away his plate. "You must think I'm being pretty dumb."

Quaid looked embarrassed. "You got a good reputation and you're junking it. I'm not even sure why except that you're unhappy. Shit, I don't even know why you're unhappy." Quaid tapped out his pipe on an ashtray. He looked like someone who had forgotten something important, like where he had put his checkbook or an important phone number. "I don't think you're dumb. I mean, you're my friend. But a lot of people will. Besides that, you're taking a big chance. If you think canceling the inquest will solve Trieger's problems, I'll bet a thousand bucks that you're wrong. DiTullio and his buddies have Trieger set up for blackmail, extortion, who knows what. If I were you, I'd just let him go. Like you say, he did something stupid. Prison's full of people who did something stupid."

"I told him I'd help him. If I let him go, it'd be like letting myself go, I mean like letting myself go for good." Lazard took out a cigarette, then reached across the table for Quaid's matches. Glancing up, he saw Quaid's wife watching him from the other side of the kitchen.

Quaid shrugged. "Then you got to figure out some way to make these guys leave Trieger alone."

"Have any ideas?"

"Not me, I'm strictly a legman."

Lazard stood up and took hold of his cane. "Then I guess I'll go see Cassidy."

"You figure he'll help you?"

"He owes me a favor. Not only that, he owns a lot of guns."

Quaid touched Lazard's arm. "Look, Frank, if you figure something out maybe I can give you a hand."

Lazard smiled. "That's okay, Teddy, you need your pension more than Cassidy does. Just keep them off my back at the office."

Lieutenant-detective Hoffness leaned against his desk chewing on his thumbnail. A gray fedora balanced precariously on the back of his head. Hoffness stopped chewing on the thumbnail, then scratched his neck. "You must think I'm a real asshole," he said to Lazard.

Sitting in a straight chair with his aluminum cane balanced across his knees, Lazard stared up at the ceiling. He felt better than he had for months. Then he returned Hoffness's stare and shrugged.

"First I bust a gut trying to set up this fucking inquest in record time. Now you got cold feet or something. The subpoenas were sent out last week, for crying out loud."

"Cancel them," said Lazard.

"What about the marshal? He's pretty worked up about this. If I tell him it's not going to happen, he'll shit ground glass. I gotta go through with it, Frank."

"Suit yourself," said Lazard, "but when Quaid and I testify we'll say our office believes the warehouse was burned by extortionists."

"That'll make me look pretty stupid, won't it," said Hoffness.

Lazard didn't answer. Through the window over Hoffness's shoulder, he saw a seagull turning in slow circles in a blue sky. It was shortly after 2 o'clock Monday afternoon. That morning Lazard had seen Flanagan and told him he saw no point in the inquest; that upon reevaluating existing evidence he felt Flanagan was correct in thinking the fire had been set by extortionists. The main reason he had pushed for the inquest, Lazard had said, was that Bascomb wanted it to build a case against Trieger so the insurance company could refuse payment. Now, however, Lazard saw little or no proof that Trieger was involved and so he wanted to call it off.

They had been alone in Flanagan's office. As he had listened, Flanagan stared out at the Boston skyline. In the end all he had said was: "So cancel it, if that's what you want." Lazard hadn't been able to tell if Flanagan had believed him or not. Sitting now in Hoffness's office, he wondered why he cared. But irrationally he knew that even though he had thrown over this particular case, he still wanted Flanagan to think he gave each investigation all his effort, that he could never be persuaded to look the other way like Phelps or O'Neill. In fact, he wanted the same kind of belief from Hoffness, wanted to be thought an honest investigator who only called a halt when the investigation reached a complete dead end.

It was clear, however, that Hoffness was suspicious. He had large hooded eyes and when he stared at Lazard they seemed barely open. "Okay," he said at last, "so we cancel it. I'll tell the marshal you got some new evidence which is leading you in another direction. Some bullshit like that. But you know who's really going to be pissed, don't you?"

"Who?" asked Lazard, although he knew perfectly well.

"Bascomb's going to want to murder you. You really picked a great time to make him mad, considering they been doin' this bribery investigation."

"I can't help that."

"What are you going to tell him?"

"Same thing I've told you." Although he tried to sound indifferent, Lazard dreaded the moment when he would have to face Bascomb. He had no regret at stopping the investigation. It still seemed that the truly guilty people could never have been brought to court, while Trieger was little more than a scapegoat. Indeed, whenever he thought that he had saved Trieger from destruction, Lazard felt considerable relief. On Saturday, he had told Trieger to go up to his cottage, but to call every night in case Lazard needed him. As it now stood, Lazard wouldn't need him until Tuesday evening.

Hoffness took off his hat, spun it around on one finger, then set it behind him on the desk. "So that's that," he said. "Is Cassidy back to work yet?"

"He'll be out for another week."

"He get in much hot water for that stunt of his?"

"A little, but the chief figured that getting shot a couple of times was hot water enough."

"Shit, if he'd done a trick like that with us, he wouldn't even be able to find a dishwashing job in this state. What's he doin' now, just loafing?"

"I guess so," said Lazard. Actually, for the past thirty-six hours Cassidy had been following DiTullio.

"Cassidy takes the cake," said Hoffness. "He was always askin' us favors, you know, like we owed him something."

Lazard put his cane on the floor and pushed himself to his feet. "Speaking of favors," he said, "I wonder if you could lend us some equipment for a couple of days."

Hoffness cupped his chin in the V of his thumb and index finger and rubbed his jaw. "What kind of equipment?"

"I want to wire a guy, and I'll need two tape recorders. One of them really small."

"Why two?"

"It's a complicated wire."

"Jesus," said Hoffness, "you guys just don't know where to get off."

Lazard and Trieger stood under a large maple tree planted between the sidewalk and street in a wealthy section of Lynn. It was just past 11 o'clock Tuesday night and the two men were staring at a brick house set back from the road about a hundred yards away. Parked at the curb between them and the house was a dark blue Ford van. In the right-hand pocket of Lazard's sport coat was a .38 Chief's Special belonging to Cassidy. Lazard found the weight unfamiliar and occasionally wondered what it was, then remembered.

"What if they just decide to shoot me," said Trieger.

"They won't."

"What makes you so sure?"

The house belonged to the realtor Julian DiTullio. It was in the style that Lazard knew as Tudor, although he doubted the house was more than twenty years old: a steep slate roof and mullioned windows. There was even ivy on the fireplace chimney. Six or seven large trees grew in the front yard and Lazard half expected to see Pugliese hiding behind one of them.

Pugliese had nearly become a serious problem. The previous afternoon, while Cassidy had been following DiTullio, he had suddenly realized that Pugliese was following him as well. His concern that Pugliese might see him had been tempered by his discovery that Pugliese was wearing a wig and false moustache.

On the chance that Pugliese might spot Cassidy and ask what he was doing, Lazard had decided to pull him off the investigation. That morning he had found Pugliese in the arson office again standing on a chair and rummaging through boxes of files on top of the lockers. He had been wearing a gray corduroy coat similar to the one which Lazard often wore.

"What are you doing?" Lazard had asked.

"I keep finding more fires this guy DiTullio's been involved in."

"Forget it," said Lazard, "we're closing the case."

"What do you mean closing the case?" asked Pugliese, balancing on the chair. "What about the inquest?"

"That's been called off so you might as well quit fooling around with the car thieves."

"It's more than just car thieves. That guy's had a lot of property go up."

"Maybe so, but there's no way to link him to the warehouse. All we have is some circumstantial evidence and a bunch of theories. I could name you twenty guys who've had more property go up than DiTullio and they're all walking around as free men today."

"So you just want me to quit?"

"That's right, take a vacation or something."

"A vacation?"

"Sure. You did a pretty good job tracing that car."

"You mean that?" Pugliese had asked each question with increasing amazement.

"What'd I just say?"

Pugliese had compiled a list, however, of twenty-five fires with which DiTullio had had some connection—DiTullio was either owner, part owner, or real estate agent. Nearly all the fires were of unknown origin.

Lazard now had the list of fires in his pocket and he thought of it as he stared across the dark street at DiTullio's house. Then he asked himself if Pugliese would have quit the case so readily if he didn't respect him. Lazard knew that Pugliese's choice of a gray corduroy sport coat was a sign of that respect, but instead of being flattered, it made him uncomfortable, as if he had stones in his shoes or his shirt were too tight.

In any case, Lazard hoped the list of fires would give him a bit of leverage. His main fear, however, was that whatever he did would give the leverage to DiTullio.

"Let's go," said Lazard. "It's getting late."

The two men walked up the street toward the van. Some of the houses were surrounded by dark hedges and all had a number of mature oaks and maples which gave the neighborhood the appearance of a manicured forest.

Reaching the van, Lazard tapped twice at the back window. The door opened and they climbed inside.

"You sure took your time," said Cassidy. "DiTullio got home around nine. That scrawny guy's with him, Weingarten, must be his bodyguard. Maybe he brushes his fuckin' teeth for him. They're in the back room drinking and watching the TV. There's nobody else in the house."

Lazard and Trieger were crouched down in the back of the van. Cassidy sat on a low chair next to a table half covered with recording equipment: a large reel-to-reel tape recorder, speakers, a cassette recorder, and a microphone. The small light above the table made Cassidy's face look especially craggy. He wore a dark brown turtleneck and brown sport coat. Separating them from the front of the van was a sliding door.

"You ready to go inside?" Cassidy asked Trieger.

"I guess so."

"I bet you're ready to wet your pants," said Cassidy.

Trieger didn't answer.

"Okay, buster, roll up your shirt. We'll stick this to your gut."

Trieger pulled up his shirt. Cassidy took a small microphone from the table and carefully taped it to Trieger's left side just below his rib cage with white adhesive. Cassidy's movements were quick and certain. As he watched, Lazard thought with admiration that Cassidy never did anything without giving the impression that he had done it successfully hundreds of times. Then he remembered he had thought something similar just before Cassidy was shot.

"All right," said Cassidy, "tuck in your shirt."

"You know what you've got to do?" asked Lazard. "Just tell them you're not going through with the inquest. You know, like we talked about earlier. You got to make DiTullio say something we could use in court, then we'll come get you out."

Trieger shook his head. The skin on his face seemed stretched tight and he kept looking from Lazard to Cassidy. "Frank, he told me before that he'd kill me."

For a moment, Lazard was suspicious of Trieger's fear, as if Trieger had been lying about the extent of his involvement. Then Lazard decided that was foolish. What experience did Trieger have with crooks? His idea of excitement was a grand-slam home run.

"If they start anything," said Lazard, "we'll be right there. Look, if this doesn't work, you'll have no way to get them off your back. They'll get every cent you own. Now go get your car and drive up to the house."

Trieger pushed his hand through his hair, then glanced at Cassidy. "Okay, open the door," he said.

Lazard drew back the curtain over the window and looked out at the dark street. Then he shoved open the back door and Trieger jumped out. Lazard watched Trieger hurry toward his car. A dog started barking, then stopped. Lazard shut the door.

"Think he'll pull it off?" asked Cassidy. Through the speakers they could just make out the sound of Trieger's footsteps.

"Maybe."

Cassidy scratched his stomach, then leaned back in his chair. "I don't see why you don't just give up on him. So what if he gets nailed or goes to jail? He acted stupid."

"He was going to kill himself."

"Big deal."

Lazard tried to think of some argument that would convince Cassidy, something to show the other man how it hadn't been worth destroying Trieger, but all Lazard could think of saying was, "Maybe he's a friend of mine."

Cassidy yawned. "He must be a complete asshole."

Over the small speakers, they heard Trieger slam his car door, then start the engine. Cassidy fiddled with the dials, adjusting the volume. Then he put the small cassette player next to one of the speakers, pushed the record button, and stopped it again with the pause control.

"I'll start it up when he knocks on the door," said Cassidy. The metal interior of the van made his voice echo. "You know what'll happen if they catch us on this?" he asked.

Lazard was lighting a cigarette. He shook out the match and dropped it on the metal floor. "You scared?" he asked.

Cassidy started to speak, then stopped as they heard Trieger pull up in DiTullio's driveway and get out of his car. There was the sound of Trieger climbing some steps. Lazard tried to picture the front of DiTullio's house. The front door had diamond-shaped windows of rippled yellow glass and a brass knocker in the shape of a lion's head. He imagined Trieger pressing his thumb against the bell.

"You know, these bastards," said Cassidy, "they could easily shoot him, just haul off and pop him."

"No, they won't." Lazard wondered if he had any real reason to think that.

"Shit, if they shot him, we'd have ourselves a great case. You ever think of that? Fuckin' Flanagan would love us."

For a second Lazard almost wished it would happen. "Start the recorders," he said.

Cassidy pushed buttons on both machines. As he did so, the sound of a door opening came over the speakers.

"What do you want?" It was a hoarse voice, more like the caw of a crow than a group of words.

"I want to see DiTullio."

"Haven't we given you enough trouble?" There was a pause. "Maybe you better come inside." More footsteps, then the sound of the door shutting and locking. "Turn around, face the wall, and put your hands over your head." Lazard thought he could hear the sound of Trieger's breathing. "Okay, wait here."

"That's Weingarten," said Cassidy. "He must of patted him down."

The small speakers made the voices sound tinny and far away. Lazard put his hand into his coat pocket to touch the revolver. It was no comfort.

"DiTullio's going to bust a fuckin' gut," said Cassidy. "I'd love to see his face when Weingarten tells him."

Again there were footsteps, then the voice of Weingarten: "He says come into the back room. You go first."

The sound of their footsteps changed as they walked down the hall, crossed a rug, then onto a wooden floor again. After about a minute, Weingarten said, "Hey, look who's here."

Lazard could just make out the sound of a television in the background. He recognized the music from a soft-drink commercial.

"What the fuck do you want?" said DiTullio.

Lazard tried to visualize DiTullio standing up and facing Trieger. His mental image, however, was of the photograph showing DiTullio and his wife in the booth of the restaurant: both heavyset and angry. He had the barest memory of the bodyguard, Weingarten, whom he had seen earlier in the day: a thin, middle-aged man with thick black hair combed back over his head.

"I've been finding out about you," said Trieger. "You've had lots of fires. I thought I'd come and say I plan to tell everything I know at the inquest."

Trieger sounded clearly scared, but stubborn and even angry. There was no response for a moment.

"Wasn't one beating enough for you?" asked DiTullio. "You think we're just playing games?" If Weingarten sounded like a crow, DiTullio's voice was of some gentler animal: a soft, pleasant voice which seemed to contradict his words.

"I guess you're serious enough," said Trieger. "I'm saying I just don't care. Your friend in Miami has got my brother for $40,000 and you both figure you can burn my warehouse and I'll bail out my brother with the insurance money. You're good at fires, right? This time you'll be lucky to stay out of jail."

There was a pause, then the sound of a bottle clinking against the rim of a glass. "You know, Mr. Trieger, you got two cute little daughters. If you don't go through that inquest like a dummy and deny everything, you'll see how good at fires I really am."

"Is that a threat?"

"Sure it's a threat," said DiTullio. "I'll burn your house right to the ground. What are those cute little daughters insured for?"

"You son of a bitch."

"Hey!" shouted Weingarten.

There was a thumping noise like empty boxes being bounced down a flight of stairs. Lazard grabbed the small cassette recorder and shoved it in his pocket. "Let's go," he said. "Leave the other tape running."

Lazard yanked open the back door. Behind him, Cassidy said: "Don't you want to wait for some better stuff?"

"They're killing him, for crissake."

By holding his cane flat against his bad leg, Lazard could almost run. Cassidy hurried ahead and disappeared into the darkness of DiTullio's yard. Lazard felt the .38 in his coat pocket bounce against his hip as he hobbled along.

Just as Lazard reached the house, Cassidy reappeared. "They're in a room around back. I could see through the window." He bent over to pick up a large white stone which must have weighed fifty pounds. A border of these stones separated the lawn from a line of small bushes beside the house.

"What's that for?" asked Lazard.

"You'll see."

"We've got to seem tough."

"I *am* tough," said Cassidy.

They went around the right side of the house by the garage. Lazard nearly stumbled against some garbage cans. The window that Cassidy had mentioned was all the way at the rear. It looked in on a den or family room: pine paneling covered the lower half of the walls. Trieger lay on the floor on his stomach and Weingarten crouched over him. Trieger's eyes were open. Lazard felt a surge of relief: at least he wasn't dead.

Cassidy pulled Lazard back from the window, then shoved the rock toward his stomach. "Take this, lift it over your head, and toss it through the window. Then get the fuck outta the way."

Lazard grabbed hold of the rock and watched Cassidy take his revolver from a clip at his belt. The window began at chest level. Balancing on his good leg, Lazard raised the rock above his head and moved back about five feet. He glanced at Cassidy.

Cassidy stood flat against the house, holding his gun above his head. "Okay, let's give 'em a scare. Throw the fuckin' stone."

Lazard heaved the rock forward. It smashed through the screen and glass, then toppled into the room. Almost before it hit the floor, Cassidy was leaning through the window with his gun in his hand.

"I'll kill the first fucker who moves," he shouted. Cassidy's shoulders were flecked with bits of glass. "Hey, Trieger, get your ass in gear and go open the front door."

Leaving Cassidy at the window, Lazard limped around to the front. Trieger was waiting at the door when he reached it. He had blood on his face and his shirt was torn. Despite his bruises, Trieger was grinning. Lazard slapped his shoulder as he went past him.

"All the way down the hall," said Trieger.

The den was long and narrow like a railway car, with several dark leather couches and chairs. A large liquor cabinet stood at one end and a large color television at the other. The television was on and tuned to some talk show. DiTullio and Weingarten stood on either side of it while ten feet away Cassidy leaned through the window pointing his revolver. Oriental rugs covered the floor. The large white rock rested in the middle of the room with a trail of broken glass leading back to the window.

"What the hell's going on here?" said DiTullio.

"I'm coming around," said Cassidy. "If either of you fuckers tries anything, I'll bust you in half." Cassidy disappeared.

DiTullio was a paunchy brown-haired man in a gray leisure suit. Weingarten was very thin and wore a blue jacket, white shirt, and black pants. The moment Cassidy disappeared he began to reach into his jacket.

Lazard had never fired a .38 before. Pointing the gun toward the television, he squeezed the trigger. There was an immense noise and the screen blew apart, showering DiTullio and Weingarten with glass. Both men ducked. Lazard's ears were ringing. "Put your hands over your heads or I'll kill you!"

Cassidy came rushing into the room, knocking Trieger out of the way. "What happened?"

"Weingarten tried to pull a gun."

"Jesus Christ," said Cassidy. He walked slowly toward Weingarten. "Didn't I tell you? Didn't I say you had to behave?" Although Weingarten was tall, Cassidy was at least four inches taller and fifty pounds heavier. Weingarten had a long cadaverous face. His mouth was open slightly as he watched Cassidy. "I hate bein' fucked with," said Cassidy.

Reaching out, Cassidy grabbed the lapels of Weingarten's jacket, yanked him forward so the two men's faces were inches apart, then hurled him back. Weingarten flew about five feet through the air and smashed against the wall. As he slid down, Cassidy took several steps forward, drew back his leg, and kicked Weingarten in the groin, doubling him over. Weingarten fell onto his face. Cassidy bent down and took a small automatic from a holster under his arm. Then he went over and frisked DiTullio.

"So what's this about?" said DiTullio. "Think I don't know who you clowns are?"

Lazard limped toward DiTullio until he stood about two feet away. The realtor's jowls and cheeks looked like two little purses. Moving quickly, Lazard reached out and slapped DiTullio twice across the face, knocking him back against the wall. Then he took the small cassette recorder from his pocket, briefly pushed the rewind button, started it again, and set it on the remains of the television. DiTullio's voice began in midsentence: ". . . burn your house right to the ground. What are those cute little daughters insured for?"

Lazard shut off the machine. DiTullio didn't say anything but seemed to be staring at Lazard's feet. Weingarten still lay curled up on the floor.

"There isn't going to be any inquest," said Lazard, "which means there's a good chance that the insurance company will pay up. When that happens, Trieger's brother will pay his debts. If after that point, either you or your buddy in Miami makes any contact with Trieger or his brother, this tape goes public."

"So what?" said DiTullio. "That tape can't prove anything." He put his hands in his pockets and moved away from the wall.

Lazard took out Pugliese's list of fires. "I've got a list of twenty-five fires here, in property you either owned or had a hand in. If we dig a little deeper, we can probably find more. You must be dealing with a lot of unhappy insurance companies. They'd be tickled pink to have this tape."

DiTullio rubbed his cheek, then looked from Lazard to Cassidy. "It still seems you boys are taking a chance. Maybe they'll get me for a fire or two, but what's to keep me from dragging you in too?"

Lazard turned to Trieger, who was standing by the door. "Show him the mike," he said.

Trieger pulled up his shirt to expose the microphone taped to his side.

"This tape is still running," said Lazard. "You haven't tried to

217

call the police or deny any of these charges. If you lay a finger on either of these brothers, the first tape goes to your insurance company. If you drag us into it, the second tape goes as well. Why make it so complicated? If you do nothing, you'll get your money. If you get greedy, well, then you'll have a lot of trouble."

DiTullio looked uncertain. He crossed his arms, then uncrossed them again. Weingarten still on the floor made a moaning noise. Cassidy looked around the room and yawned.

"It could mean trouble for you too," said DiTullio after a moment.

Lazard shrugged. "Not so much. We'd testify. I won't go to jail or lose any money. Maybe I'd lose my job. Big deal. I didn't want to be a fireman forever."

————22————

At first Lazard had thought the chairs and couches were uphol-
stered in red leather, then he decided it had to be vinyl. It was a
large room and the walls were covered with walnut paneling. Most
of the light came from small lamps on the dozen or so tables. The
waiter was more like a good servant than was common in Boston:
white shirt, black vest, black bow tie. Mounted above the fireplace
was the head of a moose. Despite such attractions, Lazard felt restless and regretted his decision to have a drink with Baxter.

The two men had come to the bar of the Hampshire House at
11 o'clock, half an hour earlier, after having sampled four others
along Newbury Street, the last being the bar at the Ritz-Carlton
Hotel. Baxter's wife was visiting their daughter in Springfield, and
earlier that evening he had telephoned Lazard to see if he wanted
to go out and hit the high spots, as Baxter called them. Baxter
knew little of how Lazard lived when he wasn't at Fire Headquarters, but he assumed he led a normal bachelor life and would have
been almost hurt had he known Lazard didn't take advantage of
his access to the young and beautiful in singles bars. Apart from
that, Lazard suspected the invitation had also been inspired by

Baxter's concern for what he thought of as Lazard's recent peculiarity.

Lazard had meant to stay at home and read, but whenever he tried to focus on his book he found himself thinking about Trieger, DiTullio, and having called a halt to the investigation. Lazard and Baxter had worked on Wednesday, the previous day. Nothing had been said about Trieger. The insurance company, in the form of David Bascomb, had relephoned several times but the calls had been given directly to Flanagan. As far as the arson office was concerned, the investigation of the warehouse fire was over.

Thursday morning, however, when Phelps and Hufnagel arrived at the office at 7:30, the subject of Trieger resurfaced. Lazard had been preparing to leave.

"I hear you finished up the Plympton Street fire," Phelps had said.

Lazard was suspicious. "Pretty much."

"You issue a complaint against anyone?"

"No, we had to close the case pending new information."

Phelps began leafing through a phonebook on top of the TV by the window. "I thought you really wanted to solve that one," he said. "You know, two firemen killed and all that. Didn't you used to be friends with that guy? What's his name, Trieger?"

Lazard was about to make an angry answer, then saw everyone watching him: Fatback, Baxter, Quaid, even two fire prevention inspectors from across the hall. They all knew he had dumped the case.

"We're still friends," Lazard said after a moment.

Phelps grinned. "There's nothing like friendship," he said.

Lazard had spent much of the day brooding about Phelps. He wished he could punish Phelps for thinking him a crook, pick him up and throw him against a wall as Cassidy had done to DiTullio's bodyguard two days before. Instead, he would have to live with it; to respond to Phelps would only keep the subject alive.

In any case, when Baxter called to see if he wanted to go out, Lazard had agreed. They would hit a few classy bars downtown and make a night of it. Baxter had called it painting the town red. One of Baxter's common fantasies concerned the bachelor life he might have had had he remained single. This had become his prime subject as they moved from bar to bar; and he had been so talkative, so impressed by his surroundings, and so impressed to be a participant in his surroundings that Lazard had begun to wish him someplace else. Of all the bars they had visited, Baxter liked the Hampshire House best.

"You know," said Baxter, "I'd give my left nut to own a room like this. Class, that's what I like. Know what my house is? It's the place I keep the stuff my wife buys. Maybe that's not fair, maybe I buy some too."

Baxter was half sprawled in a red armchair on the other side of the table. He wore a bright green sport coat and a yellow shirt. His tie was printed with a color photograph of skyscrapers and expressways against a setting sun, deep red in the smog. Lazard kept staring at it, trying to recognize the city, but the combinations of glass and cement could have been anywhere. Baxter was drinking a strawberry daiquiri, his idea of a bachelor drink. He rested the glass delicately on his large stomach.

"My cousin Willy," said Baxter, "thirty years ago right when we got out of the army, he asked me if I wanted to go in with him selling cars. Not me, I was going to be a fireman. You know, that guy, he's got a place in Newton Highlands. Every fuckin' room looks like this one. Even the kitchen. Tell me, have I been kickin' myself?"

Baxter took a large mouthful of his daiquiri, then glanced around the room. "By the way," he said, "you hear about Cassidy? He's back in the hospital."

"What for?"

"Dumb fucker must of been lifting weights or something. Bullet wound in his chest broke open and a lotta blood went into the lung."

"Will he be all right?" Lazard felt his skin getting hot, then wondered when he would stop accumulating things to feel guilty about.

"Sure, but it means he won't be back in the office for a while. Guess he's mad as a son of a bitch. Maybe he broke himself open with that big girlfriend of his, you know, sexual horseplay."

Lazard didn't answer. He was sorry he hadn't been shot instead. Then he thought that was stupid. At least they had helped Trieger, gotten him off the hook. Maybe that was stupid too. Lazard was drinking whiskey and water and had already forgotten how many he'd had. The only other customers were two women at a table overlooking Beacon Street and the Public Gardens. Near them on the wall was a portrait of Lord Byron wearing a turban. The women were thin and in their thirties.

"Speaking of Cassidy," said Baxter, lowering his voice, "know what keeps bothering me?"

Lazard drained his glass. "What?"

"When Cassidy and me went into that whore's apartment and that guy came storming out with a gun, well, it just keeps going through my head. I had my revolver in my back pocket and I couldn't get it out and I keep seeing that guy pointing his gun at me and me not able to get mine out. You know, I just fell down on the floor, I mean, he didn't hit me or anything. One minute I was standing, the next I was down on the floor. Like I been stuck in fires and scary shit like that, but nothin' was ever that bad. Know what I mean?"

"Maybe." Lazard glanced at Baxter's puffy face.

"You ever in something like that?"

The waiter brought them fresh drinks. Lazard didn't say anything until he had gone. "When I burned my leg—I kept thinking someone would come and the pain couldn't get worse, but no one came and the pain got worse."

"What happened?"

"They finally came and pulled me out."

"You think it changed you much?"

"Maybe it made me think you shouldn't make plans." Glancing around the room, Lazard was struck by how foreign it felt to him.

"I don't think havin' that gun pointed at me is goin' to change me much," said Baxter. "I've just had some bad dreams, that's all."

While they had been talking, a group of four couples had come in and taken a table to the right of Lazard under a portrait of the Earl of Portland. They were loud, laughed constantly, and had apparently been drinking elsewhere. All were in their early thirties and fashionably dressed. It soon became clear that two of them had been married to each other, were recently divorced, and were now meeting with their current lovers and friends to show themselves capable of rising above the circumstances of their lives and letting bygones be bygones.

For a few minutes Baxter and Lazard listened to their talk, which consisted of advice by the ex-spouses and a listing of small faults which the new lovers could look forward to discovering: leaving the refrigerator open and underwear under the bed. As each fault was mentioned, all eight laughed happily.

"Oh yeah," said Baxter, "I stopped by the office this afternoon, you want another piece of news?"

"What?" Lazard watched the eight people under the portrait. They looked beautiful and popular and excited with their lives.

"Pugliese got married."

"Who to?"

"That schoolteacher that kept hanging around the office. I forget her name. So what, it's Pugliese now. Fatback said we should put some money together and get 'em something, you know, a wedding present, and I said we should get them an old set of army bunk beds."

As if in response to the news about Pugliese, Lazard found himself thinking he should quit the Fire Department. Why continue doing something he neither liked nor had any belief in? Maybe he could do private work like Bascomb or something altogether different. Like what? Lazard couldn't think. As he tried to concentrate, he remembered Virginia Lufkin lying in bed in the motel room, naked except for her half-moon earrings and her watch with its small black strap. Lazard wanted to reach out and touch her. Then he shook his head and realized he was drunk.

"Jesus," said Baxter, "know where they went on their honeymoon? Fuckin' Niagara Falls. Can you believe it? Pugliese said you told him to take a vacation. Well, he took the week off. Christ, I wish you'd give me a vacation and I wouldn't go to no fuckin' Niagara Falls neither."

But Lazard wasn't listening. David Bascomb had just entered at the front of the room and was sitting down at the bar. At first Lazard thought that Bascomb had followed them but that was impossible. Bascomb had on a dark brown Harris Tweed jacket and camel-colored slacks. He greeted the bartender by name and the bartender poured Bascomb a large snifter of brandy and set it before him.

Then Lazard remembered that Bascomb had an apartment on Beacon Hill where he lived with a young woman who studied Chinese at Harvard. He probably lived only a couple of blocks away. How could he have forgotten that? Drunkenly, he wondered if he had led Baxter to the Hampshire House in hope of meeting Bascomb so they could receive the punishment that part of Lazard felt was deserved.

Baxter was still talking about Pugliese and trying to be amusing by suggesting unsuitable wedding presents. He laughed and slapped the table with his hand. "You could enroll 'em in a dirty movie of the month club or what's that place in California that has sexy underwear? Maybe get some of those panties with a lot of feathers on the crotch or the kind made out of sugar that you can eat."

Lazard watched Bascomb's face in the bar mirror. He liked the face, liked its easy smile and how it wrinkled when Bascomb talked. Bascomb cleaned his glasses on his necktie, then took out a red box of toothpicks and set it beside his glass. Lazard wished he were a hundred miles away. The only exit was the door by which Bascomb had come in. Lazard knew it would only be seconds before Bascomb noticed his reflection in the mirror.

"What the hell's wrong with you?" asked Baxter. "You look like you're gonna blow lunch."

Lazard didn't answer. Bascomb had seen him and the two men were staring at each other in the bar mirror. The detective's expression was hard, and it seemed to Lazard that Bascomb had almost put on a new face. Then Bascomb turned around slowly in his seat.

Baxter twisted his head to look over his shoulder. "Oh, oh," he said, "it's fag-locks."

Bascomb began to walk over to their table. He took his time and didn't bother looking at Baxter, who was struggling to sit up straight in his chair.

When he reached them, he put his hands in his pockets and glanced around the room as if he were bored. "So what'd they pay you?" he asked. Bascomb looked at Lazard and his expression grew angry again. "You know, Phelps gets about 750, 800 bucks. That's what your old captain used to get as well. Then there's a guy over in the marshal's office that gets about $700. That's a little low. I know a fire captain in Somerville that won't take under a thousand. Not bad for doing nothing. So what'd you get, Frank? What did they give you for letting Trieger off the hotseat?"

Lazard remained silent. His fingers were curled around the

crook of his cane and he watched them grow white. Baxter scratched his stomach and pretended not to be listening.

"I'm still recommending nonpayment," said Bascomb. "If the insurance company goes along with me and Trieger sues, I'm going to drag your ass into court and put you on the stand. What the hell, you won't be around much longer anyway." Bascomb paused to push his glasses up on his nose with his thumb. "Just tell me, Frank, what'd they pay you for letting them get away with killing two firemen?"

Lazard stumbled to his feet.

Bascomb reached out and pressed against Lazard's chest with one finger. "What're you going to do, cripple, hit me?" He stared at Lazard for a moment, then spat down at the table and turned away. Lazard watched him leave the bar. He remained standing, swaying back and forth between his chair and the table. The four loud couples under the portrait were staring at him.

Baxter looked embarrassed. He heaved himself to his feet, then glanced around to make sure Bascomb had gone. "I gotta find the powder room," he said.

Baxter half walked, half staggered from the room. After a moment, Lazard took out his wallet and threw a twenty on the table. He felt like seeing Trieger, just to talk to him, but Trieger had gone back to his cottage on Lake Sunapee. Maybe he could call Virginia Lufkin instead. Then he remembered she had married Pugilese. Why had she done a dumb thing like that? Lazard shook his head, then slowly limped toward the door. He kept thinking he wanted to talk to someone. Maybe Quaid or Cassidy, but they were both firemen.

He yanked open the front door of the Hampshire House, then tripped on the mat. Stumbling forward, he tried to grab the railing but missed. At the last moment, he reached out his hands to break his fall. His cane cluttered down into the street. Lazard landed on his stomach, then slid down three or four steps to the sidewalk. Getting to his feet, he saw his hands were scraped and bleeding slightly. They felt numb. It was hard to get his breath. He picked up his cane, then looked back and saw the waiter watching him from the door.

Lazard turned right down Beacon. It was cold and he didn't have a coat. Several cabs slowed down beside him, then moved on. He wondered where his coat was, then decided it wasn't worth going back to find it. Why bother with a dumb coat? Looking up, he saw a man in a dark jacket walking toward him. For a moment, Lazard felt afraid, but before he could gather his thoughts, the man passed him, walking steadily toward Charles. Lazard pushed himself away from the fence and turned right down Brimmer.

The streetlights were simulated gas lamps on old-fashioned iron poles. He decided they hurt his eyes. Lazard's limp added to his drunken unsteadiness and he kept hitting the fence to his right, falling off the curb to his left. In his ears was a great rushing, like water pouring through a narrow space.

To hell with Bascomb, he thought, to hell with the lot of them. At least he had saved Trieger, saved him just as if he had dived into a river and pulled him out. At least that was settled. But even as he thought this, Lazard realized it wasn't true. Sure it's true, he said to himself. Then he shook his head again. Far from having a hold over DiTullio, he had given DiTullio a hold over him. How that hold would be used Lazard had no idea; all he knew was that someday there would be a phone call or a knock on the door which would call him to account. "That's not true," said Lazard out loud. "It's over, over and done with." But even as he said the words, he doubted them.

He turned right onto Byron. It was an old narrow street. Black bags of trash had been put out for collection, along with several broken chairs and a couch with the springs pushing through the torn fabric. Lazard's eyes burned and he stopped to rub them. Then he staggered on again. As he passed one of the streetlamps, he lifted his cane and hit the crook hard against the glass. One pane broke, showering him with glass. Lazard kept hitting until the light went out. The darkness felt good on his eyes.

Pressing his cane against his leg, he continued to make his way along Byron toward the next streetlamp. The street was a long box. In his confused state, Lazard felt a great sense of purpose. When he reached the streetlamp, he began smashing his cane against the glass, hitting it over and over. The cane made a loud clanging noise against the metal. Bits of glass flew around him and at last the lamp went dark. It made Lazard feel good. He began to limp toward the next streetlamp. Someone was shouting at him. He didn't know where his car was or where he had come from.

There had been a moment in Lazard's last fire as an active lieutenant when he had almost saved himself and escaped. As he climbed the stairs to the third floor of the burning three-decker, he wondered whether he would be taking such a chance if he hadn't arrived late and felt the disapproval of the district chief. If he found the boy and the boy were alive, then it might be worth a citation. But there were no citations for dead kids. Maybe he should just give up. Lazard judged he had about seven minutes left in the tank of air on his back. He decided to keep going.

Although there was no fire on the third floor and much of the smoke had been drawn through the holes chopped in the roof, it was still extremely hot because of the fire on the lower floors. Lazard's main concern was that the ceiling beneath him had not burned through and that the floor would be safe.

The third floor appeared to be one large apartment. Truckmen had already broken the front windows. At the top of the stairs Lazard found himself in a long living room with a large braided rug and large stuffed armchairs and a sofa. After all the noise downstairs, Lazard thought the third floor seemed as quiet as a grave. Lights from the window threw his shadow on the black smoke as he crawled across the room, keeping close to the floor and pointing his flashlight ahead of him. On a small table was a television and on the television was a fishbowl. Two dead goldfish floated at the surface of the water.

Lazard crawled through a kitchen, then found a closed door to his right. It was a bedroom. The smoke was thicker here and he spent nearly a minute feeling under a double bed, then into a closet. Nothing. The floor was littered with clothing and at least fifteen pairs of women's shoes. Lazard crawled out of the room and across the hall.

The second bedroom was smaller, but even so Lazard had to go over most of the floor with his hands, reaching back under the bed and into the closet. His light swung back and forth across the walls, showing a piece of palm leaf tied into a cross and photographs of first communions. Lazard told himself he was taking too long, that the floor was getting too hot.

Out in the hall again he heard shouting from downstairs and a crashing noise as the truckmen began pulling down the ceiling, looking for extensions of the fire. A cheap brown runner covered the floor of the hall. Ahead of him was another closed door and in front of it Lazard could make out a small huddled shape.

It was a dog, a dead cocker spaniel. Lazard tried the door. It was locked. He stook up, hurled himself at the door, and it smashed open. The one window hadn't been broken and the room was thick with smoke. Lazard was almost certain the boy was in this room and that he would find him dead.

There were two single beds and a deep closet. The place he found the boy, however, was under a bureau where he had crawled and passed out. Lazard grabbed the boy's foot and pulled. The boy flopped out into the circle of light thrown by the flashlight. Lazard guessed he was about three: a little one-legged boy in jeans and a red T-shirt with short black hair. Lazard wondered how he had lost his leg. He was obviously dead. The room was extremely hot and even Lazard's air pack didn't seem to help.

He crawled to the window and smashed the glass with his helmet. He had hoped to see ladders, see the aerial tower which would rescue him. Instead, there was only a group of men on a 2½-inch line three floors below. They seemed centuries away. Through the second-story windows to his left, Lazard saw flames pushing out and licking their way up the side of the building. One of the men on the ground saw him and pointed.

Lazard ducked back into the room, grabbed the body of the boy, and made a crouching run toward the door. Out in the hall it was much hotter and he could see red behind him toward the back of the flat. He turned and ran toward the stairs, almost tripping over the body of the dog. The floor began to sag beneath his weight. It was very hot and the brown runner was smoldering, about to burst into flames.

It was in the kitchen that it happened. The floor seemed to sink, then partially gave way. His right leg broke through. Lazard lunged forward, throwing the child ahead of him. His leg sank through to the hip, while his left leg was wrenched back behind him. He could feel intense heat on the leg which had gone through the ceiling. He tried to push himself up, but the boot was caught and wouldn't come free. He had also dropped the flashlight which shone across the body of the boy. Frantically, Lazard looked for something to help him pull himself out, but the only thing was the runner itself. He began to pull at it, but it wasn't nailed down and he only began pulling it toward him. The boy had fallen half across the runner and as Lazard yanked at it, trying to free himself, he pulled the boy toward him. The boy bounced along the floor in the beam of the flashlight. His arms flopped at his sides and his one leg with its foot in a blue sneaker seemed to kick back and forth. The bell on Lazard's tank started to ring, indicating he was almost out of air, but Lazard didn't hear it as the fire in the room below burned through his boot.

Lazard wasn't even aware when he began to scream. He knew the fire was melting the rubber of his boot, had begun to eat into his leg. It was as if the hole he had toppled into was pain itself, as if his entire body had moved into his burning leg, his whole life and history and all his plans beyond that moment—all had become part of his leg which burned and kicked in the air of the room beneath him, hanging from the ceiling like a flaming chandelier.

At that moment a firefighter from Engine 52 on the tip of a 2½-inch line reached the door of the downstairs room, saw the leg and didn't even realize the flaming mass was a leg until he saw the white bone of the knee. The leg kicked and swung back and forth as if in a violent wind. Almost as if it were dancing, thought the man as he raised the nozzle toward it.

ABOUT THE AUTHOR

STEPHEN DOBYNS lives in Maine. This is his fourth novel. He has published as well four books of poetry; has received two poetry fellowships from the National Endowment of the Arts, and was chosen the Lamont Selection of the Academy of American Poets in 1971. His poems have appeared in about fifty magazines.